Faithful HEART

OTHER BOOKS BY AL LACY

Angel of Mercy Series:
A Promise for Breanna (Book One)
Faithful Heart (Book Two)

Journeys of the Stranger series:
Legacy (Book One)
Silent Abduction (Book Two)
Blizzard (Book Three)
Tears of the Sun (Book Four)

Battles of Destiny (Civil War series):
Beloved Enemy (Battle of First Bull Run)
A Heart Divided (Battle of Mobile Bay)
A Promise Unbroken (Battle of Rich Mountain)
Shadowed Memories (Battle of Shiloh)
Joy From Ashes (Battle of Fredericksburg)

A NOVEL

Faithful HEART

AL LACY

MULTNOMAH
BOOKS

FAITHFUL HEART
PUBLISHED BY MULTNOMAH BOOKS
12265 Oracle Boulevard, Suite 200
Colorado Springs, Colorado 80921

With the exception of recognized historical figures, the characters and events in this book are fictional, and any resemblance to actual persons or events is coincidental.

ISBN 978-1-60142-272-9
ISBN 978-1-60142-304-7 (electronic)

Published in the United States by WaterBrook Multnomah, an imprint of the Crown Publishing Group, a division of Random House Inc., New York.

MULTNOMAH and its mountain colophon are registered trademarks of Random House Inc.

Printed in the United States of America
2010

10 9 8 7 6 5 4 3 2 1

For Linda Sears,

one of my most ardent fans.
Her husband tells me she has "Lacy withdrawal"
between publication of my novels.

The Lord bless you, Linda!
PHILIPPIANS 1:3

FOREWORD

As Hippocrates (460-370 BC) is known as the father of organized medicine, Florence Nightingale (1820-1910) is known as
the mother of organized nursing. Miss Nightingale's rise to fame
was a result of her nursing care for soldiers of the British Army
during the Crimean War in Turkey, 1853-1856. In her thirties at
that time, she blazed a trail that led to nursing being recognized
as a profession rather than a menial service. She often spoke of
nursing as an art as well as a science. She once wrote:

> *Nursing is an art; and if it is to be made an art, it*
> *requires as exclusive a devotion, as hard a preparation, as*
> *any painter's or sculptor's work; for what is the having to do with*
> *dead canvas or cold marble, compared with having to do with*
> *the living body? It is one of the Fine Arts;*
> *I had almost said, the finest of the Fine Arts.*

For centuries the world had no organized training program
for nurses. Nurses learned while working with physicians in clin-
ics and in hospitals with experienced nurses, but not until Miss
Nightingale founded the Nightingale Training School for Nurses
in England in 1860 was there an institution established for the
express purpose of training nurses.

The aims of her school were to train hospital nurses, clinic
nurses, and visiting nurses who worked in private homes with
the sick and the aged. The length of the program was one year,
after which the nurses were placed on the staff of a hospital for
two years' further experience.

In the early nineteenth century, the status of nursing in
the United States was identical to that in England prior to the

influence of Florence Nightingale. Nurses were trained in large city hospitals, but the training was far from sufficient to equip the young women for the task they faced.

Many nurses were trained working at the sides of physicians. The American Medical Association (formed in 1847) recognized these physician-trained nurses, and by recommendation of the instructor-physicians, awarded them special certificates.

At the outbreak of the Civil War, neither the Union nor the Confederacy had an army nurse corps, but after the first battles the need for nurses became imperative. Those recognized physician-trained nurses were few and far between, but they were pushed into service as quickly as possible. Many hospital-trained nurses were sent into service for the military, and a multitude of other women served as untrained volunteers.

What few Civil War records exist estimate that some ten thousand nurses—trained and untrained—were engaged in nursing and field hospital administration during the Civil War.

The most famous of these were Clara Barton, Dorothea Lynde Dix, Mary Ann Bickerdyke, and Louisa May Alcott. Sometime during the bloody four years of the Civil War (620,000 men died), the soldiers dubbed these gallant women "angels of mercy." Nurses were labeled as such throughout the remainder of the nineteenth century and for the first few years of the twentieth century.

Following the Civil War, interest in training "angels of mercy" was high, and culminated in the almost simultaneous founding of three schools in 1873, which were approved by the American Medical Association. They were: Bellevue Training School in New York City, Connecticut Training School in New Haven, and Boston Training School.

✦

Nursing has been called the oldest of the arts and the youngest of the professions. Although many believe that nursing began with Florence Nightingale, in actuality nursing is as old as medicine itself. Miss Nightingale established the first institution for the express purpose of training nurses, but throughout human history an interdependence of medicine and nursing has produced a unique and exceptional relationship.

The history of nursing clearly demonstrates the most valuable aspect of nursing: care and caring. Caring is the essence of nursing—caring for, caring with, and caring about. But caring alone was not sufficient to nurture health, properly relieve the sick, injured, and wounded, or overcome disease. The development of nursing depended on two additional ingredients: knowledge and skill. Thus the heart, the head, and the hands were united to provide the necessary foundation for nursing to become both an art and a science.

In my creation of Breanna Baylor, I have sought to give my readers a tender, loving, compassionate young Christian woman with the heart, head, and hands of the model nurse who fulfills a need in her century, and would fill it in this century if she lived today.

It is my earnest desire that Breanna—our angel of mercy—will inspire all of her readers with the courage and compassion she portrays.

PROLOGUE

Since the Angel of Mercy series is a spinoff of Questar Publishers's Journeys of the Stranger series, and since *Faithful Heart* is the second book of the Angel series, let me lay a brief foundation for our new readers.

In *Legacy*, the first book of the Stranger series, the mysterious John Stranger met and fell in love with nurse Breanna Baylor. Breanna found herself falling in love with John also, but because she had been jilted in the past by a man named Frank Miller only days before their wedding day, she feared being hurt again and sent John out of her life.

Loving Breanna as he did, John gave in to her wishes. But he told her that though she would not see him, he would be near at times to watch over her, and that she would never be out of his heart. When he rode away from her that day in Wichita, Kansas, Breanna knew before he passed from her sight that she had made an awful mistake. She was desperately in love with him…but it was too late. He was out of earshot. She could not call him back.

In the weeks and months that followed (through the rest of *Legacy, Silent Abduction,* and *Blizzard),* John Stranger was near when Breanna faced danger and death. He delivered her from danger each time, and more than once saved her life, all without the two of them exchanging words.

Breanna was eager to tell John that she had made a horrible mistake by sending him out of her life and that she loved him with all her heart. She prayed earnestly that the Lord would bring John back so she could talk to him, but circumstances prevailed, keeping it from happening.

Then in *A Promise for Breanna,* the first book in the Angel of Mercy series, God in His own time and His own way brought them together. Breanna had experienced a recurring dream in which John had come riding across the rugged land at sunset to meet her at a cabin in the foothills of the Colorado Rockies. The dream had always ended just as she was pouring out her heart to John and asking his forgiveness for sending him out of her life.

Breanna was aboard a wagon train in Wyoming, headed for California. Frank Miller was following the train, intending to kill her. Several days previously, Lorraine Miller had been shot accidentally by Frank in South Pass City. Breanna was there filling in as town physician and had performed surgery on Lorraine.

In spite of Breanna's efforts, Lorraine died on the operating table. Frank believed Breanna could have saved her, but let Lorraine die to get back at him for jilting her. He was now bent on revenge. At the same time, John Stranger was riding toward the wagon train to look in on Breanna, though as usual, he would remain out of her sight.

A serious problem had developed for Breanna. Red Claw, a Snake Indian chief, had set his wanton eyes on her. Red Claw and his warriors had continually attacked the wagon train, and were still a threat. More than anything, Red Claw wanted to capture Breanna, and made plans to do so. Breanna's deliverance from Red Claw and her reunion with John Stranger forms the exciting conclusion to Book One of this new series.

John Stranger and Breanna were finally back together. And this time, it was no dream.

1

⬧

THE BROAD, SWEEPING VALLEY of forests and grassy meadows was turning from amber to purple as the setting sun dipped behind the distant mountains to the west.

John Stranger picked up the small pistol, put an arm around Breanna Baylor, and directed her toward the mouth of the cave. "Come, Breanna," he said softly, "let's get off this rock before darkness falls."

Breanna looked up at him and smiled. "I wish I could tell you how good it feels to be with you…and how wonderful it is to hear you say my name."

John chuckled. "I've said it a million times in my dreams."

As they stepped out of the cave, Breanna stiffened. The sight of the dead Snake chief lying with his eyes open, staring emptily toward the darkening sky gave her a chill.

John guided her around Red Claw's body, saying, "I wonder what went through his mind when he approached the cave and saw you standing there pointing this gun at him."

"The Derringer belongs to Rip Clayson," Breanna said. "He told me you traveled with the wagon train for a while when they were in Nebraska."

"Yes."

"So you got to know Rip and the others in the train?"

"Not too well. I wasn't with them all that long before I was called to Fort Boise. Commandant there needed a little help. His men were having some problems getting along."

"And they knew who to turn to for help. That's the John Stranger I know."

"Just doing my duty."

"Someday I hope to find out more about this duty of yours. Was it duty that brought you here?"

"You brought me here."

Breanna shook her head in wonderment as they continued down the crude rock "stairs." "I owe so much to you for all the times you've watched out for me, even saving my life more than once."

"You don't owe me anything, Breanna Baylor," he replied, hugging her to his side.

It was almost dark when they reached level ground and John led her to the spot where he had left Ebony. The big black gelding nickered and bobbed his head as they drew near.

"See there?" John said. "Ebony remembers you. The two of us have had many long talks about you."

Breanna was about to reply when the sound of pounding feet drew her attention. A group of men were coming through the woods from the direction of the wagon train.

"Looks like we've got company," John said. "Probably Rip and some of the men."

"You all right, Breanna?" Rip Clayson said as he emerged from the deepening shadows.

"Yes, thank the Lord! In more ways than one."

Curly Wesson, who drove the lead wagon in the train, was at Clayson's side, with five men on their heels. "Did you shoot that Injun?" the old man said.

"She did," John said.

"Good!" Curly said. "At least he won't be worryin' any more white women!"

The rest of the people were waiting at the edge of the clearing and rejoiced to hear that Breanna was unharmed. They also rejoiced to know that their tormentor was dead.

Fires winked against the darkness within the circle of wagons, and the aroma of hot food filled the cool air. Rip motioned for Carolyne Fulford to come close and introduced her to John Stranger, explaining that Carolyne had survived an Indian attack that wiped out the entire train she had been traveling with. John said he had come upon the train while on the trail.

"I fell in love with her the day we picked her up, John," Rip said, his arm around Carolyne's shoulder. "It was definitely love at first sight."

"For me, too," Carolyne said. "And Rip has asked me to marry him."

"Well, wonderful," grinned Stranger.

"We're gonna tie the knot when we get to California," Rip said.

"I'm happy for both of you. And I hope the Lord gives you a passel of children."

The happy couple smiled at each other in the firelight, then Rip said, "We haven't told you, John, but we already have one child."

"You do?" Stranger said.

"It's a long story, but the simple version is that the baby's parents were traveling in the wagon train with Carolyne and were killed along with everyone else during the Indian attack. Carolyne was holding the baby the first time I saw her, hiding in the bushes along a creek bank. The baby's name, by the way, is Breanna. Her parents named her in honor of Nurse Baylor here. I'll let her tell you that part of the story."

"It was nothing really," Breanna said. "The mother was having some complications when the wagon train stopped at South Pass City, and I delivered the little girl by Cesarean section. I hardly thought that was reason enough for them to name their baby after me, but that's what they did."

"So we're going to give the baby our name when we get married," Carolyne said. "We'll raise little Breanna Hughes Clayson as if she were our own."

Stranger grinned. "I commend you both." Then turning to Breanna, he said, "Isn't a Cesarean section something a well-trained physician does?"

"Ordinarily," she replied quietly.

John's grin broadened. "Well, I'm plenty proud of you, sweetheart."

Breanna hunched her shoulders. "I just did what had to be done. I have had a little experience in it. I just thank the Lord that precious little baby is with us."

"I'd like to meet her," John said.

"She's asleep right now," Carolyne told him. "But she'll be awake sometime after supper. You can meet her then."

John and Breanna ate with Rip, Carolyne, Curly, and wealthy widower Doral Chatsworth. During the meal, Chatsworth explained to Stranger how he offered to pay Breanna to join the wagon train and care for his wife, Hattie, who was ailing. South Pass City's new doctor had arrived, and Breanna was planning to return to Denver by stagecoach. Breanna had agreed to stay with the train all the way to San Francisco. Chatsworth had also given Breanna enough money to pay for her train ticket from San Francisco to Denver when the journey was completed. Though Hattie had been killed in one of the Snake Indian attacks on the wagon train, Rip had asked Breanna to continue on with them and give care to those who needed it.

"I consented to do so for two reasons, John," Breanna said. "Mr. Chatsworth had already paid me in full for the entire trip and wouldn't take any money back. I felt it was only right to do my part by completing the trip. And I'm eager to get to San Francisco because my sister Dottie lives near there. Do you remember me telling you about her when we first met back in Kansas?"

"Vaguely."

"I haven't seen her in almost ten years. I'm so excited!"

When the meal was finished, Doral offered to let John sleep in his wagon. John thanked him but said that he preferred to sleep on the ground in his bedroll near the wagon Breanna and Carolyne were sharing.

Suddenly there was a deep rumble on the night air. Rip Clayson rose to his feet by the fire and said, "That'll be the cavalry coming back."

Seconds later, the one-hundred-man cavalry unit thundered into the camp, drawing up just outside the circle of wagons. Rip stepped between two of the vehicles with John and Curly at his heels. The rest of the people within the circle pressed close, peering between the wagons at the cavalrymen.

As the man on the lead horse swung from his McClellan saddle, Rip stepped up and said, "My name's Ripley Clayson, Captain. I'm wagon master. You certainly put those Snakes on the run."

"That we did, Mr. Clayson. I don't think you'll be having any more trouble from that band of savages." The officer extended his hand and said, "My name's Newt Meyer."

The two men shook hands, then Clayson introduced the captain to John Stranger and Curly Wesson.

"Red Claw wasn't with the war party," Meyer continued. "We don't know what happened to him."

"We do," Clayson said. "He's dead."

"Dead?"

"That's right. I'll explain it to you later. Right now, we'd like to invite you and your men to a hot meal."

Meyer smiled and pushed his campaign hat to the back of his head. "Well, we'll just take you up on that!" He turned and called for his men to dismount, telling them they could leave their cold rations in their saddlebags. They were going to get a hot supper.

The men in blue cheered and swung from their mounts. Clayson searched the riders for the man he had sent on horseback to bring the cavalry.

"Captain?"

"Yes, sir?"

"I'm wondering where Wade Moore is."

"Oh, I'm sorry. I should have told you right away. When he arrived at the fort, he wasn't feeling well. Said he couldn't ride back with us. Asked that we tell you and his wife that he'd wait at the fort."

"I hope it's nothing serious."

"Pains in his chest. Dr. Laird, our fort physician, says he's not sure what's causing them. He's watching him close. Says it could just be pleurisy, but he's not sure."

"Well, I'm glad he made it and sent you and your men. These people have had about all the Indian attacks they can stand. Not only that, but we're totally out of ammunition. We'll need to stock up when we get to the fort."

"We've got plenty," Meyer said.

"I know there are plenty more Indians on the other side of the fort, Captain. Any of them hostile that you know of?"

"Yes. Shoshonis have been acting up in southern Idaho. We'll escort you a few miles beyond the fort, but we won't be able to go even as far as the Idaho border. We're having problems with the Paiutes due west of the fort and need to patrol it regularly. Colonel Lynch, our commandant, hesitated to send this large a unit for this mission, but your Mr. Moore told him what kind of Indian forces you've been having to fight, so he wanted to make sure your wagon train had the protection it needed."

"I'll thank him for it when I see him," smiled Rip.

When the cavalrymen filed into the circle, the people gave them a rousing cheer. The wagon master sought out Marian Moore and told her about her husband. He asked if the colonel had ever experienced pleurisy before. When Marian said he had, Rip said he was probably having a recurrence and that she shouldn't be too worried.

John Stranger went to the wagon where Breanna and Carolyne were and found Breanna feeding her tiny namesake. Stranger had a special love for infants and children. He held baby Breanna in his arms and made over her.

John and Breanna then joined Rip at the side of the wagon while Carolyne remained inside to change a diaper. Stranger drew Breanna close to him, encircling her in an arm, and said, "Rip, all this talk about the possibility of Indian trouble after the wagon train leaves Fort Bridger has me concerned."

"Yeah," sighed Rip. "Me, too."

"Since Breanna is going to stay with the train all the way to San Francisco, I've decided to do the same. I doubt there'll be any Indian trouble once the train reaches the Sierras, since the Mohaves are friendly to whites. But I want to make sure this little lady is safe."

Breanna's face lit up. "Oh, John! It'll be wonderful to have you with me!"

"It'll be more wonderful for me," he smiled.

"Well, I'll be plenty glad to have you in the train, John," Rip said. "I've never seen you use that iron on your hip or the Winchester in your saddleboot, but I've got a feeling you'd be a pretty good asset in an Indian attack."

"More than you can even imagine, Rip," Breanna said.

"You didn't do so bad yourself with that Derringer," Stranger said.

Breanna's fair skin tinted. "It was him or me."

"She has done all right during the attacks too, John," Rip said. "I put a Colt .45 in her hand, and she used it to good advantage. Where'd you learn to shoot like that, lady?"

"My Uncle Harvey taught me. Mom's brother. He taught my sister and me both how to use a handgun and a rifle. Mom, too. He said he hoped we would never have to use a gun, but if the occasion came, he wanted us to be able to defend ourselves."

"Smart man," Clayson nodded.

"Sweetheart, how about you and me taking a little moonlight walk?" Stranger said.

"I thought you'd never ask."

The couple excused themselves to Rip Clayson and Breanna slipped her hand in the crook of John Stranger's arm as they moved slowly into the woods. An owl hooted from a tree limb somewhere ahead of them, and the night breeze rustled through the branches of the towering pines. They walked slowly, moving from moonlight to shadows to moonlight.

"Oh, John," Breanna said, "I'm so glad you'll be traveling with me for the rest of the trip. It'll be so good to have you close for that long."

"I've been close many times when you didn't know it. I sure like it this way best."

As if they had practiced it, both of them stopped at the same moment, turned face to face, and looked into each other's eyes. A lock of hair had come loose and was dangling on Breanna's forehead, dancing to the rhythm of the light wind. The moon reflected in her eyes.

"I love you, Breanna. Mortal words could never express how very much I love you."

She reached up and stroked his right cheek, her fingers running over the twin-ridged scars. "And I love you, darling. Words fail me too….but in the language of the heart, we both know, don't we?"

John nodded, then lowered his head and kissed her sweetly, tenderly. They held each other for a long moment, then started walking again.

"Tell me about your sister," John said, squeezing the hand that was once again in the crook of his arm. "What little time we had together in Kansas, you barely mentioned her."

"Dottie is two years younger than me. She's my only sibling. We were both born and raised in Leavenworth. So, Mr. Stranger, you're getting a Jayhawker in this deal."

"I'll take her."

"And of course I've already told you the sad story about my parents…about Daddy running off with that other woman, I mean."

"I've not forgotten it. I know that was devastating to your mother, but it must have been hard for you and Dottie too."

"Terribly. I don't think we could have made it without the Lord's help."

"Dottie's a Christian too?" John asked.

"Yes. About three weeks after I came to know the Lord, I had the joy of leading Dottie to Him."

"I'd like to know how you came to know the Lord."

"It's sort of a long story," said Breanna, smiling up at him, "but when there's more time, I'll sure tell you about it. I was nineteen at the time. Most wonderful thing that's ever happened to me. Want to know what the second most wonderful thing that ever happened to me was?"

"Is it anything like the second most wonderful thing that ever happened to me?"

Breanna stopped, looked up at him, then said, "If your second best thing to being saved was having me come into your life…it is exactly like it."

Words were useless at that moment. John and Breanna found ecstasy in each other's arms and in the magic kiss they shared.

John took Breanna by the hand and led her to a fallen tree,

where they sat down. "I want to hear more about Dottie since I'll be meeting her at the end of this journey."

"All right. Dottie and I have a deep love for each other. I haven't seen her in nearly ten years, but we've kept in contact through letters."

"What does she look like?"

"She and I look so much alike, by the time we were in our teens, people used to ask if we were twins. Our facial features will surprise you. Our hair is exactly the same color, and we are the same size. She tells me in her letters that even though she's borne two children, she still could wear my skirts and dresses."

"Eyes?"

"Same blue as mine."

"Any inclinations toward nursing, like her sister?"

"No. All she ever wanted to be was a wife and mother. That's what caused her to answer an advertisement in the Leavenworth newspaper when she was eighteen. In her eyes, she was practically an old maid, and when she saw Jerrod Harper's ad in the paper, she jumped at it."

"You mean *mail-order bride?*"

"Yes. Jerrod is older than Dottie. About five years, I think. The ad said he was a Civil War veteran, that he owned a farm near San Francisco, and that he was a born-again Christian and was looking for a born-again wife."

John pulled at an ear. "Civil War veteran, eh? You said she went out there and married him a little less than ten years ago?"

"Yes."

"But the war was just getting started ten years ago. It wasn't quite six months old. How could he have been a veteran?"

"Dottie found out he'd been wounded at the Battle of Wilson's Creek in Missouri early in the war and was given an immediate medical release from the army."

"Oh, okay. That would tally out."

"Jerrod is from Missouri. He'd joined the Union army at the very outbreak of the War. Became a sergeant quite quickly."

"What kind of wound did he have? Does it bother him now?"

"The medical condition that put him out of the War was shell shock, according to Dottie."

"Same thing as combat fatigue."

"Yes. Jerrod sustained some physical wounds, too. A cannonball exploded close to him. Shrapnel cut him up quite a bit, but it was the combat fatigue that caused the army doctors to release him. Some men get over it, other's don't. Sometimes it will seem that a shell-shocked man has gotten over it, when he actually hasn't. It will lie latent in him for months, even years, then crop up again."

"Something stimulates it?"

"Sometimes. A sudden loud noise or flash of light. Actually anything that takes them off guard or by surprise. With many, there is no obvious cause at all that sets them off."

"Sets them off? You mean, they go berserk?"

"Yes, quite often. In the medical field we call them 'startle reactions.' When the shell shock is active in a man, he'll be easily irritated. Many become violent. They'll do things that in their normal state they would never even consider. When the startle reaction subsides, they're always very sorry for what they did. They often live under a cloud of guilt for their violent actions. They actually become two people. It's called *dementia praecox*.

Often they get so bad they have to be locked up in an asylum."

"Do you know if Jerrod has had any problems with it?"

"Dottie hasn't said. I would think if he had, she would mention it in her letters."

"So as far as you know, she's happy with her mail-order husband?"

"Yes. I tried to talk her out of going off and marrying a man she'd never met…but Dottie is headstrong."

"Like her sister."

Breanna smiled. "Her fear of becoming an old maid drove her to answer Jerrod's ad. His reply convinced her that he was a dedicated Christian and that the Lord would give them real love for each other. From her letters, I can say it's worked out exactly like that. The Lord has given them two wonderful children. James is eight now, and Molly Kathryn—they call her Molly Kate—is six. I have pictures of them at my apartment in Denver. They're adorable."

"If they're related to you, they have to be."

"Oh, you!" Breanna gave him a playful jab on the shoulder.

"You say their farm is near San Francisco?"

"They have thirty acres about twelve miles south of the city. They have orchards of various kinds, and raise strawberries and lettuce. Possibly other things, too. I don't know."

"Well, I'm sure you're eager to see them. You've never met Jerrod or the children, right?"

"Right, but I can't wait to meet them and see Dottie again."

"I'll look forward to meeting them myself." John paused, then said, "Well, we ought to head back."

"All right."

"But before we do, let's talk to the Lord together."

John and Breanna held hands, and John led them in prayer, asking the Lord to guide them and give them wisdom so they might know His perfect will and His plan for their future. He closed by thanking God for bringing them together and for giving him the love of the most wonderful woman in the world.

This brought tears to Breanna's cheeks, and before they headed back, John kissed them away.

THE STARRY-EYED COUPLE walked slowly back toward the wagon train, savoring every moment of their private time together.

Breanna told John she had prayed many times a day that the Lord would bring him back to her so she could tell him how much she loved him. She brought up the times he had been there to protect her from harm, then had slipped away, leaving her another silver medallion.

"Oh, John," she sighed, "each time I thought my heart was going to shatter with sorrow."

He patted the hand that gripped his arm. "Just doing as you told me—staying out of your life. At least, to a degree."

"I know, darling. The only person to blame was myself." She thought a moment, then said, "That day in Hay Springs when you appeared out of nowhere and made that awful brute who was manhandling me eat his cigar, I—"

"He got off lucky. I had other plans for him—that is, before that rifleman across the street knocked me out. When I came to, you were gone."

"You *do* know what happened, don't you?"

"Yes. You had an obligation in Denver, and you had to leave immediately on the stage."

"I'm glad they explained it to you. I wrote a quick note and left it with the marshal to give to you. I'm assuming you never got it."

"No, I didn't. What did it say?"

"It said for you to come to Denver and see me as soon as possible."

"Well, I guess it wasn't the Lord's time for us to get together."

"I can see that now," Breanna said, squeezing his arm. "And then there was that train ride in the Colorado Rockies—you all dressed up like a stoop-shouldered Mexican."

John laughed. "Really fooled you on that one, didn't I?"

"Well, yes and no. I kept studying you, with something scratching at the back of my mind. Then when we were told you had overcome the outlaws and were taking them down the mountain in the caboose, I knew. I just knew. You fooled me for a while…but when it was all over, I knew it was you."

"Even before Ridge Holloway put the silver medallion in your hand?"

"Yes. Even before that."

They walked silently for a few minutes, then John said, "Breanna…"

"Yes, darling?"

"There's something I need to tell you, and I guess now's as good a time as any. It's about Frank Miller."

Breanna stopped, causing him to stop also. She looked up at him in the pale moonlight with brow furrowed. "Yes? What about Frank?"

"I learned in South Pass City that he broke out of jail, bent on killing you...and what for."

"He's on the loose?"

"He *was* . But now he's dead."

"Dead? What——?"

"On the trail. He was following the wagon train, intending to kill you. The Snakes captured him, tied him to a tree, and left him for the wild beasts."

"I...know about those tactics. But are you telling me you knew Frank? You recognized him?"

"Yes. We met in Cheyenne City a few weeks ago. I heard a man call him by name, so I talked to him."

"And now you found him dead, torn apart by wild beasts?"

"I came along as he was being mauled by a cougar. I killed the cat and was going to cut Frank loose, but he told me there wasn't time. He had something to say, and he had to say it quick. He barely got it out before he died."

"What did he say?"

"He said when I found you, I was to tell you that he was wrong. That he knew you had tried to save his wife. His last words were, 'Please tell her I'm sorry...for everything.' I believe he really meant it."

Breanna nodded, too overcome with emotion to speak. She moved close, wrapped her arms around John, and laid her head against his chest. They clung to each other for several minutes, then without speaking, turned and walked toward the camp.

✦

At sunrise the next morning, wagon wheels grated on rocky ground, and the long line of prairie schooners rolled southward. The cavalrymen rode alongside them and behind them, and Captain Newt Meyer rode out front with Rip Clayson and John Stranger.

As usual, Breanna Baylor sat next to Curly Wesson on the seat of his wagon. She had her Bible open on her lap and was reading aloud to him. From time to time, she lifted her eyes to set them on the broad back of the man on the big black gelding.

They were moving into desert country, less green and more brown, more rocks and fewer trees. The bunch grass and buffalo grass dotted the sandy land with their small clumps of green. The sun gave off less heat than it had only days before, and the wind was not as warm. Autumn was making its presence known in Wyoming.

About two hours had passed when Clayson turned and trotted his horse along the line of wagons, chatting with the men who walked alongside their wagons and with the troopers. It took him about twenty minutes to make his way to the end of the line, then trot back to the front. Breanna happened to be looking up when Rip rejoined Meyer and Stranger. She saw Stranger say something to both men, then wheel Ebony about and ride toward the lead wagon. Drawing abreast, he turned Ebony around and pulled up alongside the wagon on Breanna's side and saw that she had her Bible open on her lap.

"You preaching to Curly?" he asked, returning her smile.

"Not exactly. The Lord knows he needs it, though!"

"Hah!" cackled the old man. "Now just what makes you say that, missy?"

"Nothing, Curly, I was only kidding,"

"*Have* you been preaching to him, Breanna?" Stranger asked.

"Oh, yes. In fact, you've no doubt noticed a change in him since you rode with the train for a day or two back in Nebraska."

"Not sure I know what you mean," Stranger said.

"Remember that horrible lump Curly always had inside his mouth?"

Stranger grinned. "Well, I hadn't given it any thought, but now that you mention it, he *is* a little more respectable looking."

"Tell him what happened, Curly," Breanna said.

"This little gal preached at me 'bout gittin' saved, John. Like you done when you was ridin' with us."

"Yeah?"

"Yessir! An' that's exac'ly what I did. I asked the Lord Jesus to save this ol' sinner, wash him in His blood and save his wretched soul. An' He did, John! He did."

"Hey, wonderful, Curly!" exclaimed Stranger. "Welcome to the family!"

"Thanks. Shore is good to know everythin' is all right between me and the Lord."

"Nothing can match that kind of peace, can it?"

"No, sir! An' I don't need that chew no more neither!"

"I was just reading to Curly from the book of Proverbs," Breanna told John.

"Ah, yes. The business office of the Bible," he replied, nodding. "If all of us would apply the wisdom in that book to our lives every day, we'd save ourselves a lot of heartaches and be a lot more pleasing to God."

"I don't doubt that fer a minute," Curly said. "This ol' boy shore has a lot to learn, though."

"Don't we all?" Stranger said, then rode forward and rejoined Clayson and Meyer.

When the wagon train stopped and set up camp that evening, Captain Meyer announced that they were within a day's drive of Fort Bridger. There had been no further sign of hostile Indians, for which the people were thankful.

After supper, Stranger talked with Rip and Curly at the Wesson wagon. They were discussing what kind of action to take if they ran into snow crossing the Sierra Nevada Mountains.

At the same time, Breanna sat beside Carolyne Fulford next to a small fire. Mothers prepared their children for bed, and the men clustered in small groups, talking about their futures in California. Carolyne was telling Breanna about different medical procedures she had seen her father use, and Breanna listened intently.

Their conversation was interrupted when a rugged-looking sergeant stepped up and said, "Excuse me, ladies. May I butt in?"

"It appears you already did," Carolyne said. "What can we do for you, Sergeant?"

"Pardon my forwardness, but I've been wantin' to meet the pretty nurse here, and I thought now would be as good a time as any." He looked down at Breanna, grinned, and said softly, "Miss Breanna, my name's Bill Finley. I...ah—"

"Are you not feeling well, Sergeant?" Breanna said, rising to her feet. "Tell me what's hurting. I have medicines for various sicknesses and hurts."

Finley grinned and replied, "I'm fine, ma'am, except..."

"Except what?"

"Except I'd just like to get to know you. I really have a strong feelin' toward you."

"I appreciate your straightforwardness, Sergeant," she said, smiling, "but let me say as kindly as I know how—I'm already spoken for." Breanna had been in this position more times than she could remember.

"Words ain't that bindin', ma'am. I don't see a ring on your left hand. I figure there might be a chance for a fella to come into your life and mean more to you than some fella who's only spoken for you but not made it official."

"There is *no* chance, Sergeant. You may be excused."

"Whoa! Wait a minute now," Finley chuckled, lifting palms forward. "I'm not one to back off easy. I think when a woman says no to a friendly man, she really means yes."

"You can take my word for it, Sergeant. When I say *no*, I mean *no*. Now, as I said, you may be excused."

Finley grinned, shook his head, and said, "Don't you beat all? You see, honey, it's a little feisty filly like you that really sparks interest in me. I like a gal with spirit."

Breanna's attention was drawn to the towering figure of John Stranger, who stood six feet behind Finley. She had not noticed his approach and had no idea how long he had been standing there.

"Are you hard of hearing, Sergeant?" she said. "I said you may be excused!"

Finley took a step closer to her and, grinning broadly, said, "I can tell you like me, honey. Why not drop the indignant facade and admit it. You and I could make beautiful music together."

"Not with the discord you bring, Sergeant," Stranger said. "Now move on."

Finley turned to face the owner of the voice. "What business is it of yours?" he gruffed.

"Miss Baylor happens to be *my* woman, and we both like the arrangement. I have the utmost respect for the uniform of the United States Army, and I'd hate to bloody it. But the one you're wearing *will* get bloody if you don't move on. I heard the lady excuse you twice." Few men had ever spoken so boldly to Bill Finley.

"I was only tryin' to make friends with the lady, mister. That ain't no crime."

"It is when she doesn't want to make friends and tells you to make tracks."

Neither man was aware that people were staring at them from every direction.

"Well, I just decided I ain't movin' on unless you can make me," Finley said, his eyes sparkling with the anticipation of battle.

Breanna saw Stranger bristle. She rushed around Finley to face him, her back to John, and said, "Sergeant, believe me, if you force John, you'll be sorry. You've never fought a man like him. I know what he can do, and I'm the one who'll have to try to put you back together after he's done with you. Take my word for it, you can't win."

Finley lifted his line of sight to Stranger and felt the power of those icy gray eyes.

"Listen to me," Breanna said. "I can see that you've been in many a fight. Correct?"

"Yeah."

"You win them all?"

"No."

"Well, just think of the worst beating you ever took. Would you want to fight that man again?"

The sergeant frowned. "Nope."

"Well, there's an old saying, Sergeant. *Good judgment comes from experience, and a lot of that comes from bad judgment.* You understand what I'm telling you?"

Finley raised his eyes to the man who stood eyeing him, then meeting Breanna's gaze again, he nodded and turned away. When he had disappeared in the surrounding darkness, Captain Meyer moved in quickly and said to Breanna, "I appreciate what you did, miss, but maybe you should've let the sergeant get his block knocked off. He's a good soldier, but he's got a bit of belligerence and bully in him that needs to be pounded out."

"By someone else, perhaps, Captain," Breanna said, "but not by John Stranger when he's protecting me. You wouldn't have much sergeant left."

Meyer grinned, looked at Stranger, then said, "I have a feeling you speak from experience, ma'am."

"I do. This is one man you don't want to see riled."

"I believe you, ma'am," the captain said, then touched his hat, nodded at Stranger, and walked away.

"How about another moonlight walk?" John asked. "That is, if Carolyne will excuse us."

"No problem," Carolyne smiled. "It's about time for me to go and find Rip."

Arm in arm, John and Breanna made their way outside the circle of wagons and strolled along the double-rutted trail where hundreds of prairie schooners had rolled westward in their trek to California.

"Thanks for talking sense to that soldier," John said. "I

wouldn't want to bloody his uniform, but I would've if he hadn't backed off. Any man who'd force himself on you would find himself in real trouble."

Breanna squeezed his arm and smiled as she looked up at him. "You've already demonstrated that, darling, and it means more to me than you'll ever know."

They found a moon-drenched spot and sat on a rounded boulder and talked for about an hour. Then they prayed together, asking God to give them wisdom about their future together.

The next day was a cloudy Saturday. The seventeen wagons moved at a slow but steady pace, angling southwest across the arid land. It was midafternoon when the stockade fence and the squat buildings of Fort Bridger came into view. The clouds were breaking up, and yellow shafts of sunlight shined through.

Captain Meyer galloped ahead of the wagon train with his lieutenant beside him. They reached the gate and disappeared inside. Some ten minutes later—when the wagons were within a mile of the fort—the two officers rode through the gate and galloped back.

Rip Clayson and John Stranger rode just in front of the lead wagon. Breanna and Curly listened when the two officers drew up.

"They're ready for you, Mr. Clayson," Meyer said. "You can pull all the wagons inside the fort."

"Won't that crowd the place?"

"There's room. The Shoshonis have been on the prowl, and Colonel Lynch wants the wagons safe in the stockade. One of our patrols had a battle with them earlier today. They came back carrying five dead troopers, and we've got eight men shot up pretty bad. Five of them are critical. Our post physician is working furiously to keep them alive. I—" He looked toward Breanna, then said to Clayson, "I told Colonel Lynch we have a nurse in the wagon train, and I…well, I sort of volunteered her services."

"That's all right, Captain," Breanna said. "I'll be more than glad to help."

Meyer smiled. "I knew you would, ma'am. Colonel Lynch took me immediately to Dr. Laird and we told him about you. He was mighty glad to hear that a real nurse would be helping him."

"That isn't possibly Dr. *David* Laird, is it?"

"Why, yes, ma'am. Do you know him?"

"Yes. He and I worked together in Las Cruces, New Mexico, about three years ago. There was a typhoid epidemic all over that area."

"If I'd known that, ma'am, I would've told him your name."

"That's all right, Captain. He'll find out soon enough." She paused, then asked, "Did you learn anything about Colonel Wade Moore?"

"Yes, ma'am. He's still having those chest pains. I know it'll help him to see his wife."

"I'm sure it will," Breanna said.

John tugged on the reins and slowed Ebony enough to let the lead wagon catch up to him. "There's no letup in your line of work, is there?" he said.

"No," Breanna smiled. "It's sort of like *your* work. Always someone needing help."

"I've had quite a bit of experience patching up wounded men. I'll be glad to do anything I can, sweetheart."

"I'll sure tell Dr. Laird, honey."

Curly grinned. "You two are somethin' else, you are. Real lovebirds. Just like me an' my wife used to be...from the day we met till the day she died. When you two gonna tie the knot?"

John and Breanna exchanged glances.

"When the Lord gives us the sign that it's His time for it," John said.

"Well, guess I cain't argue with that. Miss Breanna's been teachin' me 'bout how the Lord has a plan fer His children's lives, and how we hafta do a lotta prayin' and Bible readin' to be sure we don't get in His way an' mess things up."

"Well, she's been teaching you right," Stranger said. "And nobody ever had a prettier teacher than you've got."

"Hey, don't I know that! An' I'll tell you somethin', sonny. If'n ol' Curly here was a few years younger, I'd be a-givin' you a run fer yer money!"

John laughed and wiped a hand across his brow. "Whew! I'm sure glad you were born a hundred years ago!"

The three of them had a good laugh together, then John trotted Ebony forward to join Rip Clayson and the two officers.

The gates of Fort Bridger swung wide, allowing the wagons to roll inside. A young trooper directed Curly to the spot where he was to park his wagon. When it rolled to a halt, Breanna reached behind her and picked up her medical bag. John Stranger was off his horse quickly and beside the wagon to help Breanna down.

"I see they have a telegraph here," he said. "I really should let Marshal Duvall know where I am, and that I'm going to stick with the wagon train until it's safe in California. I'll find you as soon as I get a wire sent to him."

Breanna knew that John kept Chief U.S. Marshal Solomon Duvall in Denver informed of his whereabouts in case he was needed. Duvall's office had become a main contact point for lawmen and fort commanders all over the West who needed to locate him.

"All right," Breanna said. "I'll tell Dr. Laird you've offered to help."

Captain Meyer appeared with the fort commandant at his side. John and Breanna were introduced to Colonel Derek Lynch, who was in his late fifties. Just then Marian Moore rushed up and spoke breathlessly to Captain Meyer, asking where she could find her husband. Meyer told her he was being kept in a spare room in the officers' quarters. He would take her there right away. Breanna told Marian she would look in on her and the colonel later.

Lynch pointed Stranger to the telegraph room and led Breanna toward the infirmary, a small log building in the very center of the fort. Next to it stood the guardhouse, and beyond that the mess hall.

Blue-uniformed men milled about the fort, which covered about three acres inside the stockade fence. Off to one side were the stables and the corral. On the opposite side were long rows of log barracks, and at a right angle to them were the officers' quarters, the commandant's office, a large meeting room, and the telegraph room.

Though the afternoon was cool with a touch of fall in the air, the infirmary door was propped open. Colonel Lynch led Breanna to the door, then stepped in front of her, stuck his head in, and said, "Doc, I have the nurse from the wagon train here."

"Oh, great!" came a voice familiar to Breanna. "Please bring her in."

3

COLONEL DEREK LYNCH stepped back from the door, allowing Breanna Baylor to enter the infirmary, then moved in behind her. Breanna's gaze swept through the room, taking in a dozen cots lining three walls. Seven were occupied. An eighth patient lay on the examining and operating table near the back wall. A white cabinet stood flat against the rear wall, sided by a long counter where a wash basin sat next to a well pump. The odor of wood alcohol mingled with the odor of ether. Only two of the wounded men had been attended to by the doctor. The others lay in pain, wrapped in makeshift bandages, awaiting their turn.

Dr. David Laird was at the operating table working on a wounded soldier. When he heard footsteps, he turned from his work momentarily to look over his shoulder. His eyes revealed the smile concealed by his surgeon's mask.

"Nurse, you sure are a welcome sight! I—" Dr. Laird straightened up, turned all the way around with a bloody scalpel in his hand, and gasped, "Breanna!"

"Hello, Doctor," she replied, smiling. "It's good to see you again."

"Same here, dear lady," he sighed. "We'll talk later. Wash

basin is right over here. Get washed up as quickly as you can. I needed you two hours ago."

"I see you haven't changed a bit," she said.

"Can't teach an old dog new tricks, you know."

Breanna had the attention of the men on the cots as she made her way to the cupboard, her ankle-length skirt swishing. She placed her medical bag on the counter, asked Colonel Lynch to work the pump handle, and scrubbed with lye soap. Then she took her place on the opposite side of the operating table, a surgeon's mask covering her mouth and nose. Colonel Lynch was feeling a bit light-headed from the sights and smells and excused himself.

The young soldier on the table had an arrow in his chest. His bloody shirt lay over the back of a nearby chair. Breanna saw two other bloody arrows lying on the floor. She could see that the young corporal was in serious trouble. The Shoshoni arrow had come dangerously near his heart, and there was much bleeding.

Breanna steadied the arrow while Laird carefully cut around it and finally was able to remove it. Small pieces had broken off the arrow tip and had to be removed one by one. Breanna adjusted artery clamps as needed to give the doctor space to work, and dabbed at oozing blood with cotton pads to keep the opening as clear as possible.

While she worked, she told Dr. Laird about John Stranger coming into her life, that John was well-experienced with wounded men, and that he would be there to help after he had sent a wire to the marshal in Denver. Laird commented about John's last name and told her he was glad she had met the man of her dreams. He said he would welcome John's help.

"What can you tell me about Colonel Moore, Doctor?" Breanna asked as the surgery on the young soldier continued.

"I'm afraid it's his heart. At first I thought it was pleurisy, but the more I study him, the more I'm convinced he's having heart pains. He told me about the death of his son—how the boy sacrificed his own life to save him. He also told me how rough he'd always been on the boy, accusing him of cowardice. I think the heart pains may be mostly stress related, brought on by the guilt he's feeling."

"Maybe he's got a more tender heart than one might think, given his crusty manner," Breanna said.

"Well, I've told him he mustn't go on with the wagon train. He needs complete rest. I'm treating him with sedatives, but it's rest that's going to get him over it—that and reconciliation with his wife."

"He must've told you that she's been pretty cold to him since Jason was killed."

"He spilled it all to me."

"Good. I've gotten to know Mrs. Moore pretty well, Doctor. I have no doubt she'll make the effort to reconcile."

"The man is strong. With proper rest and things right between him and his wife, I feel confident he'll be all right."

Dr. Laird and Breanna worked like a precision team together. When the corporal started to come around, Laird instructed Breanna to apply more ether. He was pleased at the skill he saw in her hands, a skill he had admired since the first day they had worked together in Las Cruces.

"What's this young man's name, Doctor?" Breanna asked.

"Lenny Pinder. Farm boy from Iowa. I've gotten to know him well. In fact, I know every one of these men on the cots." He looked in their direction and said, "We're working as fast as we can, fellas."

One of them spoke up. "I wasn't in much of a hurry till she came in, Doc. Now, I can't wait for attention."

The others laughed in spite of their pain.

"With such a pretty nurse to look after me, I think I'll stay sick for a long time," another said.

They laughed again. Blushing, Breanna turned and looked at them. Her smile was hidden by the mask she wore, but they could see it in her eyes.

"Complications, Doctor?" Breanna asked when she turned back and saw the concern on Dr. Laird's face.

"Yes," he nodded, keeping his eyes on his work. "The heart has sustained some damage. I've done everything I can do. We'll close him up and leave him in the hands of God. Unless God intervenes, he's not going to make it. He could easily hemorrhage to death."

Breanna looked down at the pale, boyish face and wondered if Corporal Lenny Pinder was a Christian.

While the doctor sutured the wound, Breanna looked up to see John Stranger step through the open door. The eyes of the soldiers on the cots followed his towering figure as he strode past them, giving them a warm smile.

Breanna introduced John to Dr. Laird, who asked him a few questions to test his knowledge of bandages and bleeding. Satisfied, Dr. Laird gave him instructions on what to look for and how to care for the wounded men until he and Breanna could get to them.

Corporal Pinder was moved to a cot, and the man in the next most serious condition was laid on the table. Hours passed. At suppertime, other soldiers fed the wounded men and a couple of privates brought food and drink for Dr. Laird, Breanna, and

John Stranger. The three ate quickly, then returned to their work. It was just after nine o'clock when they finished the last of the medical work and surgeries. The first three men Dr. Laird had worked on were critical. All three had taken arrows, one in the back and the other two in the chest.

As the doctor and his helpers were washing up, Colonel Lynch and Captain Meyer came in and commended them for the excellent job they had done. Laird took the colonel and the captain aside and explained that three of the men were in critical condition. He would stay in the infirmary with them all night. If they survived until morning, they had a good chance of making it.

Laird returned to John and Breanna and said, "I want to thank both of you for your help. Without it, some of these men might be dead by now."

"I'm just glad we arrived when we did," Breanna said.

"You do well for someone who's never had formal medical training, Mr. Stranger," the doctor said. "You should have been a physician."

"Thanks, Doc, but I don't think so."

"Well, you sure have talent in that area," Laird said.

"He has talents in many areas, Doctor," Breanna said. "I never knew a man who could do so many things well. He's even a great preacher!"

Colonel Lynch's face lit up. "Is that so? Well, tomorrow's Sunday, and at present Fort Bridger has no chaplain. Mr. Stranger, would you consider preaching our Sunday services for us?"

"I think Miss Baylor's estimate of my preaching may be a little biased, Colonel, but if you can talk Mr. Clayson here into delaying the wagon train's departure for a day, I'll be glad to preach for you."

All eyes swung to the wagon master, who had entered the infirmary moments before. Rip rubbed the back of his neck for a moment, then said, "Well, we're already running nearly two weeks behind schedule, Colonel, but I've heard about John's preaching from several sources. I'd like to hear him myself. Okay. We'll pull out first thing Monday morning."

"Good!" the colonel exclaimed. "Then it's settled. I'll put the word out to the men."

Breanna quickly told John and Rip that Dr. Laird was prescribing extended rest for Colonel Moore and that the Moores would not be traveling further with the wagon train. Breanna, John, and Rip decided to go see the Moores and went together to the room in the officers' quarters where Marian sat beside her husband's bed. Marian was relieved to hear that Dr. Laird thought her husband would be fine if they wintered at the fort. The colonel smiled and said they would join the first California-bound wagon train that came through next spring.

"In the meantime," he said, "Marian and I've got a lot to talk about together. I guess the Good Lord knew what I needed more than I did."

"He always does," Breanna said. "Always."

Morning came with a few puffy clouds scudding across a clear sky. Colonel Lynch was awakened at sunrise by Dr. Laird, who told him that two of the three critical men had died during the night. Only Lenny Pinder was still holding onto life. Pinder seemed better, but the nature of his wound left the doctor wondering if he would make it.

During breakfast the sad news of the two deaths spread through the fort. The two men would be buried that afternoon. Just before the morning service, John and Breanna visited the men in the infirmary, doing what they could to cheer them up. Colonel Lynch and Dr. Laird came in while they were talking to Lenny Pinder, who was quite weak but getting some color in his face.

"I just asked Doc if you men could attend the preaching service this morning," Lynch said, "providing some of your fellow-soldiers carry you outside on your stretchers. He gave permission for everyone except Corporal Pinder. How about it?"

There was immediate response from the five wounded men. They all wanted to attend the service.

"Colonel, are you going to hold the services just outside the infirmary like usual?" Pinder asked weakly.

"Yes. It's not cool enough to move us inside the mess hall yet."

"Good," Pinder said. "Then I can hear Mr. Stranger preach, too."

Breanna leaned over and placed her hand on the corporal's shoulder. "You'll be able to hear him, Lenny. John speaks softly most of the time, but when he gets to preaching, his volume rises."

John Stranger gave Breanna a look of indignation and everyone laughed. Even Lenny Pinder.

Most of the Fort Bridger personnel attended the preaching service. They sang gospel songs and hymns by memory, then the colonel introduced John Stranger, making a few joking remarks about his name.

John went along with it, added his own touch of humor, then opened his Bible. His heart was heavy over the recent deaths of the soldiers, and he chose Hebrews 9:27 as his text: *"And as it is appointed unto men once to die, and after this, the judgment."*

He reminded all of his hearers that as death had come to their comrades, so one day it would come to them all. With tears in his eyes, John warned of hell and judgment for those who die in their sins, and made it clear that salvation comes only by repentance toward God and faith toward the Lord Jesus Christ. At the close of the message, several men, including three of the five wounded ones, responded to the invitation to receive Christ.

After the wounded men had been carried on their stretchers back into the infirmary, Corporal Pinder spoke to Dr. Laird and asked if he would tell John Stranger he wanted to talk to him. Moments later, Stranger entered the crowded log building, spoke to the wounded men on their cots, then stood over Lenny Pinder.

"Colonel Lynch said you wanted to see me," he said, smiling.

"Yes, sir. I heard your sermon. And…and I want to talk to you about it."

Stranger picked up a straight-backed wooden chair, placed it beside the cot, and sat down. "Questions, Lenny?"

"Yes, sir."

"Shoot."

"Well, sir…in your sermon you said that Jesus died for sinners, and that we're all sinners, right?"

"Yes. He sure did, and we sure are. Romans 3:23 says, *All have sinned, and come short of the glory of God.* And Ecclesiastes 7:20 says, *For there is not a just man upon earth, that doeth good, and sinneth not."*

Pinder nodded. "I believe that, Mr. Stranger, but what if...what if a man stole something from someone and never got caught? And because he never got caught, the thief never made restitution."

Stranger leaned forward, placing his elbows on his knees. "You talking about Lenny Pinder as the thief?"

Pinder hesitated, then said, "Yes, sir. I...I won't go into details, but I stole something very valuable from a neighboring farmer when I was eighteen. My conscience has eaten me alive, Mr. Stranger. I wanted to go to the man and confess my crime before I joined the army, but I just couldn't work up the courage to do it. And now...now, I'm dying."

"Lenny, Dr. Laird says you're better today, and—"

Lenny rolled his head back and forth on the pillow. "No, Mr. Stranger. I know. Somehow I know I'm not going to make it. I...I want to be forgiven for my crime, and for all my other sins. Help me. Please."

John Stranger told young Pinder the story of the dying thieves at Calvary. One thief railed at Jesus and died in his sins, but the other admitted he was getting what he deserved. Before he died, he asked Jesus for salvation, including forgiveness for his crimes and all his other sins.

When Stranger told how Jesus promised the dying thief they would be together that very day in paradise, Lenny Pinder's lower lip quivered and tears filled his eyes. "Mr. Stranger," he said weakly, "if I asked Jesus to forgive me and save my soul right now, He would do it, right?"

"He sure would, son. His Word says, *Whosoever shall call upon the name of the Lord shall be saved.* And Jesus said, *Him that cometh to me I will in no wise cast out.* You call on Him right now,

I guarantee you, He won't cast you out."

"Then…that's what I want to do. Will you help me?"

"Of course," Stranger said, laying a hand on Lenny's shoulder.

John Stranger helped Corporal Lenny Pinder word his prayer, as the farm boy from Iowa called on Jesus Christ to save him. When Lenny was finished, Stranger spoke words of assurance and comfort. Weak and sick as he was, Lenny smiled and wept for joy, knowing he had been forgiven for all of his sins and would go to heaven when he died. The other patients who had become Christians that morning rejoiced with Pinder, sharing the sweetness of salvation.

John Stranger found Dr. Laird and asked what he thought about young Pinder's chances of living. Laird said that the damage to his heart and the wound next to it could result in his death. Only time would tell.

Stranger went to Breanna, who was removing a splinter from a soldier's hand. He was part of the burial detail for the soldiers who had died during the night and had gotten the splinter from the handle of the shovel he was using. They were sitting on a bench in the sunshine. Stranger waited till she was through and the soldier had gone, then he sat beside her and told her of Lenny's conversion. Breanna was elated at the news and took John by the hand and hurried to the infirmary.

For the rest of the day, Dr. Laird kept a close watch on Lenny, fearing that his time was short. As night fell, Lenny began to grow weaker.

After the evening preaching service, John and Breanna took a stroll around the inside perimeter of the fort's stockade walls. The time spent together served to deepen their devotion to each other and to mold their hearts in a stronger bond of love. Once again they prayed together, asking God to guide them in their decisions. They also thanked the Lord for the way He had worked in hearts that day, bringing so many to Himself. They prayed too for Lenny Pinder, asking the Lord to spare his life unless, in His wisdom, He had higher plans for him.

Before retiring for the night, they went to the infirmary and found Dr. Laird sitting beside Lenny, who was asleep and resting easy. Laird still had hope that Lenny would make it. If he lived till sunrise, he most likely would be over the hump.

Dawn was a gray hint on the eastern horizon when John Stranger awakened where he slept on the ground to the whisper of a voice calling his name. He blinked and sat up and saw that it was Dr. Laird. "Yes, Doctor?"

Laird hunkered down beside him and said in a choked voice, "Lenny didn't make it, Mr. Stranger. He died ten minutes ago."

Sadness washed over the tall man as he threw back the covers of his bedroll and sighed, "It was God's will, Doctor. You did all you could."

"That I did. There comes that point when we doctors can go no further. He's in God's hands now."

"Yes," John said, rising to his feet as Laird rose with him. "I'll tell Breanna as soon as she gets up. Have you let Colonel Lynch know yet?"

"Not yet. I'm going to his quarters now. I wanted to advise you first."

Stranger thanked him, and as the doctor moved away, he

called after him, "If the burial can be right away, I'll be glad to conduct the funeral service."

There was sadness in Fort Bridger over the loss of Corporal Lenny Pinder, but the Christians also rejoiced that the boyish young soldier was now with the Lord.

John Stranger conducted the funeral service at the graveside. He and Brearina, along with Rip Clayson, went to the officers' quarters and told the Moores good-bye, then the wagon train rolled out of the fort with its cavalry escort.

4

A FARM WAGON threw up dust as it bounced and fishtailed at full speed northward toward San Francisco amid vineyards, orchards, and truck farms. The two horses pressed into the harness, running as fast as they could go. They seemed to know the trip was urgent. Foam flew from their open mouths, flecking their sweaty bodies as the young woman in the seat snapped the reins, shouting at the top of her voice to hasten them on.

In the seat on either side of her were her eight-year-old son and her six-year-old daughter. The boy's head, which lay in her lap, was wrapped in a blood-stained towel. The girl crowded close to her mother, clinging to her slender waist for all she was worth.

The mother was near panic. She could not spare the horses. Her son's life was possibly at stake.

Like many great cities of the world, San Francisco was built on a harbor which was part of a great bay extending forty-five miles inland and varying from three to thirteen miles in width. And like many boom and bust towns of the West in the early 1870s, its main streets were lined with hotels, gambling casinos, dance halls, and saloons. In the area known as the "Big Bad" Square Plaza, banks and other financial institutions crowded together with shops of every description, restaurants, clothing stores, and the like.

San Francisco, with its sixty-five thousand residents, was larger than any town between the Pacific Coast and Kansas City, Missouri. It was a busy, bustling town of fog-blurred mornings and clear afternoons, the sun shining on a blue bay flecked with white caps and a brisk, clean wind whipping the sails of the ships that passed in and out of the harbor.

Always on the minds of San Francisco's residents, and those who visited there, was the threat of earthquakes. From its earliest days (the town was founded in 1776 and named after explorer José Francisco Ortega), the area was frequently shaken by quakes. Most were minor, but some were major. The minor ones merely unnerved San Francisco's residents. The major ones shattered windows, cracked walls, and often left small crevices in yards and streets.

On one thing the seismologists agreed—the quakes were going to become more serious, and they looked for a "big one" to come sometime around the turn of the century.

The formidable coast ranges shielded the inland valleys from the fogs and winds that plagued the town and bay. The flat lands immediately south of San Francisco and the valley east of the coast ranges produced healthy orchards, vineyards, and fields of fruits and vegetables.

The young mother who raced the family wagon into San Francisco with her children beside her was from a fruit and vegetable farm several miles south of town.

Dottie Harper's wagon thundered into San Francisco on Third Street, racing northward, then threw dirt as she veered it onto Market Street and headed for Powell. The town's two hospitals were only a block apart on Powell Street, but Dottie chose to go to City Hospital. It had more doctors than Smith Memorial, and her chances of getting immediate attention for James were better there.

At the corner of Market and Powell, she almost struck an elderly couple just starting across the intersection as she whipped the wagon around the corner and raced toward the hospital's front doors. Dottie jerked on the reins and skidded the wagon to a halt, the horses blowing hard.

Her heart beat against her ribs like a caged bird bent on escape as she climbed down, catching her skirt momentarily on the brake handle. Her anxiety rose when the towel around her son's head slipped down and she saw fresh blood flowing from his left ear.

"Here, Molly Kate," she said, extending her arms to the girl. "Let Mommy help you down." Molly Kate's pallid face and widened eyes gave evidence of the fear she felt for her brother.

Dottie placed the girl on the ground, then leaned against the wagon's side and gathered James into her arms. The air was cool, but sweat trickled down the side of her face. James was conscious, but had not spoken a word since they left the farm. His eyes were dull and his mouth hung open listlessly, shock shadowing his features.

Dottie cradled James in her arms and headed for the hospital entrance. Molly Kate hurried along behind her. Dottie was almost to the double doors when one of them swung open. A young man with an arm in a sling started out, saw her coming, and held the door open.

The receptionist at the desk took one look at Dottie's face and knew something was seriously wrong. When her glance fell on the bloody towel that encircled the boy's head, she rose to her feet.

"We have an emergency here, ma'am," Dottie gasped. "My son's left ear is bleeding."

The receptionist's features stiffened when she looked at James and saw also the purple bruises on his face, the swollen left eye, and the split in his upper lip.

She glanced at Molly Kate, making sure she was untouched, then said, "Your name, ma'am?"

"Dottie Harper. My son's name is James."

The receptionist picked up a pencil and scribbled quickly on a sheet of paper. "H-A-R-P-E-R, ma'am?"

"Yes."

"And your address?"

"General delivery, San Bruno. We have a truck farm and orchard near San Bruno."

The receptionist wrote it down hastily, dropped the pencil, and said, "Come with me. You can bring the little girl, too."

As they hurried down a long hall, the receptionist studied James and asked, "Same person who beat the boy put those bruises on *your* face?"

A cold knot formed in Dottie's stomach. Her throat constricted, and she attempted to clear it.

"Sometimes in cases like these, we're told that the child fell," the receptionist said.

"No. No, he didn't fall. He—"

"Right in here." The woman stopped suddenly and pushed the door of the examining room open. "Lay him on the table. I'll get a doctor right away."

Molly Kate's eyes were wide as she looked around the room. It smelled like medicine, and there were two large cabinets with shelves full of cans and bottles. Three straight-backed chairs stood against the back wall.

The receptionist paused at the door. "Somebody gave that little fellow an awful beating. And whoever it was got pretty rough with you too, didn't he?"

Dottie bit her lip, but did not reply. The woman disappeared down the hall.

James was still conscious, but his eyes were dull. As Dottie made him as comfortable as possible, she said over her shoulder, "Molly Kate, honey, why don't you sit down on one of those chairs?"

Molly Kate, who had the same blond hair and sky-blue eyes as her mother, asked, "Is James gonna be all right, Mommy?"

"Yes, honey. The doctor will be here in a minute. He'll make James all right. You go sit down."

Dottie studied her son, thinking that he looked more and more like his father. He had the same dark-red hair and hazel eyes as Jerrod, and the same prominent cheekbones, chin, and jaw line.

People intermittently passed by in the hall, moving slowly and speaking in low tones. Their soft sounds were suddenly over-ridden by rapid footsteps, and a slender man in his late forties rushed through the door. He wore a white smock over his regular clothes.

"Mrs. Harper," he said, "I'm Dr. Glenn Olson. Mrs. Stratton—the receptionist—told me the boy had been beaten severely and that you had taken some abuse, too. Both are quite obvious."

Dottie closed her eyes and nodded. Then opening them, she said, "I'm fine. James's ear has been bleeding. You can see the towel is soaked with blood."

Dr. Olson bent over the boy, removed the towel, and did a quick examination of the ear. He then studied the facial bruises, the cut lip, and looked into the dull eyes. "It'll take me a while to assess the damage, Mrs. Harper. There's a waiting room—"

He was interrupted by a white-clad nurse who came through the door, saying, "Sorry it took me so long to get here, Doctor. We had a small emergency in the ward, and I couldn't leave right away."

"I understand. Nurse Nola Warren, this is Mrs. Dottie Harper," Olson said. "The boy, here, is James. I don't know the pretty little lady's name back there on the chair."

"Molly Kate," Dottie said, her voice barely more than a whisper.

"As I was saying, Mrs. Harper, there's a waiting room down the hall to your right. If you and Molly Kate will wait down there, I'll come and talk to you as soon as I know what we're dealing with here."

"All right, Doctor. Thank you. Come, Molly."

The little girl hurried to her mother and grasped the hand that was offered her. As they moved toward the door, Nurse Warren looked at Dottie's facial bruises and the worry in her eyes, and said, "Doctor, wouldn't it be all right if Mrs. Harper stayed while you examine James? I'm sure she'd appreciate being able to remain with him."

Dottie smiled at the nurse and held tight to Molly Kate's hand.

"Oh. Well, of course," Olson said. "That would be better in this case anyhow. I need to ask her some questions."

Molly Kate returned to her chair and Dottie moved up to the table and stood opposite the doctor. Olson told Nola that he needed to take some stitches in the boy's cut lip even though the cut was scabbing and the bleeding had stopped. He then used a reflector to examine James's ear. The boy winced when he touched it, but did not cry out.

"Sorry, son," Olson said softly, "I don't want to hurt you, but I have to see into your ear canal. Does it hurt real bad?"

James seemed only half-conscious. "Not real bad, sir," he said.

"You're just a brave young man. I think it must hurt quite a bit."

James did not reply. He looked up at his mother, who was holding his hand.

Tears misted Dottie's eyes. She managed a smile and said, "He truly is a brave young man, Doctor."

Olson finished his examination and laid the reflector aside. "I don't think there's anything serious here, Mrs. Harper. The bleeding has nearly stopped. James took a sharp blow right on the ear, enough to break the wall of the canal near the opening. Anything to do with our ears usually bleeds more freely than most other parts of our bodies. He'll be all right. I'll put some salve in there that will help aid its healing. You can take some home and apply it a couple of times a day for the next week. There shouldn't be any more problems with it." He paused for effect, then added, "That is, unless he gets another beating like this one."

Dottie's face flushed.

"Who did it, Mrs. Harper?" pressed Dr. Olson.

Dottie bit down on her lower lip, closed her eyes, and let the tears spill down her cheeks. She drew a shuddering breath, but when she tried to answer, she couldn't.

Doctor and nurse exchanged glances, then Olson placed a hand on Dottie's shoulder and said, "Your husband?"

She nodded in little jerky movements and started to weep. Molly Kate slid off the chair, hurried to her mother, and wrapped her arms around her at the waist. "Don't cry, Mommy!" she said. "Please don't cry!"

Nola took Dottie by the hand, squeezed tight, and said, "Here, come sit down."

Dottie eased down on one of the wooden chairs at the back of the room, and Molly Kate crawled up on the chair beside her. Nola went to the cupboard, picked up a square cloth about the size of a hanky, and gave it to Dottie, saying, "Here, honey. Use this."

"You stay there and rest, Mrs. Harper," Dr. Olson said. "Nurse Warren and I will get these stitches in, then you and I can talk."

The smell of ether was strong in the room while Dr. Olson took stitches in James's lip, assisted by Nola. When they were finished, the nurse began cleaning up while the doctor turned a chair around and sat on it backwards, facing Dottie.

Dottie didn't want to talk to the doctor about Jerrod. The whole thing was like a bad dream. She wished she could just wake up and it would all be gone. She would rather run and hide than tell Dr. Olson she was married to a man who was possibly losing his mind.

"Mrs. Harper, I want you to tell me exactly what happened,"

Olson said. "What caused your husband to beat on the boy like he did, and what brought on the battering *you* took?"

Dottie's chest felt heavy. Her hands were damp and she blotted them on her skirt.

"Mrs. Harper," Dr. Olson said in a tone he would use with a child, "as a physician in private practice and as a staff member of this hospital, I am bound by the law to report cases of assault and battery to the San Francisco police."

Dottie's hands shook. "Even if the assault took place outside the city—in another county?"

Olson scrubbed a hand over his face. "Well—no. The San Francisco police have no jurisdiction beyond the city limits. Where did this happen?"

"On our farm. We live near San Bruno."

"That's in San Mateo County?"

"Yes."

"There's nothing to keep me from notifying Sheriff Donner that this child was brutally beaten by his father. It would interest him, I'm sure. Ma'am, another beating like this could mean your son's life. You dare not allow him to be beaten again. Has your husband done this before?"

"Yes. Several times, but none this severe."

"And Molly Kate? Does he beat her too?"

"Not like he does James, but the spankings have become beatings."

"And how about you? Has he done this to you before?" Olson asked, eyeing Dottie's facial bruises.

Dottie nodded and swallowed hard, eyes suddenly bright with tears.

"Those look recent. You got them today, right—for trying to stop him from beating James?"

"Yes," she whispered.

"Tell me about it."

Dottie sniffed and wiped away more tears. "Well—James spilled his milk at the breakfast table. He was playing around—as boys do—he shouldn't have been playing at the table, I'll admit. But when the milk went over, Jerrod lost his temper and backhanded him. Knocked him off his chair. James was stunned, but Jerrod picked him up, yelling at him for spilling the milk, and struck him again and again. I screamed at him to stop, but he kept right on. I jumped on him, and he let go of James and turned on me. He hit me in the face. Twice."

Dr. Olson shook his head slowly. Dottie noticed that Nola was now standing over James, who was still under from the ether.

"Then what happened?" Olson asked.

"He went after James again. I was able to get to my feet, and I grabbed the cast-iron skillet from the stove and hit him on the head from behind. It knocked him out. Jerrod had already hitched the horses to the wagon before breakfast, and I just put the children on the wagon seat and headed for the hospital."

"How old is your husband, ma'am?"

"Thirty-two."

"So he's what—about four or five years older than you?"

"I'm twenty-eight."

"How long has this behavior been going on?"

"Well, off and on for about eight years. It just never was this bad, nor was it very often. It's gotten worse in the last five months. He's been having more and more of these temper fits—

that's what I call them—since late April, maybe early May. And with each one, he's become more violent. But..."

"But *what?*"

"I need to explain something to you, Doctor."

"No one's calling for me," said Olson. "I have time to listen."

"Jerrod was in the Civil War, Doctor. Union army. He was made a sergeant early on because he showed a natural instinct for fighting and a knack for leading men. But with each battle, as he saw his men getting killed and maimed, he became increasingly fearful. I assume he began to fear the same thing could happen to him. I didn't know him then, but this is what I've pieced together. He won't hardly talk about it."

"I'm beginning to get the picture, Mrs. Harper. This is what we call combat fatigue—shell shock."

"Yes, so I've learned from my sister. She's a C.M.N. We write to each other periodically. I told her about this in a letter, and she wrote back and explained it to me."

"Where does she work, Mrs. Harper?" Nola asked.

Dottie sent a glance her way. "Breanna's a visiting nurse. She works out of Denver, Colorado. Her sponsoring physician is Dr. Lyle Goodwin."

"Oh, I've heard of him," the nurse said.

"So have I," Olson said. "Dr. Goodwin has quite a reputation in the A.M.A. Excellent man. You say your sister's name is Breanna?"

"Yes. She's not married, so she's still a Baylor. That's my maiden name, of course. Breanna is two years older than me. Her work takes her all over the Rocky Mountain area—sometimes even farther than that." Dottie sighed, took a deep breath and said, "Breanna says these fits are called 'startle reactions' by you doctors."

"Yes," Olson said. "If your husband is a victim of combat fatigue, your sister has called it correctly. Was he treated for this in the army?"

"I don't know. It's almost impossible to get him to talk about it. The only other thing I know is that he was in the battle at Wilson's Creek in Missouri. I think it was in 1861—in August. A cannonball exploded quite close to him. He's got scars on his body where shrapnel hit him. He was released from the army after spending several weeks in a hospital, but it wasn't because of the shrapnel wounds. It was because of the shell shock. The army doctors said he would never be fit for combat again. Jerrod told me that much."

"After one of these temper episodes—startle reactions—is he very repentant, tearful, sorry for his actions?"

"Every one of those. He always begs the children and me to forgive him and promises he'll never do it again."

"He's like two different men, right?"

"Exactly."

"Mm-hmm. Fits the pattern perfectly. I was an army doctor in the Civil War and dealt with shell shock many times—and with its results. So many times it will develop into what we call *dementia praecox.* A split personality. Two different people living in the same body, but only one appearing at a time."

Dottie put her face in her hands, took a deep breath, then raised her head and looked at Dr. Olson through fresh tears. "Why has it taken so long for the shell shock to do this to him? It's been over nine years since his discharge."

"*Dementia praecox* can lie dormant in a man's mind for a while, Mrs. Harper. But in most cases, it eventually crops up in time, and the more often the fits occur, the more violent the victim becomes. This has been the pattern, hasn't it?"

"Yes. For a while it was only me he beat on, but in the past three months, his rage has also turned on the children. I've always backed Jerrod in his discipline of the children, but when the spankings became beatings, I had to interfere. This just made him even more angry. He—he beat a mule to death a few weeks ago in a fit of rage. Another time he beat one of the draft horses with an ax handle. Poor thing will never get over it."

"Let me ask you this, Mrs. Harper," said Olson. "Does Jerrod have nightmares?"

Dottie's lips trembled. "Yes. He's had them off and on over the eight years since his problem began to show up, but nothing like in the past five months. He wakes up screaming in the middle of the night three or four times a week."

"Does he tell you what the nightmares are about?"

"He won't talk about them. But I think he's reliving the battles he fought in, especially Wilson's Creek. One night when he sat up in bed, he used the word *cannonball*. When I told him, he denied it."

The doctor sat for a long moment, then looked Dottie in the eye and said, "Mrs. Harper, I want you to do two things. First, you should report this to Sheriff Donner—especially this most recent incident. Something must be done to prevent Jerrod from further harming you or the children. Like I said, another beating like James took today could kill him."

Dottie's face paled and her voice cracked with emotion as she said, "Doctor, I want to protect my children, but if the sheriff puts Jerrod in jail, it'll destroy him. Not only that, but our farm will dwindle to nothing. It's already suffering because of Jerrod's problem. If the sheriff locks him up, the children and I will have no money—no income."

"The second thing I was going to tell you to do is get help for Jerrod," he said softly,

"You mean *medical* help?"

"Yes. The sheriff needs to know about Jerrod's problem and what he's done to you and the children. He can work with you on this—but instead of simply locking him up, he needs to be institutionalized under the care of a psychiatrist. I'm in sympathy about your financial well-being, Mrs. Harper, but I'm more concerned for your safety. Let me recommend Dr. Matthew Carroll. He's the best psychiatrist on the West Coast. Dr. Carroll is a staff physician here at City Hospital, but he's also head of staff at City Mental Asylum. His office is near the asylum on Dupont Street, a half block from Portsmouth Square Plaza."

Dottie looked sick and afraid. "Doctor, if I—if I suggest to Jerrod that he see Dr. Carroll, he'll fly into a rage. I know it. He'll never submit to it."

"This is why the San Mateo County sheriff must be involved. He can tell Jerrod he has a choice. He can be jailed for what he did to James, or he can agree to get help for himself under the care of Dr. Carroll."

"You mean there's something that can be done to cure him?"

"A total cure, I doubt. But I believe he can be helped. Dr. Carroll is the one to tell you about that. The main thing is to do something about it immediately."

Dottie's mind was in a spin. She could not bear the thought of her husband locked up in the asylum. She loved Jerrod with all her heart. In the quiet reaches of her mind, she told herself that with extra love and care, she could help Jerrod.

"Will you go to Sheriff Donner today and tell him the situation?" Olson asked.

"I—I'll consider it."

"Mrs. Harper, don't put it off," Olson said, rising to his feet. "You get to the sheriff today and have him help you get Jerrod under Dr. Carroll's care."

Dottie licked her lips but did not reply.

Olson sighed and said, "I'll be glad to contact Dr. Carroll for you, if you'd like."

Dottie rose from the chair, took her daughter by the hand, and said, "Thank you, Doctor. I'll let you know. Right now I need to take James and head for home."

The doctor sighed again and said, "Bring him back in four days. If the lip is healing properly, I'll remove the stitches."

Dottie told him she would and thanked him for his kindness and concern.

James was now awake and listening quietly. His lip was swollen where the stitches had been taken, and there was cotton in his left ear. The doctor handed Dottie a jar of salve and urged her once more to take action right away.

Dottie took James in her arms, and with Molly Kate walking beside her, headed down the corridor, past the reception desk, and toward the double doors. When they moved out into the sunlight, Dottie's heart almost stopped, and Molly Kate ejected a tiny fearful whimper.

Standing beside the family wagon was Jerrod Harper, holding the reins of his saddle horse.

5

THE SIGHT OF HER HUSBAND and the somber shadow in his eyes struck terror in Dottie Harper's very soul. She stood there in frozen indecision. Should she run back into the hospital? Or should she stand her ground and hope passers-by would help if Jerrod became violent?

Oh, Lord, she prayed. *Help us! Don't let Jerrod—*

Suddenly Jerrod's countenance twisted in agony and tears filled his eyes. He let go of the reins and started toward his family, sobbing. His huge frame shook with emotion as he stepped onto the boardwalk. Tears spilled down his cheeks and into his neatly-trimmed beard.

The sight of him coming toward her, broken and contrite, touched Dottie's heart and aroused her sympathy for him. James gave a tiny whine of fear and Molly Kate stared up at him, eyes wide.

"Oh, Dottie, I'm so sorry!" Jerrod sobbed. "Is my…my boy all right?"

"You hurt him bad, Jerrod," Dottie said, trying to remain calm. "The doctor said as big and strong as you are, you could have killed him."

Jerrod Harper removed his wide-brimmed hat, sleeved tears from his face, and ran his fingers through his thick dark-red hair. He drew a shuddering breath, looked at the frightened boy in Dottie's arms, and said, "James. Oh, James…Daddy's so sorry! I'm so awful sorry! Will you forgive me? Please, son…forgive me."

James looked into his mother's eyes, then back at his father and said, "Yes, Daddy. I forgive you."

Jerrod wept harder, but this time with relief. He held out his arms to James. "Son, would you let me hold you for a minute? I need to hug you."

James looked to his mother for advice and saw approval in her eyes. When she released James into his father's hands, she leaned over and gathered Molly Kate into her arms. The child embraced her mother's neck and held tight.

People on the boardwalk and in passing vehicles gawked at the touching scene.

Jerrod wept bitterly, repeating again and again how sorry he was for what he had done. James touched his father's tear-stained cheek and said, "It's all right, Daddy. I know you didn't mean to do it."

"James, Daddy will never beat you like that again. I promise. It'll never happen again, son!"

James wrapped his arms around his father's muscular neck and held him tight. Jerrod looked down at his wife and daughter, and said, "Dottie…Molly Kate. Please forgive me for bein' so awful. I promise—solemnly promise—I'll never be like that again. May God strike me dead if I ever do!"

Dottie held her little girl tight and said, "I forgive you, Jerrod. And Molly Kate does, too, don't you honey?" Molly Kate nodded, still showing some fear of her father.

Jerrod's tears and sorrow touched Dottie to the quick. Then and there, she brushed aside the idea of reporting him to the sheriff or of trying to get him under psychiatric care. She took hold of his hand and brought it to her mouth and kissed it. "Let's go home, Jerrod," she said.

Jerrod placed James on the wagon seat, then took Molly Kate from Dottie and set her there, too. He helped Dottie climb up to the seat, then mounted his horse. Together, the Harper family headed south out of San Francisco into farm country and toward home.

Jerrod was overwhelmed with the joy of being forgiven by his family. He prayed silently, asking the Lord to forgive him also. Scriptures came to mind, assuring him that when sins were confessed, God forgave and cleansed them in the blood of His Son. Jerrod fought tears again, knowing that the Lord kept His Word. From his lofty place in the saddle, he set his eyes on Dottie and thanked the Lord for giving him such a precious wife.

And then there was Molly Kate. It hurt him that those big blue eyes showed fear when she looked at him. But what else could he expect? Molly Kate had seen him beat James. He remembered hearing her scream of terror this morning while he was pounding on her brother.

Jerrod Harper, he told himself, *you're the lowest of the low. If anybody deserves the wrath of God, it's you.* He remembered what Job had said when he got a good glimpse of the Lord. Like Job, Jerrod Harper abhorred himself.

James said something to Dottie and suddenly sat up. She pulled rein and quickly stopped the wagon. Molly Kate looked the other way while her brother retched with the dry heaves. The boy's face was flour-white when his mother returned his head to her lap and snapped the reins.

Only minutes ago Jerrod had been basking in the forgiveness he had found from his family and from his God. Now he struggled to control the contempt he felt toward himself. *He couldn't forgive Jerrod Harper.* He more than abhorred himself. His body tensed, and a twitch pulsed at the corner of his mouth like an irregular heartbeat.

Dottie saw him stiffen in the saddle and looked with alarm at his face. The twitch, which she had seen so many times in the past five months, always appeared just before he went into one of his fits.

"Jerrod, get a grip on yourself." Dottie's voice quivered as she said it.

He looked down at her, his face glistening with sweat. The twitch was becoming more pronounced and he was breathing heavily.

"Jerrod!" Dottie cried. "Don't let the other Jerrod take control. Fight him, darling! Fight him!"

Jerrod pulled rein and Dottie halted the horses. His hands shook as he clutched the saddlehorn and groaned. His cheeks were glazed, his breath quick and shallow, his eyes wild in mounting panic. The wagon had eased a few feet ahead of him. Dottie looked back and cried again, "Jerrod!"

His breathing grew deeper, and the twitch began to subside. Suddenly he expelled a long breath and with it went the wiretightness of his nerves. He let go of the saddlehorn and wiped his hands over his bearded face, taking several deep breaths.

Dottie slid from the wagon and hurried to him. "You did it!" she said, weeping for joy. "You drove the other Jerrod back! I love you, darling! I love you!"

Jerrod blinked against the sweat that stung his eyes and

smiled down at his wife. He slid to the ground and took Dottie in his arms. They stood in a tight embrace, holding each other as if they had been apart for years.

Dottie thanked the Lord for the victory she had just seen. Was it the words of love she had called out to her husband that pulled him through? She thought so. Yes! Jerrod wouldn't need Dr. Matthew Carroll. Dottie would love him back to the man he used to be!

That night after the children were in bed asleep, Jerrod and Dottie sat down at the kitchen table for an extra cup of coffee. They were side by side, holding hands.

Jerrod lifted the hand he held, kissed it, and spoke slowly with feeling. "Dottie, I'm so sorry for what I did to James...and to you. Those marks on your face should be mine. I wouldn't blame you if you left me and got a divorce. I don't know how you've stood it. Any other woman would have packed up the children and been gone long ago."

Dottie rose to her feet and wrapped her arms around her husband's neck, pulling him close to her heart. She toyed with his thick locks as she said, "Do you remember the day you met me at the stagecoach station when I came to be your mail-order bride?"

"How could I ever forget?"

"When I first laid eyes on you, I fell in love. It was the Lord's hand on us, and I knew it."

"I loved you *before* I first saw you," he said. "When your letter came with your picture and I saw that beautiful girl lookin' at me, I fell head-over-heels."

Dottie kissed his forehead. "You say you wouldn't blame me if I divorced you."

"Nobody could blame you."

"But, darling, I couldn't do that. I couldn't leave you. That day we stood before God and Pastor Yates, I vowed to love you and stay by your side in sickness and in health till death parted us. My vows are sacred to me. I will stay by them. Besides, you're going to get better. I'm going to pour out so much love on the good Jerrod and make him so strong that the bad Jerrod won't come back ever again."

"Thank you," he said, planting a kiss on her chin. "How can I not get better with you taking such good care of me?"

Dottie knew it would take time and that Jerrod would need all the support he could get. She wanted to propose that they go to their pastor for help, but she had suggested it a few weeks earlier and Jerrod had bristled. He didn't want the preacher or anyone at the church to know. Dottie knew to bring it up now could set him off again.

But he did need to face the fact that it would take time. She cautiously explained this to him, trying to make him realize that the potential for hurting her and the children was still there. At first he insisted that he would never hurt them again, but when Dottie reminded him of all the previous promises he had made and broken, he reluctantly agreed she was right.

It bothered Dottie that Jerrod had always refused to let her pray with him about the problem. He wanted to avoid the subject completely, as if not talking about it would make it go away. Now she was pleasantly surprised when he looked into her eyes and said, "I want the Lord to help me. Could we read the Bible and pray together?"

"Yes, let's do," she exclaimed, and went to get the Bible she kept on the kitchen cupboard.

Jerrod and Dottie read several passages of Scripture together, then with hands clasped on top of the table, they prayed. Jerrod poured his heart out, pleading with God to help him overcome the evil forces within him. He told the Lord he never wanted to hurt his family again, but he must have His help.

Dottie was much encouraged to hear her husband pray so earnestly. She told herself that though it would take time, with God's help and a lot of love from her, the bad Jerrod could be conquered. While Jerrod continued to pour his heart out, she asked the Lord to help her love him more.

Jerrod did well through the night. There were no nightmares, and both of them slept until dawn without waking. After break-fast, Jerrod read the Bible to his family and led them in prayer. He kissed all three, then went to the barn to begin his day's work.

For Dottie it was a day of housecleaning. The Harpers lived in a three-story house that was forty years old. The top floor had two bedrooms, an attic, and a small turret room with a cone-shaped roof on a front corner. On the second floor were four bedrooms, each having its own walk-in closet, dressing and bathing room, and fireplace. Jerrod and Dottie occupied the largest bedroom, and James and Molly Kate each had their own bedroom, leaving the spare as a guest room.

Molly Kate's room and the guest room were at the front of the house, facing the double-rutted lane that led to the road. Molly liked her room especially because it was near the corner next to the turret room with the cone-shaped roof. She often pre-tended she was a princess and the turret was the tower of her castle.

Dottie spent most of the day sweeping and dusting every room on the first and second floors. Later in the afternoon she climbed the steep staircase to the third floor and began her work up there. Molly Kate was in her room playing with her dolls, and

James, who was still not feeling well, was lying on his bed.

Dottie was almost finished in the turret when she heard Molly Kate call to her from the floor below, "Mommy!"

"Yes, honey?" Dottie called back.

"There's somebody coming up the lane!"

Dottie went to the latticed windows that faced the front of the house and saw two riders trotting up the lane.

Some five hundred yards to the east of the house, beyond a grove of eucalyptus trees, Jerrod Harper was cultivating a section of his strawberry field, using one draft horse to pull the cultivator. Suddenly his attention was drawn to a silver-haired woman running across the field from the south, waving her arms and shouting his name. It was Maudie Reeves. In their late sixties, Will and Maudie Reeves were his closest neighbors. Their farm bordered the Harper place on its southern side. The Harpers were close friends with the Reeveses, who belonged to the same church in San Bruno.

Jerrod halted the horse and began running toward Maudie. He could see that she was frightened or upset.

"It's Will!" Maudie shouted as they drew close. "He had the wagon up on blocks, putting on a new axle, and it somehow came off. He's pinned underneath. I can't get it off him!"

"Where is he?" asked Jerrod, starting toward the Reeves place.

"On the back side of the barn. In the corral."

Jerrod took off running. It took him less than four minutes to reach the split-rail fence that separated the two farms. He hurdled the fence and headed toward the barn. He ran into the barn and out the rear door into the corral, and found Will Reeves pinned to the ground.

The wagon was larger than most and quite heavy. Will had been replacing the rear axle, and the back end of the wagon was on his chest. His face was beet-red as he struggled to lift the dead weight off him.

"Oh, thank God!" he grunted when he saw Jerrod. "Help me, Jerrod! It's squeezin' the life outta me!"

"Just hold on, my friend. I'll have you out of there in a jiffy."

Jerrod backed up to the end of the wagon, got a good grip underneath the bed, and hoisted it upward. When he saw that Will had rolled free of the wagon, he eased it down, then let it fall the last six inches. It hit the ground with a heavy thud. Will sat down on the edge of the nearby water trough as his cows and horses looked on inquisitively.

"Are you all right?" Jerrod asked. "You shouldn't be tryin' to put that axle on by yourself, Will."

"I've always done it before."

"Yeah, but you were younger then. You know I would've come and helped if I'd known you needed me. I asked if you're all right."

Reeves looked up at him, rubbing his chest. "Yes, I'm fine. No bones broken, though I'm sure I'll be sore for a few days. Glad Maudie found you home. If you hadn't come when you did, I'd have died."

"Tell you what, Will," Jerrod said. "Tomorrow I'll come over here and put that axle on for you. Okay?"

"You sure you've got time?"

"I'll *make* time. What are friends for, anyhow?"

Will grinned, shaking his head. "You're a real friend, Jerrod. Okay, I'll give you a hand, and we'll have it done in no time."

Maudie appeared at the barn door and breathed a prayer of thanks when she saw her husband sitting on the edge of the water trough.

Dottie stepped out on the front porch with Molly Kate beside her. When she saw the sun flash off the riders' badges, she knew it was the sheriff and his deputy.

"Are they coming to arrest Daddy?" Molly Kate asked.

"I don't know, honey," Dottie said. "They might be if some-body told them what Daddy did to James yesterday."

The lawmen drew up, and the older man touched his hat brim and said, "Afternoon, ma'am. I assume you're Mrs. Harper."

"Yes, I'm Dottie Harper."

"I'm Max Donner, San Mateo County sheriff, ma'am. This is my deputy, Myron Hall."

Hall touched his hat brim, nodded, and smiled tightly. "My pleasure, Mrs. Harper," he said.

Donner looked down at Molly Kate and said, "And what's your name, honey?"

"Molly Kate," came the timid reply.

"Molly Kate, huh? My, that's a pretty name. Of course it'd have to be, wouldn't it? For such a pretty girl, I mean."

Molly Kate leaned against her mother and did not answer.

"Dr. Glenn Olson contacted me by wire, ma'am," Donner said, looking back at Dottie. "Told me about you bein' there at the hospital yesterday with your son."

"I see," Dottie said.

"From what the doc said, ma'am, your boy was beaten quite severely by your husband."

Dottie pulled her mouth tight and gave a short nod.

"Dr. Olson's wire said he strongly advised you to contact me about the beating…but he had a feeling you weren't going to."

Dottie said nothing.

"Dr. Olson feels somethin' should be done so's Mr. Harper doesn't hurt the boy anymore."

"Jerrod and I had a long talk last night, Sheriff," Dottie said. "We're working together on it. Things will be different now."

"Where is Mr. Harper, ma'am?" Hall asked, adjusting his position in the saddle and making the leather squeak.

"He's working in the fields He'll…be out there till milking time."

"You can direct us to where he's working, can't you, ma'am?" Donner asked.

"Yes. Of course. But really, Sheriff, everything's fine. Believe me, it won't happen again."

"I intend to make dead sure it doesn't, ma'am," Donner said as he swung from his saddle. "We'd like to see the boy, then you can direct us to where Mr. Harper's workin'."

"All right," Dottie said, casting a furtive glance toward the strawberry field. "I'll take you to my son."

Molly Kate ran ahead, and Dottie led the lawmen through the parlor and up the stairs to the second floor. The sight of the boy appalled both men.

Sheriff Donner set steady eyes on Dottie and said, "Mrs. Harper, this kind of thing has to stop. Dr. Olson said your husband had beat you, too, and I can see the evidence on your face."

Dottie touched the purple mark on her temple, but said nothing.

"We've seen all we need to, ma'am," the sheriff said. "Now, you can tell us how to find your husband."

"Are you going to arrest him?"

"Right now, I just want to talk to him."

"Come outside. I'll show you how to find him," she said reluctantly.

Molly Kate preceded her mother down the stairs. Donner and Hall were behind Dottie. When the little girl moved out onto the front porch, she hollered, "Look, Mommy—Daddy's here!"

Dottie and the lawmen saw Jerrod coming from the barn toward the house. He looked grim as he set his eyes on Donner and Hall.

O, dear Lord, please don't let the bad Jerrod surface now! Dottie prayed.

6

SHERIFF MAX DONNER stepped off the porch with Deputy Myron Hall on his heels and fixed Jerrod Harper with a level stare as he drew up. "Mr. Harper, I'm San Mateo County sheriff Max Donner, and this is my deputy, Myron Hall. We'd like to talk to you."

Jerrod looked questioningly at Dottie.

"Sheriff Donner received a wire from Dr. Glenn Olson, Jerrod—the doctor who took care of James yesterday," Dottie said. "Dr. Olson felt the sheriff should investigate what happened."

Jerrod nodded, then looked Donner in the eye and said, "Sheriff, it was an unfortunate incident. I...lost my temper and—"

"You must have done more than lose your temper, Mr. Harper," Donner said. "We were just up in James's room. Little fella took a real battering."

"Yes, Sheriff, I realize that, but—"

"As sheriff of this county, sir, I cannot and I *will* not allow that kind of thing to go on if it's in my power to stop it."

Jerrod felt his other self trying to surface. He struggled against it, and suddenly the overpowering force was gone.

He pressed a slight smile on his lips and said, "Sheriff, I've had some problems because of combat fatigue I suffered in the Civil War. Dottie and I had a long talk after what happened yesterday. Things are gonna be better. I'm ashamed of what I did to my son, but it isn't gonna happen again, I assure you."

"I know about your problem," Donner said. "Dr. Olson explained it to me, and said he had told Mrs. Harper you need to get professional help. Suggested you see someone at City Mental Asylum."

"*City Mental Asylum!* I'm not goin' to any insane asylum!"

Dottie bounded off the porch and took hold of her husband's arm, praying in her heart for God's help. "Honey, Dr. Olson was very concerned when he saw what James had suffered. He simply doesn't want anything worse to happen."

"Mr. Harper, you need professional help," Sheriff Donner said. "I know a little about combat fatigue. My brother was in the War, and he had symptoms much like yours. He brutalized his wife and was always sorry afterward, but it didn't stop. He did it repeatedly for two years."

"Did he ever get over it, Sheriff?" Dottie asked.

"Yes, ma'am—when he killed himself. He went wild one day and almost beat his boss to death. He lost his job, and his wife left him. It was all he could take. He took a shotgun and—well, he's been gone now for six years. I can't make you get professional help, Mr. Harper, but there's tragedy coming if you don't. You need to see Dr. Carroll."

"Dottie and I will work through this thing, Sheriff," Jerrod said.

"Not without the right kind of help, you won't."

Dottie was holding Jerrod's arm and could feel him trembling. The lawmen saw a change come over him, and both took a step back.

Dottie shook him and said, "Jerrod! Jerrod get hold of yourself."

Jerrod took a deep breath and patted the hand that held his arm. "We're going to whip this thing, Sheriff," he said calmly. "Believe me. I don't need this Dr. Carroll. I have the Lord, and I have my wife and children who love me. We'll make it."

Max Donner sighed and fumbled with one end of his thick, droopy mustache. "Well, Mr. Harper, I can't force you to get the help you need. I could jail you for what you did to your son, but I couldn't legally hold you for very long. So...let me make it very plain. If there are any more child beatings, I will come after you, and I'll have you declared unfit to run free in society. You'll see the inside of a cell, be it a prison or the asylum. What's more, if I learn of you beating your wife like you did yesterday, I'll be all over you like fur on a grizzly. You understand?"

"I understand, Sheriff. I don't want to ever hurt my family again. And I'm not going to. Dottie and I are going to work together, and I'm going to be like I was before the War."

Donner took a deep breath, glanced at his deputy, and let the air out slowly through his nose. "You won't ever be like you were before the War, Mr. Harper. That's about as possible as a man losin' an arm and growin' a new one. You need to put yourself under Dr. Carroll's care, and I urge you to do it."

With that, the sheriff turned and said, "Let's go, Myron."

When the two lawmen had ridden out of earshot, Jerrod turned to Dottie with fire in his eyes. "Why did you tell that Dr. Olson so much? He didn't have to know everything that goes on in our lives!"

Dottie heard Molly Kate eject a tiny whine. She turned to see her begin to back across the porch toward the front door, her eyes wide with terror.

"You shouldn't have done that, Dottie!" Jerrod bawled. "What goes on in our family is none of his business!"

"Molly Kate, go on inside the house," Dottie said. "See what James is doing. I didn't just up and tell Dr. Olson everything, Jerrod. He figured most of it out by himself, and simply asked me if it was so. Would you want me to lie?"

"You didn't have to answer his questions! You could've told him to mind his own business!"

Dottie could hear Molly Kate whimpering behind her. She glanced at her daughter, who was at the door but frozen to the spot and staring at her wild-eyed father.

"Go on, honey," Dottie said. "See what James is doing."

Molly Kate burst into tears. "No, Mommy, I can't leave you! Daddy will hurt you!"

"Jerrod! Look at Molly Kate!" Dottie cried. "You're terrifying her! Don't do this to us!" Dottie wanted to run, but she knew Jerrod could easily catch her.

"You deserve to be punished, Dottie! Do you hear me? That doctor wants to put me in the asylum, that's what he wants! And it's your fault because you told him things you shouldn't have. You must be punished!"

Jerrod took a step back and raised both fists over his head as if to strike her.

"Daddy-y, don't! Don't hurt Mommy! You promised you wouldn't ever hurt her again!" Molly Kate screamed.

Jerrod froze and looked past Dottie to the quaking, weeping little girl. His chest was heaving and his breath was rasping in and out. Molly Kate saw it and moved toward the edge of the porch, crying, "Please, Daddy! Don't you love Mommy? If you love her, you won't hurt her!"

"That's right, Daddy," came a fear-filled voice from above. "You love Mommy, don't you? Don't hurt her! You promised you wouldn't!"

"James!" Dottie gasped, turning to see him standing at the window in Molly Kate's room.

Jerrod stared at James in the upstairs window, then looked again at Molly Kate. He studied her for a moment, still breathing hard, then looked at Dottie. He strained to gain control. An ache began as the pressure built behind his right eye, clouding his vision.

Dottie shuddered and stared at him. "Jerrod," she said softly, "I love you."

Jerrod ejected a wild cry, shook himself, then turned and ran toward the barn.

Dottie looked up and said, "Come down, James. Quickly. I'm taking you and Molly Kate to Grandpa and Grandma Reeves's house."

Maudie Reeves left the kitchen, carrying a cup of hot coffee, walked into the parlor, and stood over her husband, who lay on the couch.

Will painstakingly worked his way to a sitting position. "Thank you, sweetie," he said.

Maudie handed him the steaming cup. "I really think we ought to go to town and let one of the doctors at City Hospital take a look at you."

"No need, honey. I'm okay…just bruised and sore. I'm sure nothin's broken."

"Not even some ribs?"

"Man's lived in his body as long as I've been in this one, he knows it pretty good. I'll be fine in a couple of days."

"Well, praise the Lord Jerrod was home or there's no telling what might've become of you."

"Amen to that."

Maudie smiled. "Jerrod and Dottie are such precious kids. I don't think there's anything they wouldn't do for us."

"Man couldn't ask for better neighbors," Will said. He blew on his coffee; it still wasn't cool enough to drink.

Maudie saw movement in the yard through the large parlor window that faced onto the front porch. She moved across the room to the window to get a better look. "Well, I declare! It's Dottie and the children, Will."

Will wanted to get up and follow his wife as she headed out the door, but the pain and stiffness in his body made him decide to stay where he was.

Maudie knew something was wrong when she stepped out on the porch and saw the looks on their faces and James in his pajamas. She hurried down the steps to meet them. "Dottie, what happened? What's wrong?"

Dottie Harper was on the verge of tears. "Could we go inside, Maudie? I'll tell you in there."

"Sure, honey," nodded Maudie, taking the hand of a child in each of hers. "C'mon. Let's go in the house."

Maudie and the children moved through the parlor door ahead of Dottie. Will set his coffee cup down and began to work his way off the couch.

Dottie saw that he was hurting and said, "Will, what happened to you?"

"Jerrod didn't tell you?" Maudie asked.

"No. Tell me what?"

Will was unsteady on his legs. He held his hand to his chest and said to Maudie, "You tell her, honey. I've got to sit down."

Maudie told Dottie about the wagon falling on Will less than two hours before. She explained how she had run to the Harper place for help, found Jerrod in the strawberry field, and sent him to lift the wagon off her husband.

"Shouldn't we take you to the hospital so they can check you over?" Dottie said.

"I'm okay," he said with a tight smile. "Coupla days' rest and I'll be good as new. What I want to know is, where did you get those bruises…and where did James get his?"

Dottie sighed, backed to a chair that faced the couch, and before easing onto it, looked at Maudie and said, "You'd better sit down. What I'm about to tell you is going to jolt you."

James and Molly Kate sat on either side of Will, edging up close. He was the only grandfather they knew, and they loved him dearly.

Dottie had never told the Reeveses about Jerrod's problem. It had been difficult to keep it from them, especially in the past five months when it had gotten progressively worse. She could no longer remain silent, nor, she found, did she care to. She broke down several times as she told them.

When she finished, Dottie wiped tears from her cheeks and rose to her feet. "If it's all right, I'll leave Molly Kate and James here while I go back to Jerrod. When it's safe for them to come home, I'll come and get them."

"Dottie, from what I've just heard, it isn't safe for you to go home either," Will said. "You stay with Maudie and the kids, and I'll go get Sheriff Donner. Jerrod's got to be locked up."

"I have to go to Jerrod. He needs me. And besides, Will, you're in no condition to sit in a saddle."

"Then I'll walk home with you. From what you've told us, Jerrod could be very dangerous. I can't let you go there alone."

"Please, Will. I appreciate your concern, but I'm not afraid. Jerrod and I need some time alone."

The old man sighed. "Well, young lady, I won't interfere since you put it that way. But if you get home and find him still out of control, you get out of there and hurry back here. You understand?"

"I understand, Will." She kissed both children, telling them she would be back soon to get them. She thanked Maudie and Will for their help and headed across the fields toward home.

Jerrod leaned against a post that held up one corner of the hay loft, the words of his children echoing though his mind. A sheen of sweat filmed his face. His throat was dry from hard breathing. He felt relief that he had been able to turn and run before he struck Dottie.

An earth-shaking sound suddenly assaulted his ears. He raised his head and looked through the open barn door that led to the corral. Instead of sunlit corral, lined by split-rail fence, he saw Rebels coming across steaming grassy fields. He stumbled to the door and used its frame to steady himself.

Sergeant Jerrod Harper was back at Wilson's Creek on that

hot August day in 1861. The thunder of battle roared in his ears. He looked around for his squad. He was alone. Where were his men? Had the Rebels killed them all?

"Hey!" he yelled, running his gaze around the deep-shadowed interior of the barn. "Maynard! Wilson! Dougherty! Girard! Where are you?" Were his corporals all dead?

A cannon shell exploded a few feet from the barn door. The blast of it took Jerrod's breath. Muskets were barking from the field before him. He could hear the slugs tearing into wood all around him. Hundreds of Confederates were coming across the field in a swarm of gray. He looked around for his musket. Where was it? It was in his hand only a moment ago.

Again, he searched the interior of the barn. *Where had his men gone?* They wouldn't have deserted him. Not those brave— Suddenly there were dozens of bloody bodies crumpled, heaped, sprawled all around him.

The Rebel yell mingled with his scream. They were closing in on the run. Jerrod swung his head back and forth, trying to find a weapon. All these dead men...they had muskets. What happened to their muskets? The wild-eyed Rebels were almost to the door of the barn. He wouldn't go down without a fight. He would find something—

His eyes fell on the double-bladed ax he kept with some garden tools near the barn's front door. His head was hurting, as though it would split apart. His feet felt heavy, but he shuffled to the ax and closed the fingers of both hands around the handle. The screaming Rebels weren't going to get him without paying a price.

Louder and louder the chorus of voices beat at him, punctuated with the boom of cannons and the rattle of musketry. The men in gray taunted and yelled as they poured through the door, their eyes bulging with hatred for Yankees. Jerrod clutched the ax handle and swung it with all his might at the first line of soldiers who came at him, bayonets cutting the air.

The ax struck the milking stanchions, sending splinters in every direction. To Jerrod Harper, the sharp blade cut into Rebel flesh.

The battle continued. Hissing through his teeth, Jerrod swung the ax over and over and over again. Most of the time, it cut only air. Sometimes it struck a wall, a post, the gate of a stall, a feed bin.

Jerrod drove the enemy troops backward through the door that led to the corral. Then the sharp blade chewed into the heavy post that sided the door frame and buried itself deep. Jerrod struggled to free the blade, but it wouldn't budge. He jerked on the handle till it broke, then used it to drive the remaining troops backward.

Abruptly, the enemy disappeared. The Rebel yells stopped. Jerrod was at the door frame, swinging the ax handle at thin air. He was all alone. He blinked in amazement and could see the horses and the family cow huddled together at the split-rail fence a hundred feet away, staring at him and swishing their tails.

He turned about and searched the barn interior for the bodies of his men. They were gone. He was suddenly very weary. His throat was parched, and he was breathing as if he were climbing a mountain at a run above timberline. He dropped the broken ax handle and sank to his knees.

He began to weep. Tears streaked his cheeks as he sobbed heavily, mumbling, "Dottie! Dottie, where are you? I need you!"

Dottie Harper prayed as she crossed the fields, asking the Lord to show His power in Jerrod's life. Certainly God could reach down and make Jerrod's problem go away. Her heart cried for her husband. He had seemed to be getting better, and then this happened.

As she drew near the barn, she heard Jerrod's voice, coming from inside. She lifted her skirt and ran to the door, pulled it open, and found him a few feet inside on his knees, weeping and calling her name.

Dottie knelt in front of him, cupped his face in her hands, and said, "Jerrod, I'm here! See? It's me, sweetheart!"

Jerrod opened his eyes and tried to focus them on her face. He breathed her name and threw his arms around her, begging her to forgive him.

"It's all right, darling," she said. "Come on. Let's go to the house."

When they rose to their feet, Dottie noted the broken ax handle, the blade stuck in the heavy post at the door frame, and the splintered posts, gates, feed bins, and walls. She told herself Jerrod had fought a gallant battle in the war going on inside him.

She was unaware he had again fought Rebels.

7

THE NEXT DAY WAS SUNDAY. As usual, Jerrod Harper was up before the sun to do the chores. Sunrise came while he was milking the cow and pondering the horrible experience he had lived through the day before.

The battle he fought at the barn had been so vivid and real. Its effect still haunted him. Seeing the lifeless bodies of his men strewn around the interior of the barn brought back memories he wished he could forget.

Jerrod thought of how the children remained withdrawn from him when Dottie had brought them home late yesterday afternoon. But could he blame them? Not in the least. What a horrible thing for James and Molly Kate to have to see—their father acting like a wild man, threatening to punish their mother for telling too much. Jerrod lashed himself. Dottie had never been one to talk too much. Dr. Olson had figured things out for himself and simply asked for verification of his assumptions. Certainly Jerrod did not want Dottie to lie.

"Lord," he prayed, while streaming milk into the bucket, "please don't let all this become public knowledge. It's an embarrassment for Dottie and the kids…and it certainly is for me. Help me, Lord. Please help me overcome this other man who lives inside my body. You well know that I've never wanted to hurt Dottie and the kids. I love them with everything that's in me. You know my heart, Lord, and You know it's the truth. Help us as we go to church today to gain strength from You to overcome this awful thing in our lives."

Jerrod continued to pray for God's help while he finished milking. Moments later, he carried the full bucket to the back porch of the house and poured the milk through the strainer into another bucket. He could smell breakfast cooking as he neared the kitchen door and went inside.

Dottie was at the stove, scrambling eggs, and Molly Kate was seated at the table in her robe. She gave her father a fearful look as he crossed the kitchen to the cupboard and carefully poured the milk into a metal container. He put the lid on the container and turned around to find the little girl staring at him. She quickly avoided his eyes. Dottie saw it as she set a plate of steaming eggs on the table.

"I don't blame her, Dottie," Jerrod said. "She has every right to be cautious of me." He turned to his daughter and said, "I know that when I let the bad man inside me take control, I frighten you. I don't blame you for shying away from me. I love you, and I hate it when I act so bad. All I can ask is that you try to understand that I can't help what happened to me in the War, and that I'm doing everything I know how to get better."

"I heard that sheriff man say you should go to that Dr. Carroll," Molly Kate said.

Dottie smiled at her daughter, leaned close to her, and said, "Well, honey, we're trying to make Daddy better without him going to Dr. Carroll. It costs money, and right now, our funds are sort of low."

"But if Jesus wants Daddy to go to Dr. Carroll, won't He give us the money? Pastor Yates preaches all the time that God will supply all of our needs."

Dottie glanced at Jerrod, then said, "Well, Molly Kate, maybe Jesus wants to make Daddy well all by Himself."

Molly Kate tilted her head, squinted at her mother and asked, "Then how come He hasn't done it?"

Dottie looked again at her husband, who gave her an I-don't-know-how-to-explain-it-to-her look and shrugged.

"Jesus likes doctors," Molly Kate said matter-of-factly. "He sent Dr. Luke to travel with Paul because Paul didn't feel good. Since Jesus likes doctors, shouldn't Daddy go to Dr. Carroll like that sheriff man said, so he can get well?"

A probing thought passed through Dottie's mind. Was the Lord using the mouth of a child to tell them they should put Jerrod under Dr. Carroll's care? Jerrod would never submit to it, especially if it meant being admitted to City Mental Asylum.

"We'll just have to pray harder so we'll know, won't we?" Dottie said, patting Molly Kate on the head.

"I guess so," the little girl said.

Jerrod moved toward the table and said, "James is going to have to hurry if he's going to eat with us."

"He didn't feel good at bedtime last night," Dottie said.

"Well, what about church?" Jerrod asked.

"You'll have to go by yourself today. James is definitely not up to it, so I'll keep him home. Molly Kate can stay here with us."

"You sure he's that sick?"

"Not really sick, but pale and weak. The walk to and from the Reeves place yesterday was pretty hard on him. The stitches in his lip are giving him some discomfort, too. He'll get them out

Tuesday, and I'm sure he'll be feeling better in a couple more days. We can all go to church together next Sunday."

"All right, but there's no sense in Molly Kate missin' church. She can go with me."

For the first time, Dottie realized she was afraid to let Jerrod be alone with her daughter. She tried to keep her voice from betraying her fear. "Jerrod, she's been through a lot lately. It's probably best that she stay here with James and me."

"Haven't we always gone to church unless we were sick?"

"Well, yes, but—"

"Well, Molly Kate's not sick. I want her to go to church with me."

Dottie cleared her throat softly and spoke carefully. "Jerrod, she's been through so much lately. She's apprehensive about you. Can you blame her?"

Tears filmed Jerrod's eyes. He knelt beside his daughter and laid his hand on her shoulder. "Honey," he said, a quaver in his husky voice, "Daddy loves you with all his heart. I wouldn't hurt you, no matter what. I'd like for you to go with me to church. Would you really be afraid to go?"

The child bit her lower lip and studied her father's tear-filled eyes. She loved her father as much as any six-year-old could, and his tears touched her tender heart. She looked at her mother questioningly but got no answer. The decision would be hers.

Molly Kate rubbed her hands on her robe, licked her lips, and said, "I wouldn't be afraid to go to church with you, Daddy."

Jerrod wiped the tears from his face with his hand and folded his daughter in his arms. "Thank you, sweetheart," he said, choking on the words.

An hour later, Dottie stood on the front porch of the farmhouse and waved as Jerrod and Molly Kate drove away in the family wagon. They waved back, and soon turned at the end of the peach orchard and passed from view. Dottie hurried into the house and fell on her knees beside the couch in the parlor. She prayed earnestly for Molly Kate's safety, asking the Lord to bring her home without harm. She also prayed, as she had hundreds of times in the past five months, for Jerrod to be made well.

James came down from his room and stood at the parlor door. He waited quietly for his mother to finish, then entered the room. Dottie smiled at him and stood up.

"Well, there's my little man. I thought you were going to sleep the whole morning away."

"I wasn't asleep," he said. "I started down the stairs when Daddy was trying to get Molly Kate to go to church with him. I thought it would be best if I stayed in my room, so I went back up."

Dottie ran loving fingers through his dark-red hair. "Hungry?"

"A little."

"Well, let's see if ol' Mom here can rustle her boy up some grub."

After breakfast, Dottie and James read the Bible and prayed together, then James went up to dress while Dottie cleaned up the kitchen. Dottie could tell he still wasn't feeling well. When he came back down, she asked if he would like to go into the parlor, sit on the couch with her, and look at the family picture album. They hadn't looked at the album together since James was Molly Kate's age.

James was delighted to have the time alone with his mother. As they sat side by side looking at the album, James asked many questions about his maternal grandparents.

There were pictures of James when he was a baby, and also of Molly Kate when she was tiny. Soon they turned a page and James saw a picture of his mother and her sister when they were in their late teens. It had been taken shortly before Dottie made the trip to San Francisco to be Jerrod Harper's mail-order bride. James had almost forgotten the picture.

"Mommy, you and Aunt Breanna sure do look a lot alike," he exclaimed. "You could be mistaken for twins!"

Dottie smiled. "You're right. Many people used to ask if we were twins, especially about the time your Aunt Breanna was eighteen and I was sixteen."

"She never has gotten married, has she?"

"No. At least she wasn't as of the last letter I got from her a few months ago. She was engaged once, but it never worked out."

"How come?"

"Well…the man she was to marry broke off the engagement only days before the wedding and married someone else. I think your Aunt Breanna's heart was broken so bad, she's never gotten over it."

"That was a mean thing to do."

"Yes, it was."

"Do you think she'll ever get married?"

"Oh, I have a feeling that day will come. She mentioned a man named John in the last couple of letters, but didn't tell me much about him. From the way it sounded, he was away some-where, and they hadn't gotten to be together a whole lot."

James studied the picture carefully and said, "You and Aunt

Breanna were real close, weren't you?"

"Yes," she smiled. "As close as sisters could be. She's a wonderful person, James. So sweet and kind. Full of compassion and love. She makes a wonderful nurse. Breanna has always loved to do for others."

"Like you, huh, Mommy?"

Dottie pulled him close. "Thank you, sweetheart."

"I sure hope I get to meet Aunt Breanna some day."

"Well, the Lord willing, that day will come. You'll love her, I assure you."

Talking about her sister stirred Dottie's heart toward Breanna and made her miss her terribly. She decided to have James lie down and rest while she reread some of Breanna's letters.

The morning sun was pleasantly warm as Jerrod and Molly Kate made their way toward San Bruno. Dust clouds roiled up behind the wagon. Birds sang in the trees as if they were holding services of their own to give glory to their Creator.

Jerrod looked down at the small girl who sat beside him and marveled at how much she resembled her mother. Speaking softly, he said, "Honey, it would be best if you didn't tell anyone at church about what…about what Daddy did to James and to Mommy. Understand?"

"Yes, Daddy."

"If somebody asks you why they're not at church, you just tell them it's because James isn't feeling well. Okay?"

Innocent blue eyes looked up at him. "Okay."

"You won't be lying, Molly Kate, because James really isn't feeling well."

"I know, Daddy."

The bell in the steeple was ringing as father and daughter pulled into the churchyard. People were leaving their vehicles and hurrying into the white frame building. When Jerrod stepped to the ground and lifted Molly Kate off the wagon seat, he reminded her of what to say should anyone ask about the rest of the family.

Jerrod and Molly Kate sat in the same pew with Will and Maudie Reeves. Jerrod asked Will how he was doing, and the old man said he was quite sore through the chest and in his back, but he was sure no bones had been broken. Jerrod brought up his promise to help Will put the new axle on the wagon, and said he would be over the next day. Will thanked him once more for coming to his rescue. Maudie asked how James was feeling, and Jerrod said that he was better but not up to coming to church. The service began just then, and no more was said.

The music was inspiring and the preaching eloquent. After the service, the congregation filed out the door, shaking hands with the preacher and his wife. Reverend and Mrs. Howard Yates greeted Will and Molly Kate, who had a grip on Grandpa Will's hand, then shook hands with Maudie. When Jerrod stepped up, Louella Yates extended her hand and said, "I missed Dottie and James this morning, Jerrod."

"Me, too," the preacher said.

"James isn't feeling well," Jerrod told them.

"Anything serious?" Louella asked.

"No. He'll be all right in a day or two."

"Well, you tell them we missed them."

"I'll do that," Jerrod nodded.

Will and Maudie spoke a few parting words to Jerrod and Molly Kate, then joined friends who had brought them to church and would deliver them home, since the Reeves's wagon was under repair.

Jerrod took Molly Kate by the hand and headed for the wagon. They passed two middle-aged couples who were in friendly conversation. Jerrod knew Duane and Betty Ferguson and Webster and Darlene Michaels very well. Web Michaels first caught sight of father and daughter and lifted a hand in greeting. "Hello, Jerrod. Hello, Molly Kate."

Jerrod and Molly Kate slowed, and Jerrod replied, "Hello, Web."

"Where are Dottie and James?" Betty asked.

"They're home. James isn't feeling well."

The two women converged on Molly Kate, complimenting her on her beautiful dress and saying she looked more like her mother every day. The two men said they had heard how Jerrod saved Will Reeves's life. Duane asked Jerrod what was wrong with James at the same time Darlene asked Molly Kate the same question.

"He...ah...he came down with a fever during the night," Jerrod said.

"He's got a cut lip and some bad bruises on his face," Molly Kate said.

Duane and Web heard Jerrod's words, but also overheard what Molly Kate told their wives.

"Molly Kate, how did James get cut and bruised?" Betty asked.

"He fell down, ma'am," she replied, reasoning that when her

father beat James, her brother *had* fallen down.

Both replies hung in the air. Somebody was lying.

Molly Kate had heard her father's lie. Her eyes were drawn to his like a magnet. She saw a flicker of anger there and her heart leaped in her breast.

Jerrod's face flushed as he chuckled, grinned nervously, and stammered, "Well, James did have a fall. Possibly his minor injuries brought on the fever."

Jerrod's explanation fooled no one.

"Well, you tell that little guy we hope he'll be healed up real soon," Web Michaels said.

"That's right," Duane nodded.

"And tell Dottie we missed her," Darlene said.

"I will," Jerrod responded weakly, taking Molly Kate by the hand.

He hurried his daughter to the wagon, hoisted her into the seat, and quickly headed out of the churchyard. If he had looked back, he would have seen the foursome staring after him, puzzlement etched on their faces.

Molly Kate ventured a glance at her father's hard features. His mouth was set in a straight, rigid line. He turned and gave her a look that mixed anger with disgust.

Jerrod snapped the reins and screamed at the horses to go faster. People on the streets of San Bruno looked on in amazement as the wagon barreled past them, throwing up dust.

It took only moments to reach the edge of town. As the wagon raced westward into the country, Jerrod fixed blazing eyes on his daughter. Rage raked his voice as he yelled, "Molly Kate, you were bad back there. *Real bad!* You shouldn't have told those women about your brother's bruises and cut lip. If you'd kept your mouth shut, they wouldn't know about them. Now, you've got to be punished!"

Molly Kate's face turned the color of gray stone. She blinked, unable to tear her gaze from her father's fiery, penetrating gaze.

Jerrod saw the wild-eyed dread staring back at him from his daughter. She was terrified to the bone, and he was glad. She had it coming.

"Why did you do that?" he demanded. *Why?*"

The child's lips quivered, but she managed to say, "Daddy, you and Mommy always taught me to tell the truth. I answered Mrs. Ferguson and Mrs. Michaels the best I could without lying."

Molly Kate's last sentence cut through Jerrod. It was *he* who had lied to the Fergusons and the Michaelses—and his daughter had heard him. He fought against the urge to punish Molly Kate. She did *not* deserve to be punished! She had told the truth, yet had worded it so as to obey the instructions he had given her before they arrived at the church.

The speeding wagon was approaching a wooded area. The war between the Jerrods was on. He aimed the wagon into the wooded area, and when it was out of sight from the road, he yanked back on the reins, drawing the vehicle to a skidding stop.

Sweat beaded his face as he turned to the frightened girl and said, "Molly Kate, you stay in the wagon!"

He jumped down and ran into the woods, wanting to get as far from his daughter as he could before he lost control.

Molly Kate sat frozen on the seat, her entire body clammy with cold sweat. She wanted to take the reins and gallop the team for home, but she was afraid to try it. When her father finally caught her, he might beat her to death. She took a deep breath, let it out with a shudder, and remained fixed on the wagon seat.

Jerrod Harper threaded his way among the trees, running like a rabbit from a hound, scared and out of breath. He opened his mouth to release a high-pitched wail, filling the woods with an eerie sound.

A stab of pain lanced through his head. He stopped, breathing hard, and leaned against a huge oak tree. Battle sounds were prickling the outer edges of his mind. He was going back…back to Wilson's Creek.

Muskets barked and cannons boomed. There was smoke everywhere. His men were shouting that Rebels were coming through the woods. He heard a spine-tingling Rebel yell and turned to see a dozen or more men in gray closing in fast with bayonets fixed.

Sergeant Jerrod Harper wheeled and fired his musket from waist level. The long-barreled gun roared and a Confederate soldier took the bullet square in the chest. Jerrod gripped his musket by the barrel and took out the next Rebel by using it as a club. Behind the charging Rebel came another, screaming, wild-eyed, and lunging at him with a bayonet. He sidestepped the bayonet thrust in the nick of time, wheeled, and struck the Rebel in the head with the butt of his rifle.

All around him, amid thunderous cannon fire and roaring muskets, men were wailing, screaming, dying. Another fierce stab of pain drilled into his head. Dizziness claimed him. A cannon shell exploded within a few feet of him. He felt the shrapnel ripping into his body. A shower of stars swirled through his mind, leaving a trail of fading light.

Then blackness claimed him.

8

IN THE PAST FIVE MONTHS, Jerrod Harper's hallucinatory spells had taken him back to the battle at Wilson's Creek more than a dozen times. Only once before had he blacked out. He had been alone at the time, and had never told Dottie about it.

His first indication of awareness was the sound of a small voice crying, "Please wake up, Daddy! Please, Daddy, wake up!"

His eyes fluttered for a moment, then he focused on the tear-stained face of his little girl, who was kneeling beside him. Molly Kate's pinched features relaxed some when she saw his eyes come open. "Oh, Daddy!" she gasped. "Are you all right?"

The love Jerrod had for his sweet daughter flooded his heart. He lifted a shaky hand and stroked the full length of the blond tresses that fell halfway down her back.

"I'm okay, darlin'," he said in a half-whisper.

"I'm sorry I left the wagon when you told me not to, Daddy," she said, "but I got worried when you didn't come back."

"It's all right, honey. I understand." He used both hands to raise himself to a sitting position.

Molly Kate felt a wave of relief wash over her. The look in his eyes and the tone of his voice told her the bad Daddy was gone.

Jerrod's hat had fallen next to him. He picked it up, placed it on his head, and rose to his feet. "C'mon, honey," he said softly, "let's get to the wagon. Your Mommy'll be worried about us."

As they walked hand-in-hand through the dappled shade of the woods, Jerrod glanced up at the sun. By its position, he knew he had been out for at least an hour.

When they reached the wagon, Jerrod bent over and picked Molly Kate up to place her on the seat. Before he did, he held her close, wrapping her snugly in his arms. "I love you, Molly Kate. The bad man inside me tried to make me hurt you, but my love for you was too strong. He couldn't do it."

Molly Kate was apprehensive, but yearned for her father's affection. She cuddled her head close to his neck and said, "Then you aren't mad at me for what I told Mrs. Ferguson and Mrs. Michaels?"

Jerrod closed his eyes and bit down on his lower lip. "No, darlin'. I'm sorry for the way I talked to you. It...it wasn't me, really. It was the bad man inside me."

Molly Kate hugged him tight. "I don't like him, Daddy. He scares me."

"I know, honey. I know. He scares me, too."

"Don't you think you should go to the doctor? Maybe he could take that bad man out of you."

Jerrod bit his lip again and placed her on the wagon seat. "Let's head for home."

At the Harper house, Dottie paced the kitchen floor, praying aloud while her worried son looked on from the table. Sunday dinner sat on the table, cold. James had eaten a half-hour earlier and now sat at his place, chin cupped in his hands. He hated to see his mother so upset. As she talked to the Lord and paced the floor, he asked God to bring his father and sister home quickly and safely.

Dottie's imagination ran wild. Had Jerrod gone into one of his fits? Where was he now…and was Molly Kate all right? Why had she let him take Molly Kate with him? Maybe if she had used just the right words in just the right tone, Jerrod would have relented and allowed their daughter to remain at home.

Finally, Dottie stopped pacing, looked at James, and said, "I can't stand this. I'm going to saddle the bay gelding and ride to the church. I've got to find them. Will you be all right, here alone?"

James nodded. "I'll be fine, Mommy. You go on. I'm worried about them, too."

The boy followed his mother to the back door of the house, then watched as she hurried to the barn and vanished through the door. Seconds later, he saw her come around the corner of the barn inside the corral, leading the bay gelding, which was bridled and saddled.

Dottie led the bay through the corral gate, then closed it. She was about to mount the animal when she heard the rattle of a wagon in the yard at the front of the house. James heard it too and hurried onto the porch.

Dottie's heart leaped in her breast as she turned and saw the wagon bearing Jerrod and Molly Kate coming around the corner of the house. She hoisted her skirt calf-high and ran toward them. James was still quite weak, but he was so excited and relieved to see his father and sister that he bounded off the porch and ran to meet them.

Jerrod drew rein and jumped down from the wagon, and husband and wife opened their arms to each other. Dottie burst into tears, sobbing, "Oh, Jerrod, I was so frightened! I thought something bad had happened!"

"It almost did, honey," Jerrod said. "I'll tell you about it after you hug Molly Kate."

James drew up, breathing hard, and wrapped his arms around his father's waist. Dottie took Molly Kate from the wagon seat, held her, and told her how thankful she was that she was all right.

James went to his little sister and hugged her, saying, "Mommy and I were really scared, Molly Kate. We prayed that Jesus would take care of you. I'm sure glad He did!"

The family worked together to unsaddle and unharness the horses and turn them loose in the corral. Once that was done, they moved toward the house.

"Dinner's cold, but I can heat it up again," Dottie said. "Can you tell James and me what happened?"

Jerrod began by telling of the incident with the Fergusons and Michaelses. He held nothing back, admitting that he had lied to them. He told about the shame he felt for lying and the anger he had toward Molly Kate for telling the women about James's bruises and cut lip.

"I began to lose control and told Molly Kate she would have to be punished," he said, stoking the fire in the cook stove as he spoke. "I tried to fight it, but the urge was overpowering. Actually, my little girl only did what we've always taught her to do—tell the truth."

Molly Kate had begun helping her mother clear the cold food from the table. She was carrying the mashed potato bowl and the gravy bowl to the cupboard by the stove when she said, "I was really scared when Daddy started yelling at me."

"I assume this spell began to come on after you left the Fergusons and the Michaelses at the churchyard and started home."

"It started comin' on the instant I heard what Molly Kate said to the women, but we were almost to the woods near the Baker farm when I realized I wasn't going to be able to fend it off. I drove the wagon into the woods and told Molly Kate to stay in it till I came back. I ran as fast and as far as I could so I wouldn't do anything to hurt her."

Dottie moved to her daughter, put an arm around her shoulder, and said, "Thank the Lord He protected you." Then to Jerrod, who had the fire going and was setting the heavy lid in its place, "What happened then?"

"I had another one of my spells, but I really don't want to go into that," Jerrod said. He removed his hat and hung it on its hook by the back door.

"It must have been a long one," Dottie said. "You were more than an hour late getting home."

Jerrod moved to the table and sat down. His features were somber. "Yeah. It was a long one."

"When Daddy didn't come back to the wagon for a long time, I was afraid something bad had happened to him," Molly Kate said. "So I went and found him. He—"

"Molly Kate, that's enough," Jerrod said. He didn't want to upset the child, but he would rather Dottie didn't know about the blackout.

"Jerrod, husbands and wives shouldn't keep things from each other," Dottie said. "I want to know what Molly Kate was going to tell me."

"I just don't want to upset you and worry you any more than I already have with this awful thing."

"I appreciate that," she said, "but I'm your wife, Jerrod. I love you. You must let me share it with you. What happened?"

Jerrod sighed, pulled at his beard, and said, "I blacked out."

"You mean...you went unconscious?"

"Yes. I'd say for about an hour. When I came to, Molly Kate was kneeling beside me, crying and begging me to wake up."

"Is this the first time you've blacked out while having a spell?" his wife asked.

"No. I did it one other time."

"How long ago was the other one?"

"Oh, I don't know. A month, maybe."

Dottie stepped to the chair where he sat, laid a tender hand on his shoulder, and said, "Darling, blacking out is serious. I think you better go see Dr. Olson."

She felt Jerrod stiffen, then he took hold of the hand that was on his shoulder, looked up into her deep-blue eyes, and said, "Maybe I won't have any more."

"And maybe you *will.*"

"But we agreed we'd work this thing out between us and the Lord," he argued.

"That was before I knew about the blackouts."

"Let's give it a little time," he said, squeezing her hand. "Okay? Let's see if I have any more. If I do, we'll talk about my seein' a doctor. If I don't, then there's no good reason to."

Dottie went back to the stove where the food was reheating. "I guess I'll have to go along with you, Jerrod, but I'd rather you went tomorrow to see Dr. Olson." She looked back at him and said, "You did understand that I said Dr. Olson and not Dr. Carroll?"

"Yes. But Olson would no doubt want me to see Carroll. Dottie, I'm not goin' to that asylum. I'm not crazy. I just have a problem to work out."

"What about Duane and Betty and Web and Darlene? Are you going to talk to them...tell them you lied?"

"It was quite obvious I was lying. They knew it. I could see it in their faces."

"Then you know what the Lord would have you do. You must go to them and ask their forgiveness."

"I know." Jerrod nodded and looked at the floor. Then lifting his eyes, he looked at his children and said, "I did wrong, kids. I did the very thing I've taught you not to do...and what I've disciplined you for doing. Please forgive me." Both children quickly assured their father he was forgiven.

Dottie put the food back on the table, steaming hot, and when Jerrod gave thanks for the meal, he also asked the Lord to forgive him for lying.

Jerrod was unusually quiet during the meal. Finally, Dottie looked at him across the table and asked, "Something worrying you, Jerrod?"

"Yeah," he sighed as he mopped gravy with a piece of bread. "If I go to the Fergusons and the Michaelses to ask their forgiveness, I'll have to tell them how James got his bruises and cut lip. I...I just can't stand the thought of everybody in the church knowin' about it."

"You don't have to tell them about the shell shock. Just tell them you lost your temper and beat on James. That's enough, and it's the truth."

The sound of a carriage rattling into the yard caught Jerrod's attention. He left the table to peer through the lace curtains in the parlor.

"Dottie, it's the preacher and Louella," he said, hurrying back to the kitchen.

"Well, let's go welcome them."

"I don't want to see them right now. The Fergusons and the Michaelses probably told them what happened."

"We can't just ignore them," Dottie said.

"You talk to them. I can't," Jerrod said as he headed for the back door.

The knock came at the front door at the same time the back door closed behind Jerrod. Dottie told the children they might as well follow her to the parlor. The pastor and his wife would want to see them.

James and Molly Kate stood a few steps behind their mother as she opened the door and greeted Reverend and Mrs. Yates with a smile. "Hello," she said. "Sorry James and I couldn't make it to church this morning, but he wasn't feeling up to it. Please, come in."

The preacher removed his hat and followed his wife into the parlor. They both greeted the children, noting James's bruises and cut lip. Dottie's facial bruises did not go unnoticed, either. Dottie led them to the couch, then she sat on the love seat with her children flanking her.

"To what do we owe this Sunday afternoon visit?" she asked, looking across the coffee table at her guests.

The preacher cleared his throat and said, "Before Louella and I left the church this morning, Duane and Betty Ferguson and Web and Darlene Michaels approached us. They…ah…they indicated that there might be a serious problem in your household, and they thought as your pastor, I should know about it."

"And what did they tell you, pastor?" Dottie asked, unable to cover her nervousness.

Yates looked toward the rear of the house. "Is Jerrod here?"

"Well...yes, but when he saw you drive into the yard, he left through the back door. He guessed that the couples you just named had told you about his conversation with them. He just can't handle facing you right now."

"I see," nodded the preacher. "Well, let me tell you what Louella and I were told."

It took Yates only a few minutes to reveal that he and his wife knew about Jerrod's lie and Molly Kate's conflicting explanation. "James may have fallen," he said, setting compassionate eyes on the boy, "but by what I see, it was while he was being beaten."

Dottie pulled her children close to her and said, "Pastor, the bruises on James and me came from Jerrod. But before you conclude that he's a violent man who should be punished, let me explain it to you."

Yates and his wife listened intently as Dottie told them the whole story, including Jerrod's battle with *dementia praecox* from combat in the Civil War.

"When Dr. Olson treated James for his cuts and bruises, and I told him the story, he urged me to get Jerrod to Dr. Matthew Carroll, whom you probably know is chief of staff at City Mental Asylum."

"Yes," nodded Yates. "I know Dr. Carroll. Quite well, I might add. He's an excellent psychiatrist, and best of all, he's a born-again Christian."

"Really?"

"Yes. He belongs to a good Bible-believing church in San Francisco and is very active in service to the Lord."

"That's good to hear!" Dottie exclaimed. "I can't help but feel the Lord allowed things to happen exactly like they did today. Jerrod feels so bad about lying to our friends and about the way he frightened Molly Kate. Maybe between the two of us, we can convince him the time has come to see Dr. Carroll."

The tall, slender preacher stood to his feet and said, "How about letting me see if I can do the convincing?"

"Certainly," Dottie said. "Jerrod loves and admires you very much, Pastor."

"Where do you think I can find him?"

"My first guess would be the barn. If not there, he may be walking somewhere out in the fields."

"I'll be back," he said and hurried out the door toward the barn. As he walked, he looked around at the fields that surrounded the house and outbuildings to see if there was any sign of Jerrod. All was still and undisturbed in the Sunday afternoon sunshine.

He reached the barn and opened the wide door. The interior was dim, lit only by the light from the small windows at both ends of the barn and by tiny threads of light that seeped through cracks between the boards. The smell of hay, leather, old wood, and dry manure touched his nostrils in a full mixture.

He paused to allow his eyes to adjust to the darkness and called out, "Jerrod? You in here? It's Pastor Yates. I'd like to talk to you."

"Over here, Pastor." Jerrod's voice came from somewhere under the hayloft.

Yates left the door open for light and found Jerrod sitting on an old wooden box beneath the loft. As the preacher drew near,

Jerrod stood and waited for him to speak.

"Can we talk?" Yates asked.

"It's about what Duane and Web and their wives told you, isn't it?"

"Yes, it is."

"I don't want to talk about it. That's why I came out here when you drove up."

"Jerrod, you need to talk about it. You need to get help before someone gets seriously hurt. Dottie told Louella and me the whole story. It's not your fault that you suffered combat fatigue in the War. For the sake of your family, Jerrod, let alone for your own sake, you need to place yourself under professional care. I know Dr. Carroll personally. He's the best in his field, and he's a fine, dedicated Christian. I know he can help you. How about if I take you to him?"

Jerrod stiffened, shaking his head. "No. First thing he'll do is lock me up in that asylum. I'm not goin' to any asylum, Pastor."

"Jerrod, you don't know that's what he would do. All I'm asking is that we go and have a talk with him. You owe it to the Lord, too. You can't serve Him like you should with this problem hanging over you. Dottie tells me it's getting worse. She loves you. She only wants you to get better."

"No," Jerrod growled, his eyes beginning to widen. "Dottie and I are gonna work it out with the Lord's help."

"The Lord gave us doctors, Jerrod. He uses doctors to help people. You need help."

"I'm not goin' to that doctor! He'll lock me up! Get outta here, preacher! I'm tellin' you—go!"

"Calm down, Jerrod," Yates said, moving closer. "You've got to consider your wife and children. I saw what you did to James and Dottie. Big and strong as your are, you could kill one of them. Is that what you want?" Yates took another step toward him, reaching out and saying, "Take my hand, Jerrod. Just take my hand. Let me help you."

Jerrod lunged at the preacher and swung a fist at his jaw. Howard Yates had been in hand-to-hand combat in the Civil War and was able to dodge the fist. He did not try to strike back, but he stepped close and said, "Calm yourself, Jerrod. You need help, and I'm going to see that you get it."

Jerrod growled and threw himself at the smaller man. They collided, and both went down. Jerrod leaped on him like a madman, swinging both fists at the preacher's head and face. Yates gamely fought back, but Jerrod's size and strength overwhelmed him. Finally, Yates managed to roll away from Jerrod and made a dash for the open door. Jerrod roared like a bear and came after him.

Dottie Harper dashed into the barn just then and screamed, "No, Jerrod!" She placed herself between the preacher and her wild-eyed husband. "Leave him alone! He's your pastor!"

Jerrod didn't even hesitate. He struck Dottie on the jaw with his fist, and she went down hard. He looked down at her for a brief moment, then wailed and ran out the door. He passed Louella Yates, who stood just outside, frozen with fear. Louella watched him run between the chicken shed and the privy and into the nearest field.

Louella hurried inside and found her husband kneeling beside Dottie, who remained unconscious. The preacher carried Dottie into the house and laid her on the couch in the parlor. James and Molly Kate stood by in tears while Louella worked at reviving their mother. Yates was in the kitchen cleaning himself up and trying to stop his cuts from bleeding.

Dottie came to after a few moments. Her children embraced

her when she sat up and told them she was all right. The pastor entered the room, dabbing at his face with a wet towel.

"I'm sorry, Pastor," Dottie said. "When Jerrod's spell wears off, he'll weep and say how sorry he is for what he did to you."

"Dottie, Jerrod's got to be put where he cannot harm anyone…especially you and these children. I'm going to send Louella for Sheriff Donner right now. I'll stay with you and the children in case Jerrod comes back right away."

"Are you going to press charges against him, Pastor?"

"No. Of course not. But he must be locked up or he's going to hurt someone seriously, maybe even kill them."

Louella hurried to the Yates carriage and drove away. Dottie was still a little dizzy, but she sat the preacher down and put iodine on his cuts and salve on his bruises.

While her children clung to her, Dottie asked Yates why God would allow a Christian family to suffer as the Harpers had.

"And why would He allow a Christian man to become the victim of something as awful as combat fatigue?"

"I don't have a ready-made answer for you, Dottie. But I can say, and we can see from the Bible, that just because people are Christians doesn't exempt them from tragedies and heartaches. The Lord uses these things to draw us closer to Him. Just think of Paul's thorn in the flesh, of Job's loss of property, family members, and health, of David's persecution by Saul, of John's banishment to Patmos—all these trials were used by God for His own special purposes. And they were made better servants of the Lord because of it."

Dottie was thanking the preacher for helping her to understand when heavy boots were heard on the front porch, and Jerrod entered the parlor. He was surprised to see the preacher, since the carriage was gone. Both children clung hard to their mother as Howard Yates rose to his feet and braced himself for another onslaught.

Jerrod looked at Yates, then at his cringing family, then back at Yates. Tears flooded his eyes and he moved toward the preacher sobbing, "Pastor, I'm sorry! I didn't mean to hurt you! I'm so sorry—please forgive me!"

Before Yates could make any kind of reply, Jerrod turned toward the love seat where Dottie sat with her children. The preacher stepped up beside him, ready to intervene if the big man showed any sign of aggression.

Face wet with tears, Jerrod sobbed, "Dottie, I'm sorry I hit you! How could I have hit you? Please forgive me!"

Dottie sat with an arm around each child, looked up at him, and said, "Jerrod, this cannot go on. We can't handle it ourselves. I see that now. Surely you must see it, too. You've got to have professional help. You must go to Dr. Carroll."

"But I—"

"You did a horrible thing, Jerrod! You battered your own pastor. Look at his face!"

Jerrod turned and set searching eyes on the preacher. He turned back to Dottie and said, "I'm sorry."

"Being sorry's not enough, Jerrod. I know you're sorry, but the damage is done. You've got to get help."

Jerrod sleeved away tears from his cheeks and started to say something else when he heard the sound of a carriage and horses pulling up in front of the house. He headed to the door to see who it was. He recognized Louella in the carriage, but his attention was drawn to the two riders on horseback. Sheriff Max Donner and Deputy Myron Hall were soon out of their saddles and headed for the porch.

Jerrod went rigid, clenching his fists. Howard Yates laid a hand on his shoulder and said in a subdued voice, "Take it easy, Jerrod. They're here because it's necessary."

Sheriff Donner preceded his deputy to the door, stepped in without being invited, and gave Jerrod a hard look. "Jerrod Harper, I'm placing you under arrest for assault and battery. Mrs. Yates told me what you did to her husband, and I can see the evidence with my own eyes."

"Is Reverend Yates pressin' charges?" Jerrod asked.

"I don't know if he'll press charges or not, Jerrod," Donner replied, "but right now we're takin' you to jail for beatin' up on him. We'll see later about charges."

"Sheriff, I'm not goin' to jail. I told the man I'm sorry, and I know he'll forgive me." He looked at Yates. "Right, Pastor?"

"Jerrod, it doesn't make any difference whether he forgives you or not," Donner said. "You've proven yourself to be a menace to society, and you're going behind bars until I say different. I warned you about this before."

Dottie drew up beside her husband, touched his arm, and said, "I don't like to see you go to jail, honey, but Sheriff Donner has to take you in so you don't hurt anyone else. We'll get this all worked out. Help is available, and we'll get you the best there is."

"I'm not goin' to jail, Dottie! You hear me? I'm not!"

Max Donner set his jaw and said, "Preacher, you take Mrs. Harper and the children to another room, will you?" As he spoke, he pulled a pair of handcuffs off the back of his belt.

Reverend Yates glanced out the door at his wife, who cautiously waited on the steps of the porch. "Dottie, let's take James and Molly Kate and go outside," he said.

Dottie gave her husband a fearful look and motioned for the children to come to her. "Jerrod, this is best for all of us right now. I know you don't want to hurt anyone, but something has to be done so you won't."

Jerrod ignored Dottie as Yates led her and the children out onto the porch. His eyes were on the handcuffs in Donner's hand. He backed away two steps and braced himself. "I'm not goin' to jail, Sheriff," he said.

"You can go the easy way or the hard way," Donner said. "Choice is yours. I suggest you choose the easy way and hold out those wrists."

Jerrod Harper's pent-up fury exploded. He lunged at the sheriff with his fist. Donner dodged the blow, and as Jerrod set himself to throw another punch, Myron Hall moved in and brought the barrel of his revolver down hard on the back of Jerrod's head. Jerrod went down in a heap, unconscious.

Dottie rushed in, face pinched, and knelt beside him, stroking his face. "Oh, Jerrod, I love you. It's going to be all right, honey. You'll see. We've just got to get you some help."

Jerrod was still out as Donner and Hall draped him over the saddle of Hall's horse, hands cuffed behind his back. When the two lawmen sat doubled up on Donner's horse, the sheriff looked down at Dottie and said, "You're welcome to visit him anytime, Mrs. Harper."

"Thank you, Sheriff," she said, holding the children close to her.

"You gonna talk to Dr. Carroll?"

"Yes. I'll go to his office tomorrow morning, then I'll let you know what he wants to do."

"All right, ma'am," Donner nodded. "See you tomorrow."

Jerrod Harper was beginning to stir as the two lawmen rode away, leading the horse that carried him. The preacher patted Dottie's arm and said, "The Lord will work it all out for the best, Dottie. Remember Romans 8:28."

"Yes," she smiled through her tears. *"All* things is what it says, doesn't it?"

9

RIP CLAYSON'S WAGON TRAIN traveled for three days out of Fort Bridger with the cavalry escort before the men in blue had to turn back. Five days later, the train veered off the Oregon Trail onto the California Trail, and on September 25, the jagged, towering peaks of the Sierra Nevada Range came into view.

It was now September 27, and the Sierras still seemed as far away. Clayson told those who had never traveled in mountain country that it was merely an optical illusion. In a few more days, it would seem that God had suddenly pushed the mountains their direction, and they would be climbing into the foothills.

There had been no Indian trouble since leaving Fort Bridger, for which all were thankful. They were nearing Mohave Indian country, but the Mohaves were friendly toward whites. This was good news to the weary travelers.

Night after night, John Stranger and Breanna Baylor had taken walks together, and on this night, the moon was full and countless stars twinkled in the vast heavens above.

About a half-mile from the camp, the pair found a large round rock at the edge of a bubbling stream. Breanna sat down and John stood over her, looking down into her moon-struck face. They were in tall timber now, and the night breeze sang to them in the treetops. Somewhere in the distance a coyote howled. Its cry was long and lonely. Moments later, the cry was answered from another direction.

John smiled, looked at the surrounding forest, and said, "Sounds like boy and girl, doesn't it?"

"It does," Breanna said. "And I think they're going to meet somewhere out there in the moonlight."

John's thoughts rushed forward to the day when he and Breanna would part again. His heart went heavy. He stepped to the grassy bank of the stream and watched the moon dance on the rippling surface. Then he turned and looked again at Breanna. He let his gaze absorb the picture she made in the silver moonlight, with the deep of the forest behind her. He loved this woman more than he ever knew he could love someone.

"The Lord sure went out of His way when He made you, Breanna," John said.

"You flatter me," she said, smiling.

"It's not flattery, my lady," he responded, walking toward her. "It's fact."

Breanna reached for his hand, took it, and pulled him down beside her. They looked into each other's eyes for a moment, then John gently folded her in his arms.

"I love you, Breanna," he said. "There's no way you could know how much I love you."

Breanna laid her hand against his cheek and said, "And there's no way *you* could know how very, very much I love *you* my darling."

The kiss was sweet and tender, then they held each other for a long moment.

"The Lord has been so good to give us a love like this," Breanna said.

"I've thanked Him in every way I know how ever since He brought us back together. I treasure you, little lady."

All was quiet for several minutes as John and Breanna savored the sweet moment together, then John broke the silence.

"Sweetheart..."

"Yes?"

"We've prayed that the Lord would give us direction about our future together."

"That we have."

"The Holy Spirit has been speaking to me in that still, small voice."

"He's been speaking to me also," Breanna said, easing back in his arms so as to meet his gaze. "May I tell you what He's been saying to you?"

John smiled and playfully cuffed her on the chin. "You really think you know?"

"No, I *know* I know. Our hearts beat in the same rhythm, John, and because the Lord Jesus lives in both of our hearts, He's revealed His plan to both of us."

"Okay. Let's hear it."

"Let's stand by the water," she said, taking him by the hand.

John rose to his feet, helped her up, and put an arm around her as they stepped to the edge of the stream. Breanna looked up at him and said, "We both have our special callings from God, John. And as much as we love each other, it's His will that we carry on in our work for the time being."

"Yes."

"You're so very much needed in this Wild West, darling. People not only need to hear the gospel you preach wherever you go, but they also need the help you give in so many ways. The Lord has His hand on you, and I know that for now, you must continue to travel and let Him lead you to those you are to help."

John nodded and smiled. "And for the time being, you are to continue your medical work and share the gospel with your patients whenever possible."

Breanna smiled in return. The night breeze toyed with her hair, dropping a lock onto her forehead. "So we both know," she sighed.

"Yes. But at least we can be together from time to time. And then..."

"Then?"

"When it's God's time, I want you to become my wife."

Tears glistened in Breanna's eyes. "Oh, John! That will make me the happiest woman in the world!"

"And it will make *me* the most fortunate man in all the world!"

They kissed, embraced, and headed back for the camp, their hearts filled with the peace of God about their present work, and about the future.

On September 30, the wagon train was winding along the trail in tall timber, nearing the foothills of the Sierra Nevadas. As usual, Curly Wesson's vehicle was in the lead, and Breanna sat beside him. It was almost noon, and the sun bore down from a clear, azure sky. A cool wind swept off the ragged peaks to the west, stirring the treetops. A half-dozen broad-winged hawks could be seen overhead, riding the currents, their shrill screeches echoing across the uneven land.

Rip Clayson and John Stranger rode side by side some fifty yards ahead of the Wesson wagon. Rip admired John's black gelding and asked him how he had come by the horse.

"Was up in Montana," Stranger said, smiling. "I happened upon a ranch on the Yellowstone River a few miles southwest of Billings. Horse I owned at the time had a bad leg, and I needed to buy a new one. Found the rancher and his hired hands all gathered at the corral. Seems they had this black gelding that nobody could ride. Just as I came upon the scene, the black was throwing the toughest bronc buster in the territory—at least that's what a couple of the cowhands told me.

"I took one look at the big black as he bounded all over the corral, back arched, head down, stirrups flying from the empty saddle. He was a mean one. His eyes bulged with fire and his nostrils flared as he snorted triumphantly, having thrown another would-be rider."

Rip squinted at something he saw on the trail some distance ahead, but it was too far away to make out what it was. He looked at Stranger and said, "I know what you're gonna tell me. You rode him, and the rancher sold him to you."

"Not quite. After seeing the top bronc buster in those parts get thrown, the rancher cursed the horse and said it was useless. The only thing he knew to do was take him to an auction and let some poor sucker buy him."

"But you—"

"Yep. I stepped up and asked the man if he'd let me try riding

131

him. He laughed and said, 'Tell you what, long, tall, and grue-some. If you can ride 'im, you can *have* 'im.'"

"And you rode him."

"Well, I don't want to brag, you understand."

"Oh, of course not," Clayson said with a smile.

"I *did* ride him, and I'm the only mortal who's *ever* ridden him." Stranger leaned forward in the saddle and patted Ebony's neck. "Isn't that right, big fella?"

Ebony nickered and bobbed his head.

Rip's attention was drawn once again to the spot on the trail ahead, and this time John noticed him squinting.

"What is it?" he asked.

"I think there's somebody down and hurt up ahead."

"Let's check it out," said Stranger, touching heels to Ebony's sides.

Curly and Breanna's conversation suddenly broke off as the two riders galloped ahead.

"Wonder what that's about," Curly said.

"They must've seen something up there. They're in a plenty big hurry." Breanna shaded her eyes from the sun and added, "They're stopping up there by those boulders. Looks like a person lying by the side of the trail."

Seconds later, they saw John mount Ebony and ride toward the wagons at top speed. He thundered to a skidding halt beside Curly's wagon.

"We've got a man up here who needs you real bad," he said to Breanna.

"What's the nature of the problem?" she asked as she reached into the wagon for her medical bag.

"Some kind of epidemic in a village nestled in the foothills," John said, sliding from the saddle. "He's running a high fever and almost delirious. Says more than half the village is either dead or dying." He lifted his hands to help her down. "I figure you ought to take a look at him before we let the wagons even get close."

"You're right," Breanna said. "He could be highly contagious."

Stranger led Breanna to Ebony and lifted her up behind the saddle. As he was swinging up in front of Breanna, she said to Curly. "Don't let anyone come any closer."

"Wouldn't think of it, ma'am," he said.

Stranger took the medical bag from her and said, "Get a good hold around my waist." Then he put Ebony to a gallop toward the spot where Rip Clayson knelt beside the sick man.

As Ebony skidded to a halt, Rip stood up and watched John slide from the saddle, then help Breanna down. She took her medical bag and knelt beside the man who lay on the ground.

"So now there are *two* mortals who have ridden Ebony," Rip whispered to John.

"She's been on him with me before," John said. "I guess I didn't phrase it right. I'm the only mortal who's ever ridden him *alone*."

Rip grinned. "I have a feeling Ebony would let Breanna ride him alone."

"I'm sure he would."

Rip and John drew close as Breanna bent over the sick man. She was talking to him in a low tone and unbuttoning his shirt.

"The headache is real bad?" she asked.

"Yes'm," he replied weakly. His eyes were dull, and there was a sheen of sweat on his face.

Breanna took one look at the red blotches on his chest and began buttoning his shirt. "How long have you had this?" she asked.

The man licked his dry lips and choked, "Week."

"Did you have an immediate loss of appetite?"

"Yes."

"Headache came on at the same time you started feeling ill?"

"Yes." His teeth were chattering from the chills in his body.

"What's your name?"

"Wayne Zeller," he said. Then his eyes closed, and he slipped into unconsciousness.

Breanna rose to her feet and turned to the men. "Did either of you touch him?"

"I did," Rip replied. "Why? What does he have?"

"Typhus," she said. "How far is the village?"

"About a mile. Just around the next bend."

"Since you've already touched him, Rip," Breanna said, "I'll need you to put him on your horse and take him to the village. I'll go with you, then I want you to go to the train and wash your hands thoroughly in kerosene and lye soap. Be sure to clean under your fingernails."

"You're not going into that village alone, Breanna," John said. "I'm going with you. Rip can go wash right now. I'll put the man on Ebony's back, and we'll walk there together."

Breanna knew by the look in John's iron-gray eyes that to argue with him would be a waste of time. "All right," she said with a sigh, "let's go."

John moved to the man, bent to pick him up, and noted that there was no rise and fall to his chest. His head lay to one side, and his mouth hung open.

"He's dead," John said, turning back to Breanna.

She hurried to the man, knelt beside him, and felt for a pulse. There was none. She stood and said, "Let's take the body to the village. Did he say what he was doing out here, Rip?"

"Trying to get help. He was heading for a ranch somewhere this direction."

Breanna nodded. "You go get washed as I told you. John and I will be back to the wagon as soon as I can assess the situation in the village. Don't touch anyone in the camp until you've washed. You're carrying the bacteria on your hands. And when you're done, rub some udder salve into your hands. It'll offset the damage done by the kerosene to your skin."

"All right," Clayson said. "Is…is typhus something like typhoid fever?"

"I'll explain when I come back so everyone in the wagon train will understand," said Breanna. "Right now, John and I must get to the village. I've got to do what I can to stop the epidemic before everyone there dies."

Rip mounted his horse and rode toward the wagon train. John placed the body over Ebony's back, then he and Breanna headed toward the village.

Rip was met by a large number of people when he arrived at the wagon train. While he washed his hands, he told them the man beside the trail had died of typhus, and that John and Breanna were taking the body to Sierra Springs.

The word *typhus* struck fear in the hearts of the travelers. Carolyne Fulford, whose father was a medical doctor, told the people that typhus was highly contagious and usually fatal, but she knew little else about it. They would all have to wait till Breanna came back to learn the details.

The people gathered at the front of the train, watching for John and Breanna. A full hour after Rip had returned, they saw the couple riding toward them. Moments later, John and Breanna dismounted, and Breanna called for kerosene and lye soap. As she and John washed, she said to the wagon master, "Nearly half the village has been affected. Ninety-two have died, including Wayne Zeller, and just over a hundred are ill." Breanna paused, then said, "I'm going to have to ask you to delay our moving on until the day after tomorrow. I need time to help the villagers stop the typhus before it kills them all."

Rip knew it was possible to run into severe weather high in the Sierras the first week of October, but he also had compassion for the people of Sierra Springs. He would have to chance it. "Okay," he said. "We'll make camp about a quarter-mile outside the village and pull out at sunup day after tomorrow."

"Thank you," Breanna said, then she looked on the circle of faces and continued, "John and I need to eat something, then we're going back to the village. No telling how long till we can return to the wagons. I want to explain why all of you must stay away from there. Typhus is highly contagious, and it is a deadly killer."

Carolyne left Rip's side and moved close to Breanna. "I want to go with you if you think I can be of help."

"I'm sure you can be. I'll take you up on your offer."

As John and Breanna picked up towels to dry their hands, Carolyne asked, "Isn't typhus related to typhoid fever?"

"Well," Breanna said, "the two diseases resemble each other in that the victim runs a high fever and usually dies. Typhus, however, causes an eruption of red spots on the body, and often causes mental disorder in addition to high fever, chills, severe headaches, and loss of appetite. It's spread by lice, fleas, bedbugs, and rats. Humans are commonly infected when the little creatures go from one person's body to another. That's why it's so important for those of us who touch an infected person to wash our hands thoroughly. Typhoid comes from a totally different source. It's caused by the typhoid bacillus *Salmonella typhosa*, and is acquired through contaminated food and drink."

"What will we be able to do for those already infected?" Carolyne asked.

"I'm afraid there's nothing we can do for them. Some of the stronger ones may survive, but most of them will die. I'm sure the day will come when medical science will come up with a cure, but the only thing we can do now is stop the spread of the disease."

"And how do you do that?" asked a young mother of four.

"Well, I found that the people in Sierra Springs, like most everyone else, think that if they isolate the infected ones, placing them in rooms with doors closed and windows shut, they'll stop the spread of the disease. It works just the opposite. The best thing to do is open all the windows and doors. Fresh air is the key to cleaning out the houses—that and good, old-fashioned washing, scrubbing, and common-sense hygiene."

"You said something too about smoke," John reminded her.

"Oh, yes. In Europe, they now burn fires in the towns when there's an epidemic. Some French doctors think smoke purifies the air. I'm going to suggest this to the people in Sierra Springs, also. I don't know if the French doctors are right or not, but it's worth a try. I'm also going to see that they burn all clothing, blankets, sheets, and the like that have been infected."

"Breanna, you all be careful," an older woman said. "Please. We don't want the three of you getting typhus."

"We'll be very careful," Breanna told her. "Other than Wayne Zeller's body, John and I touched nothing when we were in the village. We'll take every precaution."

Under Breanna's instructions, some of the women made special aprons and crude masks of heavy cloth for John, Breanna, and Carolyne. The three ate a good meal, not knowing when they would eat their next one. Carolyne rode Rip's horse, and Breanna rode Ebony with John as they headed toward Sierra Springs. The wagon train moved to the designated spot a short distance from the village and set up camp.

The trio entered Sierra Springs and went to work. John and Carolyne followed Breanna's instructions and did what they could to make the typhus victims more comfortable. Doors and windows were opened in infected houses, fires were built and maintained all over the village, and those not infected began washing, scrubbing, and cleaning with vigor.

The work went on all night long. By morning, Sierra Springs was scrubbed clean. Three more people had died during the night and had to be buried. John Stranger offered to hold services for them, and the grateful survivors gladly accepted. Preaching from the Bible he carried in his saddlebags, John gave a clear gospel message and invited those who wanted to be saved to receive Christ. Several responded. Breanna and Carolyne found Bibles in some of the homes, and along with John, visited all the victims who were lucid. Many of those also received Christ.

John, Breanna, and Carolyne worked till almost noon, then made ready to go to the camp for some much needed rest. A group of those who were not infected gathered at the edge of the town to thank them and bid them good-bye. One elderly gentleman, whom Breanna had led to the Lord, approached her with tears in his eyes and said, "You've been sent to us by God, Miss Breanna. You're an angel...an angel of mercy."

10

AT THE SAN MATEO COUNTY JAIL, Sheriff Max Donner followed Deputy Myron Hall into the cell block an hour after sunrise. Hall was carrying a tray bearing a hot breakfast for their only prisoner.

Jerrod Harper was sitting on his cot when they appeared and rose to his feet, rubbing the back of his head. The fire that had been in his eyes the day before was gone. He was calm and showed no tendency to give the lawmen trouble.

When Hall saw the serene look on Jerrod's face, he said, "Got some fried taters, scrambled eggs with sausage, and hot coffee for you, Jerrod. Y'hungry?"

Donner put his key into the cell door, turned it, and pulled the door open.

"Yeah. A little," Jerrod said.

Hall set the tray on the cell's small table and backed out, saying, "I asked for extra-large portions at the café. Told 'em you're a good-size feller."

"Thanks," Jerrod said as Donner closed and locked the barred door.

Hall noted that Jerrod was gingerly rubbing the back of his

head and said, "I hated to clobber you so hard, but you didn't give me any choice."

Tears surfaced in Jerrod's hazel eyes. His lower lip quivered as he said in a broken voice, "I'm sorry for how I acted, gentlemen. The...other man inside me got control. I hope you'll find it in your hearts to forgive me."

Donner stepped close to the bars. "We both understand a little about your problem, Jerrod. Forgivin' you is no problem. But this situation goes deeper than that. When the 'other man' takes control, you're dangerous. You've got to get some professional help. Your wife is gonna see Dr. Matthew Carroll this mornin'."

Jerrod's face stiffened.

"Now, just get a grip on yourself," Donner said, raising a hand palm-forward. "You're either gonna place yourself under Dr. Carroll's care, or I'm gonna throw this key away."

"You can't keep me here," Jerrod said, wiping tears. "I've got a farm to work...a family to support. You gotta let me out!"

"So you can pound on your wife and children when the 'other man' takes over? Not on your life. When your wife gets here, we'll see what Dr. Carroll had to say, and go from there."

"But my farm," Jerrod cried. "Dottie and the kids need me, Sheriff. It's my duty to provide for them."

"And it's my job to protect them, Jerrod, and I'm goin' to do my job. Eat your breakfast. It's gettin' cold."

After a long night with little sleep, Dottie Harper left James and Molly Kate with Will and Maudie Reeves and drove the family wagon into San Francisco. She was greeted warmly by Flora

Downing, Dr. Matthew Carroll's receptionist, and told there were four patients ahead of her, but that the doctor would see her as soon as possible.

An hour and a half later, Flora ushered Dottie into the doctor's office. Dottie was a bit surprised. She had expected a much older man, but the man who stood behind the desk smiling warmly at her was no more than four or five years older than she.

"Good morning, Mrs. Harper," Dr. Carroll said.

"Good morning, Doctor," she responded, smiling in return. He had a certain warmth about him and a winsome smile. He could help Jerrod, she was sure of it.

"Please sit down," he said, gesturing toward a chair that stood in front of the desk.

He waited until Dottie was seated, then eased down in his own chair, leaned forward with his elbows on the desk, and said, "Dr. Glenn Olson mentioned you to me, Mrs. Harper, and told me a little about your problem. I want you to know that if your husband will agree to see me, I'll do everything I can to help him."

"Thank you, Doctor," Dottie replied. "I...I'd like to ask you something right off, if you don't mind."

"Of course I don't mind. What is it?"

"I've been told that you're a saved man...a born-again Christian. Jerrod and I are Christians, and I need to know if this is true about you."

"It most certainly is. I put my faith in Jesus Christ some ten years ago. My life has never been the same—praise the Lord—and I rejoice in my salvation."

Dottie gave a sigh of relief. "It's reassuring to know my husband will be in the hands of a Christian doctor."

"I can appreciate why you'd feel that way, Mrs. Harper. Now, I need to hear the whole story on your husband... *Jerrod,* right?"

"Yes. But before I tell you the story, I have to say, Doctor, that I was expecting a much older man."

"Oh? Any special reason for that?"

"No. Just an image I made up in my mind, I guess."

"Psychiatrists *do* get old eventually," he laughed, "but like everybody else, we have to grow that way."

"Well, you've certainly done well to be so young and yet be entrusted with the responsibilities of head of staff at the asylum."

"Thank you. I appreciate your kind words."

"Your wife must be very proud of you."

"She was, Mrs. Harper. She died two years ago. Consumption."

Dottie's face blanched. "Oh, Doctor, I'm sorry! Please forgive me!"

"It's all right—you had no way of knowing."

"Please know that my heart goes out to you, Doctor," Dottie said. "Do...do you have children?"

"No. Clarissa became ill early in our marriage. Having children just wasn't possible. I love children. It would've been a wonderful thing if we'd been able to have some, but the Lord had other plans for us. I understand you have two children."

"Yes. James is eight, and Molly Kate is six."

"Well, I hope I get to meet them. Any other questions before we talk about your husband?"

"No. That's it."

"All right. How about starting at the beginning? Tell me

Jerrod's story. Try not to leave out anything significant."

Dottie told all, beginning with Jerrod's Civil War duty and ending with the events that led to his arrest. When she finished, Dr. Carroll said, "Mrs. Harper, I wish I could tell you there was a cure for Jerrod's problem, but the truth is, there isn't. The problem is only going to get worse with the passing of time."

"You…you mean there's nothing you can do for him?"

"To *cure* him—nothing. But I can help him. I can put him on sedatives that will make his angry episodes less severe. Of course, he'll have to submit himself to my care in order for me to do this."

"After what he did yesterday, Doctor, I think he might be willing to do that. You *are* talking about doing this sedative thing with him living at home. Right?"

"Yes. That is, if he gets out of jail. But let me tell you what else I can do."

"All right."

"Jerrod's problem—as you may know—is called *dementia praecox.* We have no cure for it, but there's a good chance I can help Jerrod to a degree with mental therapy. But again, I can't help him unless he will let me."

"Mental therapy?" Dottie said, her brow furrowing. "You mean you could do this with Jerrod coming here to the office on a regular basis?"

Carroll shook his head. "No. This therapy can only be done by institutionalizing him."

Dottie's heart went cold and her face lost color. "You mean at the *asylum?*"

"Yes. Dr. Olson said he had mentioned that possibility to you."

"I guess he did," she said, putting fingertips to her temples.

Dr. Carroll saw the fear in her eyes. "From what I've heard, Mrs. Harper, Jerrod can be very violent."

"Yes," she said.

"He's a large man, I understand."

"Yes, and very strong. And when this…this *thing* takes control of him, it's bad. Really bad. But…"

"But what?"

"I can tell you already, Doctor, Jerrod will never submit to being admitted to the asylum. Never. Are you sure you couldn't do this therapy in your office? I might be able to talk him into doing that much."

"A program of sedatives, yes, but not the therapy. He'll need to be monitored by trained people between my sessions with him."

"Well, could we try the sedative program, at least?"

"If he'll come and see me. I can't do a thing until he and I sit down together."

"All right. I'm going to see Jerrod right after this, and I'll talk to him about it."

"It's a start."

"Doctor, can you help me understand something?"

"I'll try."

"Jerrod is a Christian. How can this be happening to him? The Bible says the Christian's body is the temple of the Holy Spirit."

"That's right."

"Well, since He lives in Jerrod, shouldn't He be able to control Jerrod's mind?"

"I think probably the best response to—"

Carroll's words were cut off by a deep rumble; the building began to shake. The floor seemed to undulate, and Dottie's chair slid sideways.

"Earthquake!" exclaimed the doctor, bounding out of his chair and around the dancing desk.

Dottie was on her feet, wide-eyed. Her heart was racing, pounding so hard she could feel her pulse in her temples. Dr. Carroll wrapped an arm around her and hurried her to the nearest door, which led to a walk-in closet. He flung the door open and held Dottie within the door frame.

It seemed the quake was going to be a long one, then it stopped as suddenly as it had started.

Dottie was trembling in the doctor's arms, fists clenched at her sides, her face sheet-white. A few seconds passed. Suddenly Matthew Carroll realized he was still holding her. He blushed and let go.

"I'm sorry, Mrs. Harper. I didn't mean anything by holding you like that, I assure you."

"I know you were only trying to protect me…and I appreciate it," she said with a smile.

The door to the reception room came open. "You all right, Doctor? Mrs. Harper?" Flora Downing's features were a sickly gray.

"Yes, Miss Downing. Everything all right out there?"

"Just some furniture that needs rearranging," she sighed. "I'll take care of it."

"Let me do it," he said, heading toward the door.

"No, no. It's no problem to slide a few chairs around. My desk stayed put."

The doctor first put Dottie's chair back in place, then shoved the heavy desk where it belonged. He scolded himself while doing so. He had enjoyed holding Dottie, but knew it was wrong to have such feelings toward her. *Lord, You know there was nothing impure in my thoughts, but I was wrong to let myself be attracted to her. Please, forgive me.*

He sat down behind his desk and cleared his throat. "I don't know if I'll ever get used to these quakes. I know it's a part of living in San Francisco, but they always unnerve me."

"We don't get them quite so strong in the valley," Dottie said, "but I don't like them, either. There's always the possibility for a real devastating one."

"I try not to think about it," he said, scratching at an ear. "Well, let's see. Where were we?"

"I was asking you why the Holy Spirit cannot control this quirk in Jerrod's mind since He lives in his body."

"It isn't that He can't, Mrs. Harper," the doctor replied. "God Himself asked Abraham, 'Is any thing too hard for the Lord?' So it's not that He can't, but sometimes the Lord allows things to come into our lives that we don't always like or understand. This is where faith comes in. We're saved by faith, and we walk by faith. We must trust God and believe that He never makes mistakes."

Dottie nodded slowly, taking it in.

"God allowed Jerrod to suffer a serious mental wound in the Civil War, just as He allowed him to suffer physical wounds. The wound in his mind is as real as the wounds he sustained in his body. We must face the plain and inescapable fact that though the Christian's body is the temple of the Holy Spirit, our bodies know pain, illness, and defects. Just so, the mind of the Christian can know *mental* pain, illness, and defects. Our bodies came under God's curse on this earth when Adam sinned. In God's higher thoughts, He sees fit to let us suffer, both physically and mentally. Are you following me?"

"Yes. That makes sense."

"You see, God can heal any of our bodily or mental defects if He so chooses, but it's not always His will to do so."

"But why wouldn't it be His will to heal?"

"That's where His higher thoughts come in. His thoughts are different than ours. But we have examples in Scripture where God could have healed bodily sicknesses and defects, but chose not to." Dr. Carroll opened a drawer, pulled out a Bible, and began flipping pages. "Let me show you what I mean. Was there ever a greater man of prayer and faith than Paul?"

"Not that I know of."

"All right. Look here at 2 Corinthians 12:7. Paul tells of his thorn in the flesh, which was given to him by Satan to buffet him." He handed her the Bible, open to the passage, and said, "Read me verses eight and nine."

Dottie took the Bible and read aloud, *"For this thing I besought the Lord thrice, that it might depart from me. And he said unto me, My grace is sufficient for thee: for my strength is made perfect in weakness. Most gladly therefore will I rather glory in my infirmities, that the power of Christ may rest upon me."*

Dottie met the doctor's gaze. "So God said no. He didn't want Paul healed."

"That's right," Carroll said. "Yet what a great man of faith and prayer Paul was! If it's always God's will to heal if a person only has enough faith, certainly Paul could have prayed away his fleshly thorn. Turn over to Colossians 4:14 and read it to me."

Dottie flipped there quickly. *"Luke the beloved physician, and Demas, greet you."*

"See that? Dr. Luke traveled with Paul for a reason, don't you think?"

"Because he was a physician and Paul needed his care?"

"You're catching on. One more passage—2 Timothy 4." Carroll waited till she had found the page, then said, "Read me verse twenty and see what Paul says."

Dottie's eyes scanned down the page. *"Erastus abode at Corinth: but Trophimus have I left at Miletum sick."*

"See? Paul—a great giant of the faith, a man of prayer—couldn't pray his friend Trophimus well because it wasn't God's will for him to be healed. This is for the Lord to decide, not us."

Dottie was nodding. "My sister has shown me some of this. Her name's Breanna. She's a C.M.N."

"Oh, really?"

"Yes. Perhaps you know of Dr. Lyle Goodwin in Denver?"

"I not only know *of* him, I know him personally. He minored in psychiatry and has spoken at many A.M.A. conventions I've attended."

"Well, Breanna is a visiting nurse and works out of Dr. Goodwin's office."

"Wonderful!"

"She really knows her Bible. One time when I was with her she got into a discussion with a woman who insisted that the blood atonement guarantees our physical healing here and now."

"And what did your sister say?"

"She didn't have to say a whole lot. The woman argued she had perfect health because of Jesus' stripes. After a while, Breanna reached up and gently removed the woman's spectacles, saying, 'Then you certainly don't need these.' I think it startled the woman enough that she finally saw the truth."

"Your sister sounds like quite a woman," Dr. Carroll said with a grin.

"That she is," Dottie said. "Breanna also told the woman that as a nurse, she's qualified to say that everybody who dies— Christian or non-Christian—dies of some malfunction of the body. If Jesus' stripes were for the healing of Christians' bodies, we would never die. Only people outside of Christ would die."

"Good thinking," nodded the doctor. "And absolutely correct. All of God's children eventually die, no matter how strong their faith. Except for Enoch and Elijah, of course. I sure hope I get to meet this sister of yours sometime."

"Maybe someday you can. Between the two of you, I've learned a lot. And I thank you."

"You're welcome. I think with Jerrod it boils down to this— though it's taken several years for the shell shock to affect his mind to the degree you've seen in the past five months, it's just as real as if he had consumption or a diseased heart. Being a Christian doesn't make us immune to mental illnesses any more than it makes us immune to physical illnesses."

The building shuddered slightly, and the windows rattled. The doctor and Dottie looked at each other, ready to make another dash to the closet door. Then the shuddering stopped.

"Aftershock," said the doctor.

Dottie nodded with a touch of fear in her eyes.

"I haven't told you what the sheriff said to me last night," Dr. Carroll continued. "He said he can hold your husband only two days unless he's charged with assault and battery. Since your pastor isn't going to press charges, he'll have to let him go unless you file a complaint and ask that he be held longer. If you file, a county judge will decide how long he can be held."

"Does Jerrod know this?"

"No. Sheriff Donner isn't going to tell him a thing until he talks with you to see what I've suggested. I want to help Jerrod, but I don't want you or your children in danger. If Jerrod will let me treat him, at least with the sedatives, I can make his spells much less severe. Since you say he would refuse to be treated as a patient at the asylum, I strongly suggest that you make his release contingent on his promise to come and see me immediately. He *will* keep a promise to you, won't he?"

"Of course."

"Get the promise before the key is turned, then get him here as fast as possible. If he won't promise, for Jerrod's sake as well as yours and the children's, you'll have to file and see the judge."

"I'll do as you suggest, Doctor," Dottie said, rising from the chair. "I want Jerrod to get all the help he can. I just wish there was a way to cure him."

"Me, too," replied the doctor, also rising. "Maybe someday we'll learn how to cure mental illness, not just treat it."

"Thank you, Doctor," said Dottie, smiling warmly. "You've been a tremendous help already. Ah…may I ask a favor?"

"Of course," nodded Carroll.

"Would there be a time I could see the asylum…just in case one day Jerrod would have to be admitted?"

"Yes, of course. In fact, I need to head over there right now. If you'd like, I could give you a tour."

Dottie was a bit uneasy at the thought of entering the asylum, but she felt it was important that she see it. Together, she and Dr.

Carroll left the building and headed down the busy street toward the asylum. City workers were cleaning up debris from the quake, and people on the street were talking about it. She overheard someone say they were relieved it wasn't the big one seismologists were predicting would hit San Francisco within the next thirty or forty years.

Dottie shuddered at the thought as she and Dr. Carroll proceeded toward the asylum.

11

JERROD HARPER SAT ON HIS BUNK in cell number one in the San Mateo County Jail. On the opposite side of the same cell, Marty Tillman lay on his bunk, smoking a cigarette. There were three other cells, but since Harper and Tillman were the only prisoners, Sheriff Max Donner put them together. It saved Deputy Myron Hall from having to clean two cells.

Tillman was as hard and tough as they come. He had robbed the San Bruno bank at opening time that morning, and a twist of fate had the sheriff and deputy directly in front of the bank when Tillman came charging out with his revolver in one hand and a bag of money in the other. The two lawmen had their guns on him in a flash, and Tillman chose to surrender rather than fight it out. He had already been in prison twice for armed robbery, and he knew that when he went to prison this time, they would throw away the key.

"If you don't help me break outta here," Tillman said, "I'm goin' up for good, and who knows how long you'll be in here? After what I heard the sheriff say you did to your preacher and your wife, you just might be here for quite a spell."

Jerrod fixed him with a stern glare. "I told you to forget it, Tillman. I'm no criminal, and I'm not helpin' put you back out there so you can rob more banks and stages. And if you don't put that stinkin' cigarette out, I'm gonna make you eat it."

Tillman blew smoke toward the ceiling, sat up, and snarled, "Look, pal. It ain't my fault we got stuck in this cell together, but I got a right to smoke if I wanna."

"Not as long as I have to breathe it, you don't." Jerrod rose to his feet and went and stood over Tillman. "Snuff it, or eat it."

Jerrod Harper's size and obvious strength made Tillman decide to snuff it. He dropped the cigarette on the floor and ground it out with his boot. "Ya happy now?" he asked.

Jerrod said nothing and returned to his cot.

Tillman let out a sigh. "I'm gonna break outta here whether you wanna go or not."

Just then the door that led to the sheriff's office rattled and came open, and Deputy Hall and Reverend Howard Yates entered the cell block.

"Your pastor's here to see you, Jerrod," Hall said.

Marty Tillman mumbled a string of swear words, and said, "Oh, boy. Now we get to hear a sermon."

"Shut your mouth, Tillman," Jerrod said. "You've no right to talk that way about my preacher, and I don't want his ears filled with your foul language."

Yates moved close to the barred door and offered his hand to Jerrod. Jerrod took it, his gaze taking in the cuts and bruises on Howard's face. "Preacher, I sure am sorry for what I did to you."

"What's done is done," Yates said. "The main thing now is to get help for you so something like this doesn't happen again."

"Reverend," Hall said, "I'll go on back to the office. You can stay as long as you wish."

"Thanks, Myron." Yates watched the deputy move through the door and close it behind him. He then turned to Jerrod and said, "I went to Dr. Carroll's house in San Francisco late last night. He was gracious enough to talk to me and showed keen interest in your problem. Said he's willing to help if you and Dottie will let him."

"Pastor Yates, I'm grateful that you didn't press charges against me, and I thank you for that…but I'm not goin' to any brain doctor."

Yates saw the fire in Jerrod's eyes, and reached into his coat pocket and pulled out a small Bible. He opened it to Psalm 113 and began reading aloud.

"Praise ye the LORD. Praise, O ye servants of the LORD, praise the name of the LORD. Blessed be the name of the LORD from this time forth and for evermore."

Jerrod's breathing eased and he began to grow calm.

"From the rising of the sun unto the going down—"

"Hey!" Marty Tillman shouted. "This ain't no church, and I don't have to listen to that holy Joe stuff!"

"Excuse me, Pastor," Jerrod said, and he whirled on Tillman, eyes blazing.

"I got my rights, Harper!" Tillman gusted. "I hate that Bible stuff, and I don't have to listen to it!"

Jerrod reached down, sank steely fingers into Tillman's shirt, and lifted him off his feet with one hand. "One more word outta you, and I'm gonna tie you in a knot so tight you'll have to spread your toes to eat. You got that?"

"Okay, okay," Tillman said, trying to mask his fear. "Put me down. I ain't sayin' anything else."

Jerrod dropped him like a rock. Tillman hit the floor hard,

his legs buckling under him. He quickly stood up and returned to his cot. The preacher smiled to himself and finished reading the psalm aloud. Marty Tillman sat on his cot and pouted.

Yates closed the Bible, laid a hand on Jerrod's shoulder, and said, "Let's pray together."

Tillman sneered at the two men and mumbled profanities under his breath as they prayed.

When the amen was said, Yates squeezed hard on Jerrod's shoulder. "I hope to hear that you let Dr. Carroll see you, my friend."

"I…I'll consider it , Pastor."

Yates patted Jerrod's shoulder and headed for the office door. When he reached it, he turned and said, "Give the doctor a chance, Jerrod…for the sake of your family."

Dottie Harper was sure she would find the City Mental Asylum loathsome and unpleasant. She had heard plenty about insane asylums and their unsanitary conditions, mistreatment of patients, bad food, and the wailing and screaming of the inmates.

When Dr. Carroll escorted her through the main door into the lobby, she learned quickly that what she had heard about the wailing and screaming was true. Hideous sounds, though muffled, assaulted her ears.

She saw nothing that appeared unsanitary. The lobby was clean, well-lighted by large windows, and decorated with paintings of still life and countrysides.

Dr. Carroll introduced Dottie to the male receptionist and a big husky man in white who worked as an attendant. He then guided her through a pair of double doors into an open area with a counter, and long, narrow halls that went in three directions. The building was constructed of stone and mortar, and the depressing, colorless stone was visible on the inside also.

Dr. Carroll paused near the counter and said, "Mrs. Harper, as we tour the building, I want you to notice that our place is not like other asylums. We keep it scrubbed clean. And I assure you, the food is good and nourishing."

"That's nice to know," she said with a faint smile. The wails and screams were not muffled now, and they sent cold chills down her back.

"The worst patients are in that section." Carroll pointed to the hallway on their left. "We'll tour the other two first."

Dottie wasn't sure she wanted to go down that hallway at all. In fact, she wasn't sure she wanted to go down *any* hallway. She suppressed the desire to turn and run. She had to know what Jerrod would face if he ever came here.

All three halls were busy with white-clad male attendants moving in and out of the rooms that lined both sides. Dottie spotted two nurses carrying trays, their feminine forms looking out of place among the muscular attendants. She shuddered to think of Jerrod in this place at the height of one of his spells. She was sure it would take three or four men to subdue him.

"Take a look in here," Dr. Carroll said as they approached the first cell door.

Each cell had a steel door with a small open window. Dottie glanced down the hall and saw a man's arm reaching through a window, as if he were trying to grasp something. She hesitated before going any closer to the first door.

"Why don't they have glass in the windows?" she asked.

"The inmates would ram their fists through the glass and cut themselves."

"What about wire mesh? I mean, should they be allowed to reach into the hallway like that?"

"There's no harm done as long as you don't get close enough for them to grab you. We have to have the windows so we can see inside at any time. They would only cut themselves on wire mesh, too."

Dottie steeled herself and peered through the small opening of the first cell. Two elderly women sat at a tiny table, drawing on pieces of cardboard with chunks of charcoal. They looked up and smiled, but their eyes appeared hollow, empty.

Dr. Carroll leaned close to the window and spoke as he would to small children. "Hello, Sadie. Hello, Matilda. Are you having fun with your artwork?"

Suddenly, one of them stood up, anger on her wrinkled features, and threw the piece of charcoal against the stone wall. Her eyes were wild as she ran to the door screaming, "You did it again! You hate me, don't you? That's what it is! I know it! You hate me!"

"I'm sorry, Matilda," the doctor said. "I forgot. I should have said 'Hello, *Matilda*' first this time."

Matilda's gray hair stood out in every direction. She shook her head and screamed, then thrust her arm through the window. Dr. Carroll stepped back out of reach. Matilda screamed obscenities at the doctor and tried to grab him, her fingers curled into claws. An attendant came up behind them, grasped the woman's wrist, and gently pushed her arm back inside.

"Quiet down, Matilda," he said quietly. "Go back and play with Sadie."

Matilda gave the doctor a murderous look, shifted it to the attendant, then turned away. As she moved back to the table where her cell mate had remained, she hissed, "They're all against me, Sadie! They hate me because I'm smarter than they are, and they know it! They should be in here, not me!"

Dr. Carroll patted Dottie's arm. "Don't be afraid. You're safe."

Dottie shuddered and moved along as he led her down the hall. The ceilings were high throughout the building, and the howls and screams and moans resounded off the stone walls.

As they slowly passed cell after cell, Dottie said, "I noticed Matilda's fingernails were clipped really short."

"We keep all the inmates fingernails trimmed like that so they can't scratch anyone...even themselves. We can't let them have pencils either or they'd be jabbing each other's eyes out."

Dottie nodded, but her eyes betrayed her alarm.

"This asylum is far better than most in the United States, Mrs. Harper," Dr. Carroll said. "I spent a month at Bethlehem Royal Hospital in England before taking charge here. They taught me a lot. I've made many changes in my four years as staff chief."

Another man had his arm out a window, shouting that he needed water. An attendant was headed his direction, carrying a tin pitcher.

"Bethlehem Royal Hospital...isn't that the one known as Bedlam?" Dottie asked.

"Yes. It's hardly called that any more, though."

"It's been there a long time, hasn't it?"

"It was founded by Simon Fitz-Mary, sheriff of London, in 1247. It was the first asylum for the insane in England, and with the exception of one in Grenada, Spain, the first in Europe.

Actually it was called Hospital of St. Mary of Bethlehem when Fitz-Mary founded it, and the name Bedlam apparently came from an old English word for Bethlehem. During the next three hundred years, the asylum was infamous for the brutal treatment of inmates—and we got our word *bedlam* to describe any scene of uproar or confusion."

"I assume it's no longer called Bedlam because the patients are treated much better now," Dottie said.

"It's the best facility for the mentally disturbed in the world, as far as I'm concerned. They taught me so many good things that I've put into practice here, or am planning to put into practice as soon as possible."

The tour continued, and the sight of blank-eyed patients drooling on themselves or talking to themselves in meaningless phrases almost made Dottie sick. She couldn't bear the thought of admitting Jerrod there.

The second hall consisted of wards instead of cells. The wards contained those patients whose families or estates could not afford to pay half the cost of a semi-private cell.

Dottie was jittery as they turned the corner to begin the tour of the final hall, which was lined with cells that held one person each. Pads were attached to the walls to a height of seven feet, and the floors were padded from wall to wall. These inmates were dangerous and had to be isolated from all others. The wails and screams were louder here and more frequent. Dr. Carroll eased up to the first door on the right and motioned for Dottie to draw near.

"You won't have to worry about anyone reaching for you in this hall," he said. "They're all in chains."

Dottie moved up beside Dr. Carroll and peered through the

small window. What she saw made her skin crawl. A man about Jerrod's age was kneeling on the padded floor, eyes glistening with amusement as he clamped his hands around the throat of an imaginary victim. His wrists were shackled with chains linked to a steel ring imbedded in the wall at the rear of the cell. The chains gave off a metallic rattle as the man shook his imaginary victim and hissed through his teeth.

Dottie turned away, throwing her hands to her face, and gasped, "Dr. Carroll, I don't need to see any more."

Dr. Carroll put an arm around her, then thought better of it. "All right. I'll have one of the attendants walk you back to the office."

They were just turning to leave when there was a loud bang at the end of the hall, followed by a scream. The door of the last cell on the left flew open. A wild-eyed man bolted into the hall with an attendant on his heels. Two more attendants burst through the lobby doors and ran down the hall.

Dottie stood mesmerized. The escapee's face had an expression of mindless rage as he ran from his pursuer emitting harsh, animal-like cries. The attendant chasing the madman tackled him, and it took only seconds for the three men to subdue him and carry him back toward his cell.

"Sometimes an attendant will get careless and try to work with the patients without chaining them," Dr. Carroll said. "Too dangerous. I don't think that young man will make that mistake again."

Dr. Carroll ushered Dottie toward the double doors. When they reached the lobby, he looked into her eyes and asked, "You all right?"

"Yes," she nodded, pinching the bridge of her nose. "Just a bit unnerved." She took a deep breath and said, "Those attendants are to be commended for the way they handled that poor man. I could tell they were being as gentle as possible."

"I've drilled it into them that the patients must be treated humanely. We have to remind ourselves that though sometimes they act like beasts, they are human beings. It does get a little touchy now and then. Sometimes for the safety of the patients, as well as that of the workers, the wild ones have to be dealt with firmly."

Dr. Carroll could see that Dottie was troubled. "This has upset you, Mrs. Harper," he said softly. "I'm sorry. Maybe I shouldn't have let you see the place."

"Oh, no. It's best that I *did* see it. I know now that I could never let Jerrod be admitted here."

"But Mrs. Harper, you and the children are in danger. Can't you see that?"

"Yes, but…but I love my husband, Doctor, as much as a wife can love her husband. I just couldn't let him come here. And I'm afraid. Afraid that if I get him to come to see you for the sedative treatment, you might see that he's admitted by force."

Carroll sighed. "Mrs. Harper, am I understanding correctly? Are you going to go to San Bruno and tell Sheriff Donner to release your husband? Are you going to go back to the same old thing?"

"Well, I—"

"Please, listen to me. If you can't bring yourself to leave Jerrod locked up, and you won't make him come to me, at least leave him in that jail long enough to pack up your children and go back to Kansas. Certainly you have family back there who would take you in, don't you?"

"You mean leave Jerrod and go back to Kansas?"

"Well, if that's too far, isn't there somewhere you and the children can go where you'll be safe?"

"Dr. Carroll, I took a vow when I married Jerrod to stay with him till death parts us. My vows are sacred to me. I can't just go off and leave him!" Tears filmed Dottie's eyes and her lower lip quivered. A sob forced its way from her throat. "It isn't Jerrod's fault that he's this way. The real Jerrod is a kind, good man who loves me and loves his children."

"Mrs. Harper, I understand about Jerrod. I also understand about *you*. He has a wounded mind, yes, but you have a wounded *heart*. You're carrying much more than you should. You've endured this pain longer than any wife should have to. You must do something to protect yourself and your children."

Dottie was quiet for some time as she wiped away her tears. Finally, she said, "All right, I'll go to the jail. If Jerrod will promise to come see you, I'll have Sheriff Donner release him."

"And if he won't promise?"

"I don't know. I guess I'll cross that bridge when I come to it. I'll be praying that he *will* promise, but you have to promise me that you won't try to put him in the asylum."

"All right," the doctor said reluctantly, "but only if I see improvement. If not—"

"You *will* see improvement, Doctor. I'm sure of it. I must go now."

"I'll have one of the attendants walk you to your wagon."

"That's not necessary," she said, smiling thinly. "I can make it all right."

"I have a staff meeting in just a few minutes or I'd walk you myself," he said, moving along with her as she headed for the door. Dottie stepped onto the boardwalk and told him he would hear from her by tomorrow.

Dr. Matthew Carroll stood and watched her walk away. He admired her resolve to stick by her marriage vows and love her husband with everything that was in her. His heart went out to her. She bore a load few women would hold up under.

12

DEPUTY MYRON HALL looked up from the sheriff's desk and smiled as Dottie Harper came through the door. He thought she looked awfully tired as he rose to his feet and said warmly, "Good afternoon, Mrs. Harper."

"Good afternoon, Deputy," she said, trying to smile. "I've come to talk to Jerrod about putting himself under Dr. Carroll's care. If he'll agree to see the doctor—which I'm sure he will—I'll take him with me."

"Oh, I'm sorry, ma'am, but I don't have the authority to release him. Only Sheriff Donner can do that. He won't be back until quite late this afternoon. Five o'clock, at least."

"I see," she said. "Well…first things first. I'll go ahead and talk to Jerrod about it, then come back at five."

"Sure, ma'am." The deputy nodded and moved toward the door to the cell block. "There's another prisoner in here now. In the cell right next to Jerrod's."

"Oh?"

"Yes'm. As a matter of fact, we had 'em both in the same cell till I decided to change things."

"And what made you decide to change?"

"It was your preacher, ma'am."

"My preacher?"

"Yes'm. He was here this mornin' to see your husband, and while he was visitin' him, the other prisoner caused a little trouble. The reverend told me about it when he come out. Said it looked like Jerrod was gonna mop up the floor with him, so he suggested I move the other guy into another cell. The reverend was afraid Jerrod might lose control and hurt the man real bad. I think he didn't want Jerrod in any more trouble than he's already in."

"I appreciate that," she said.

"Anyway, ma'am, you won't have any privacy back there…that's the point I was tryin' to make."

"Thank you, Deputy. I guess it doesn't make any difference if the other man hears me talking to my husband."

Myron allowed Dottie to pass through the door first, then moved past her and led her down the narrow corridor. Jerrod was on his feet at the bars when they entered the cell block.

Marty Tillman was in cell number two, sitting on the cot with his back against the wall. His face carried its usual dour expression. He watched as Dottie rushed to her husband and kissed him through the bars.

"Stay as long as you want, Mrs. Harper," Hall said. "I'll be in the office if you need me."

"Thank you," she said, then turned and reached through the bars to grasp Jerrod's hands with her own. "I understand Reverend Yates was here."

"Yeah," nodded Jerrod. "Was mighty nice of him to come."

"So what did he say?"

"Not a whole lot of talk, honey. He read the Bible to me, and we had prayer together."

"He didn't talk to you about…your problem?"

"Well, I suppose he did a little."

Tillman left the cot and walked to the bars that separated the two cells. "Excuse me, crazy man. Tell your missus there what the holy man said. You know…'bout how important it is that you see that brain doctor. What's 'is name? Carroll, or somep'n like that."

"Mind your own business, Tillman!" Jerrod snapped.

Tillman shrugged and tilted his head to the side. "Just thought your missus should know that the holy man thinks you got a bolt loose an' you need it tightened."

Jerrod stepped up to the bars that separated them and said, "When I want your advice, I'll ask you. Otherwise, keep your mouth shut!"

"My, my! Testy today, ain't we? I just thought—"

"I don't care what you think! Leave us alone!"

"I'd love to, pal, but they won't let me outta here."

Jerrod burned Tillman with flaming eyes until the outlaw turned and went back to his cot. Dottie was frightened when she saw the look in Jerrod's eyes. She reached through the bars and took his hands again.

"Jerrod, listen to me. I love you. Do you hear me? I love you very, very much."

He seemed to look right through her for a few seconds, then the fierceness and the fire began to diminish. She repeated her words of love and felt the tension go out of his hands and arms.

Jerrod swallowed hard, worked at calming himself, and said,

"I love you too, Dottie. You're the best wife a man ever had."

"Then why'd ya put them bruises on her pertty face?" Tillman said. "You'd think a man as lucky as you'd treat his woman like a lady!"

Jerrod whipped his head around as though stung by a hot iron. "I feel bad enough about what I did to her. I don't need the likes of you shootin' off your mouth."

Tillman chuckled and said, "And just what're you gonna do about it?"

"Jerrod!" Dottie cried, squeezing his hands. "Ignore him! Please, honey, look at me!"

Jerrod's features were trembling as he brought his head back around and looked into her eyes.

"Don't give in!" she said. "I love you, Jerrod! Tell me you love me."

Jerrod's muscular frame trembled as he fought his other self. He gripped Dottie's hands so hard she thought he would crush them.

"Say it, darling! Say it!"

Jerrod's lips quivered, but he choked out, "I love you."

"Jerrod, do you *really* love me? With all your heart?"

"Of course," he said, nodding slowly. "You know that."

She licked her lips nervously. "All right, then. I'm going to ask you to do something because you love me." Dottie freed one hand and reached up to stroke Jerrod's bearded cheek. "Darling, I went to see Dr. Carroll this morning. He says he can treat you if you'll come into his office on a regular basis. He'll put you on sedatives that'll help you not become so violent when…when the spells come on you."

"That's not all he'll do, Dottie. He'll lock me up in that asylum."

"No, honey. We discussed that. He promised me it would just be visits in his office."

"But I don't want to be treated like I'm crazy."

"You're not going to be treated like you're crazy. I explained what happened to you in the War. Dr. Carroll understands. He can help you."

"I can't do it!"

"Jerrod, listen to me. You love James and Molly Kate, don't you? I know you do. Remember how terrible you felt when you beat James the other day? What would you do if some other man had done that to your son?"

Jerrod's eyes went wide at the thought.

"Was it you who beat James or was it the other Jerrod, the one inside you?"

"It was *him*…the other Jerrod."

"Then why don't you beat the other Jerrod by letting Dr. Carroll help you?"

While this thought was sinking in, Dottie said, "Sheriff Donner will only release you upon my say so."

"He can't hold me more'n a day or two unless Reverend Yates presses charges."

"He can if I go before one of the county judges and say I fear for our safety if you're released. The judge could confine you here indefinitely, Jerrod."

"But…you wouldn't leave me locked up in here!"

Dottie cleared her throat and moved back from the bars a step. "Jerrod, I cannot subject James and Molly Kate to the fear of being beaten by you any longer. I see the terror in their little faces. I'm their mother, and I must protect them. If you won't promise to go to Dr. Carroll with me, I'll have to ask a judge to keep you locked up. Do you understand what I'm saying?"

Tears filmed Jerrod's eyes. "Yes. I understand. Dottie..."

"Yes, darling?"

"Tell Sheriff Donner I'll go see this Dr. Carroll."

"That's a promise?"

"That's a promise."

"Oh, Jerrod!" she exclaimed, rushing back to him and kissing him through the bars. "Thank you!" She raised her eyes heavenward and said, "And thank *You*, Lord!"

"Go tell the sheriff, honey," Jerrod said, smiling. "Let's go home. I'll see Dr. Carroll today, if he has time."

"Sheriff Donner isn't here right now," Dottie said. "He won't be back till about five o'clock, and Deputy Hall can't release you. I'll drive back into San Francisco and set up an appointment with Dr. Carroll for tomorrow. Then I'll be back here at five so you can be released."

"All right," Jerrod said.

They kissed through the bars again, and Dottie hurried to the office. "I'll be back at five o'clock," she said to Myron Hall. "In case I'm a little late, don't let Sheriff Donner leave again. I want to get Jerrod out today."

Hall cleared his throat nervously and said, "I'm sorry, ma'am, but Sheriff Donner just sent a message to me by wire from San José. He won't be back until morning."

"Oh, no. Well, I guess there's nothing we can do about that. I'll go back and tell Jerrod I'll be here first thing in the morning."

Jerrod had just sat down on his cot when he heard Dottie's footsteps once again. He stood and went to the bars. "Back already?" he said with a smile. "What time's the appointment?"

Dottie smiled broader than she had in a long time, then explained that the sheriff wouldn't return until morning. She would be back then to get Jerrod and take him to San Francisco.

Dottie went away for the second time, and Jerrod returned to his cot and sat down. The stench of a cigarette met his nostrils. Jerrod glowered at Tillman, but said nothing.

Tillman rose from his bunk and moved toward the bars between them. "You oughtta be ashamed of yourself, Harper," he said. "Those are some mean lookin' bruises you put on her. Somebody bigger than you oughtta take you out behind the barn and beat you till there's nothin' left. I've robbed banks and stagecoaches, but I've never hurt a lady."

"Shut up, Tillman!" Jerrod said.

"Such a sweet little lady. I'd like to horsewhip you myself!"

"I told you to shut up!" Jerrod yelled, leaping to his feet and pressing his face to the bars.

Tillman stayed out of reach. "You know what? Dottie oughtta divorce you and find a man who'll love her and treat her right."

Jerrod gripped the bars till his knuckles turned white. Then, slowly, he lowered his head and began to weep. Tillman took another step closer.

"You don't understand!" Jerrod sobbed. "The War…it did somethin' bad to my mind. It's like another person lives inside me. An evil person. Sometimes he takes control of me, and I can't help what I do. I can't help it!"

"You're a stinkin' liar, Harper! You just use that shell shock stuff as an excuse to beat up on people and get away with it!

You're a bully, that's what you are!" He took another step forward and blew smoke in Jerrod's face. "I hope your wife comes to her senses, leaves you in here, and divorces you! That's what you deserve!" He drew on the cigarette and leaned close to exhale again in Jerrod's face.

Jerrod shot both hands through the bars and seized Tillman by the shirt. Surprise widened the outlaw's eyes, and the cigarette fell from his mouth, tumbling to the floor in a shower of tiny sparks. There was a flame in Jerrod's eyes. His lips pulled back into a wicked smile.

"Look, Jerrod," Tillman stammered, "I...I didn't mean it! I was only joking! I—"

"*You're* the liar, Tillman! You meant every word of it! So you like to blow smoke in people's faces, eh? Maybe I need to rearrange your face a little!"

Jerrod yanked Marty Tillman forward, smashing his face into the bars.

In the office, Deputy Hall heard a heavy thud and a shriek like he had never heard before. He dashed into the cell block to see Jerrod repeatedly yanking Tillman toward him, smashing his bloodied face against the bars.

"Jerrod! Stop it!" Hall shouted.

Jerrod continued as if he had not heard him at all. The deputy quickly unlocked the cell door, rushed in, and cracked Jerrod over the head with the barrel of his revolver. Jerrod dropped in an unconscious heap.

Marty Tillman slumped to the floor. Hall left Harper's cell, locked it, and entered Tillman's cell. He found the outlaw conscious but dazed. Blood was coming from his nose and mouth. Hall half-carried Tillman to the cot and laid him on it, then began washing the blood from his face. He didn't appear to be seriously hurt. Jerrod came to and rolled, groaning, onto his hands and knees. He struggled to rise, his head still filled with swirling fog, and managed to stumble to his cot.

Hall moved out the barred door, locked it, and said, "What brought this on?"

Jerrod eyed the deputy from where he sat rubbing the back of his head. "He blew smoke in my face and shot off his mouth about things that're none of his business."

"So what'd you say anyhow?" Hall asked, looking toward Tillman.

Tillman sat up, grimacing in pain. Before he could speak, Jerrod cut in. "He said Dottie oughtta leave me and find a man who'll treat her right."

"Well, she *should!*" Tillman said.

Myron Hall sighed and said, "Well, let's just say she deserves better than she's been getting. I'm glad you've agreed to put yourself under Dr. Carroll's care, Mr. Harper. You've made your wife very happy…and she has some happiness comin'. Now you two see if you can't be a bit more civil to each other. If nothing else, maybe you could try ignoring each other."

Hall then returned to the office. Jerrod laid down on his cot and quietly stared at the ceiling, his head throbbing.

Marty Tillman lay there and cursed under his breath. Twice when Hall was tending to him, he could have grabbed the deputy's gun, but his vision was blurred and he was too woozy to have tried a break.

The outlaw grinned to himself. He would find a way to get

another opportunity. He looked through the bars at Harper, who lay in silence on his cot. Hatred boiled in him toward the big brute. He imagined how good it would feel to put a bullet in him.

13

THE AFTERNOON SUN slanted through the latticed office windows, lengthening the shadows of the cross-pieces as they stretched across the polished hardwood floor.

Flora Downing looked up as the door came open and smiled when she saw Dottie Harper enter. "Back so soon, Mrs. Harper? What can I do for you?"

Dottie's eyes were dancing with delight. "I need to make an appointment for Dr. Carroll to see my husband in the morning, Miss Downing."

"All right," said the receptionist, sliding the black appointment book toward her from the corner of the desk. "Is one time better than another?"

"Late morning would be best."

Flora ran the blunt end of the pencil down the page. "Well, I have 10:15, or I have 11:30."

"Let's make it 11:30."

"All right," Flora said, "11:30 it is. Your husband's name?"

"Jerrod. J-E-R-R-O-D."

"Mm-hmm," she hummed, writing it down. "H-A-R-P-E-R. Same as yours."

Dottie laughed. "Most husbands spell their last name the same as their wives." It felt good to laugh. Things were looking better. Jerrod was going to get help, and Dr. Carroll was the man to do it.

At the Reeves farm, James Harper was in the barn, watching Grandpa Will milk the big rawboned Holstein. They had fed the chickens together earlier, and would soon go to the house for supper.

The sun was setting over the low-lying hills that led to the ocean, giving an orange-red cast to the land. The big barn door that faced the house was open, and James took a moment to admire the sunset. The sound of the two milk streams hitting white foam in the bucket was a familiar one to the eight-year-old.

"Daddy says he'll let me learn to milk when I'm twelve, Grandpa," the boy said.

"Well, now, that's a good age to learn," the old man said cheerfully. "Your hands won't be big enough to do the job till about then. In fact, come to think of it, I learned to milk when I was twelve."

"That was quite a while before the Civil War, wasn't it?" James asked.

Will chuckled. "Yeah, you might say so. Quite a while!"

James heard a faint rattling sound and turned to see a wagon coming across the field from the west. "Hey, Grandpa! Look! A wagon!"

Will Reeves's eyes weren't that good anymore without his spectacles, which he had left in the house. "I reckon you're right," he said. "Can you tell if there are two people in the seat?"

James moved to the door and focused on the moving vehicle. "Just one person," he said, calling over his shoulder. "My mother. I can tell by the color of her hair."

"Well, I hope she's got good news for us."

"Me, too," the boy said.

Will finished milking and picked up the milking stool with one hand and the bucket with the other. "Okay, partner," he said, "you can open the stanchion and let ol' Bossy out."

A few minutes later, man and boy entered the kitchen to find Molly Kate in her mother's arms, with Maudie looking on and smiling.

James rushed across the room and gave his mother a kiss and a hug. "So what about Daddy?" he asked, fearful that she might say the sheriff was going to release him.

"Well...Grandma's asked us to stay for supper. So let me help her get it on the table, and I'll tell everybody at the same time!"

"Is Daddy getting out of jail, Mommy?" Molly Kate asked.

"Let's wait for the good news, honey," Dottie said, bending over and kissing her daughter's forehead.

Horrifying images of her father in a mindless rage flashed into Molly Kate's mind. She hoped the good news was that he would see Dr. Carroll, but that the doctor could visit him in the jail. She was afraid the nightmare would start all over if her father came home.

Soon Dottie and her children were seated at the Reeves table with the elderly couple. Will led in prayer, then as they began to eat, Dottie told them the latest news about Jerrod. Tears spilled when she came to the part about Jerrod agreeing to see Dr. Carroll.

Brother and sister eyed each other furtively, wondering if the "good news" meant that their father would be coming home before the doctor had cured him.

"Dottie, are you sure Jerrod won't back out at the last minute?" Maudie asked.

"I'm sure," she smiled. "He *promised* he would do it, and with Jerrod and me, when we make a promise there's no backing out."

"So when does he start?" Will asked.

"Tomorrow morning," Dottie said with a lilt in her voice. "I've made an appointment for him to see Dr. Carroll at 11:30. I'll be at the jail shortly after Sheriff Donner arrives for the day. That is, if the children can stay with you while Jerrod and I go to the doctor's office."

"Of course they can," Maudie said. "You know they're always welcome."

"So after the doctor sees him, is he coming home?" Will asked.

"Yes! Isn't it wonderful? Jerrod's going to get better. I just know it!"

"Mommy, wouldn't it be better if Dr. Carroll would just go to the jail and see Daddy?" James asked.

"The doctor wouldn't have time for that, James," Dottie said. "He's too busy. Psychiatrists don't make house calls, or jail calls, anyway. People have to go to their offices to see them."

Dottie saw alarm in James's eyes. She reached toward her son and took hold of his hand. "Sweetie, you don't have to be afraid of Daddy anymore. Dr. Carroll is going to put him on some sedatives."

"What's sedratives?" Molly Kate asked.

"Sedatives—that's medicine, honey. Medicine that will make Daddy better."

"You mean there won't be the bad man inside him anymore?"

"The doctor said Daddy can't be completely cured, but he will be a whole lot different when he takes the medicine. We won't have to be afraid like we have been."

"Can't Jesus make Daddy all better?" Molly Kate asked.

Dottie was taken aback for a moment. Praying for just the right words, she said, "Jesus can make Daddy all well if He wants to, yes. But sometimes He has reasons for not making us all well when we have things wrong with us. The Apostle Paul had a sickness in his body that he prayed to Jesus about, asking Him to make him well, but Jesus told him it was in His plan for Paul's life that he keep that sickness. And you know what?"

"What?"

"The Bible says Paul was a better Christian and servant of the Lord because he kept that sickness in his body. We must understand the same thing about Daddy. Maybe Jesus wants Daddy to have his sickness to better use him for His glory…and to draw our family closer to Him than we would be if Daddy was made completely well."

"Oh," Molly Kate said.

To James, Dottie said, "Do you see what I'm saying, son?"

"I think so. So even though Daddy won't be all well, he won't beat on us anymore when he's taking the medicine?"

"Well, honey, that's what Dr. Carroll hopes. But we love Daddy enough to give it a chance, don't we?"

"Yes. He's a good Daddy when that bad man inside him isn't showing."

"Well, we'll all be praying that the medicine will work," Will said. "In fact, as soon as we're finished with supper, why don't we have a time of prayer for him?"

All were in agreement. When the meal was over, Will led them in prayer, asking God to give Dr. Carroll wisdom as he cared for Jerrod, and that the sedatives would accomplish the doctor's intentions. He also asked the Lord's special protection on Dottie and the children.

Dottie intended to stay and help with the dishes, but Maudie told her to take the children and head on home. They needed some time together, and Dottie needed to get to bed early.

Eager about what the next day would bring, Dottie embraced the elderly couple, thanked them for all they had done, and drove her children home.

Dawn came on August 10, 1861, with a gray reluctance. Jerrod Harper and his fifty men-in-blue were part of the left flank in the two-pronged surprise attack on the Confederate forces positioned along the banks of Wilson's Creek. Harper's unit was under the direct command of Brigadier General Nathaniel Lyon, who led the main body of Union troops. Colonel Franz Sigel led an enveloping force that would strike the Confederates from the rear.

A heavy mist drifted through the treetops and choked the surrounding fields and woods with suffocating humidity. It had been blistering hot the day before, and the night had hardly cooled at all.

The Union troops crept toward the Rebels through the mists that appeared ghost-like on the surface of the moist, grassy fields.

General Lyons was in the lead some fifty or sixty yards ahead of Sergeant Harper's unit. The signal to commence firing into the Rebel-infested thickets along the creek would come when Colonel Sigel opened up on them from the rear.

It was zero hour. The Yankees were so close, they could hear the rippling of the creek and the Confederate troops talking among themselves.

Suddenly Sigel's guns opened up, both muskets and artillery. General Lyon's forces commenced firing, and the battle was under way. The Confederates had been surprised, but were ready for the fight. Both sides of the creek were swept with fire and smoke.

Sergeant Harper and his men were to converge on a cluster of Confederate artillery imbedded in a heavy stand of trees on the creek bank closest to them. The fifty yards that lay between them and the line of enemy artillery was partially covered with patches of trees surrounded with heavy brush.

Harper gave the signal and led out. They were to wait until they could see the whites of Rebel eyes before firing. The Union soldiers knew they were charging into the teeth of Confederate artillery and that certain death awaited many of them as they followed their big husky sergeant.

Shrapnel exploded in deathly puffs of smoke, and Rebel musketeers rained bullets on the advancing Yankees. Harper ejected a wild cry and heard the cries of his men as they charged. The thunder of battle roared in his ears. Suddenly a second line of Confederate artillery appeared off to their right a few yards up the creek bank.

Harper's heart almost stopped. He and his men were about to be caught in a deadly crossfire. Bullets were already whipping around them like sleet in a northeaster. The cannons to their right opened up, and Harper's men began to drop like flies. The field was filled with smoke, and the sergeant lost sight of his unit as cannon shells exploded all around him.

A bullet whizzed past his head, its hot air kissing his ear. He staggered, slipped on the wet grass, and fell.

A gust of hot wind abruptly cleared the smoke, and there was a break in the firing. Jerrod staggered to his feet, reeling about, and saw Rebels coming from the creek brush across the grassy field. He looked around for his squad. He was alone. *Where were his men?* Had the Rebels killed them all?

"Hey!" he shouted. "Maynard! Wilson! Dougherty! Girard! Where are you?"

A cannon shell exploded a few feet from him. Shrapnel whistled dangerously close, and the blast of it took his breath. Hundreds of Confederates were coming at him now in a swarm of gray.

There was more smoke, then it cleared again. When it did, his eyes fell on dozens of blue-clad bodies, sprawled all around him. "No!" he screamed. "No-o! All my men are dead! No!"

"Harper! Hey, Harper, wake up!" came the voice of Marty Tillman.

Jerrod's mind came clear, and he sat bolt upright on his cot. The vague light from a street lantern showed him where he was. He was bathed in sweat, and he was breathing hard.

"Shut up, crazy man!" Tillman yelled. "I'm tryin' to get some sleep!"

Jerrod jumped off the cot and charged across the cell. *"You* shut up, Tillman! You think I asked to have these nightmares?"

Myron Hall lived in an apartment directly above the jail. Jerrod Harper's voice first brought him awake with the soul-wrenching cry that all his men were dead. Then he heard Marty Tillman shouting at the top of his voice.

"Oh, no," Hall mumbled groggily, "Harper's got his hands on Tillman again."

Hall hurriedly pulled on his pants, slipped into his boots without taking time to put on his socks, and darted for the door, pulling his suspenders up over his long johns. He put his hand on the door knob, then stopped and wheeled around. "Never go out the door without your sidearm," he whispered, quoting his boss.

Quickly, Hall strapped on his gunbelt and headed down the stairs. He made his way into the office and heard Tillman and Harper still shouting at each other.

Hall fired a lantern, adjusted the flame, and hurried into the cell block. Tillman heard Hall's heavy footsteps in the corridor and fell to the floor, doubled up in a fetal position with his hands covering his face, and moaned as if in great pain.

Hall glowered at Harper. "Now what did you do to him?"

"Nothing!" Jerrod said.

The deputy shot Harper an angry look, moved to Tillman's cell, and inserted the key into the lock. The cell door swung open, and Hall hurried in with the lantern. He set it down on the small table and bent over Tillman.

"Let me see, Marty!" Hall said. "What'd he do?"

"Rammed his fingers into my eyes!" Tillman said, peeking to see if Hall was wearing his gun.

"I did not!" Jerrod yelled. "I never touched him!"

Myron turned, pointed at Jerrod, and hissed, "Sit down and shut up!"

Tillman yanked the deputy's revolver out of its holster, snapped back the hammer, and lined it on Hall's face. "Get back!" he commanded. "And put those hands in the air!"

Hall blinked in disbelief. Tillman had tricked him, and he fell for it. Or had both prisoners tricked him?

Tillman rose to his feet and said, "Turn around."

"Now look, this isn't gonna get you anywhere. You—" The gun barrel came down on Hall's temple, dropping him like a rock.

"You won't get far," Jerrod warned. "They'll hunt you down like a hound hunts a fox."

"We'll see about that," grinned Tillman, lining the gun on Jerrod through the bars. "You're goin' with me, wife-beater."

Tillman left the unconscious deputy in the cell and locked the door. Still holding the gun on Harper, he unlocked cell number one, swung the door open, and growled, "I'm gonna give you what you deserve, pal. Only it ain't gonna be a mere horsewhippin', and it ain't gonna be here. A gunshot here might alert somebody. C'mon. Let's go."

Deputy Hall opened his eyes and tried to figure out where he was. His vision was blurred, and his head felt like it had been split open. A trickle of blood ran down the side of his face.

Marty Tillman!

Hall sat up, shook his head to clear his vision, and winced at the pain it caused. Slowly his eyes began to focus, and he looked around. Both men were gone. He struggled to his feet and staggered to the cell door. It was locked. He sat down on the cot and pressed Tillman's pillow against his temple to stay the flow of blood.

So they both tricked me, he thought. *Made friends in spite of what Jerrod did yesterday, planned the escape, and it worked.* All Deputy Hall could do now was wait for Sheriff Max Donner. He dreaded that, too. His own stupidity had led to the escape.

At sunrise, Dottie Harper was up and preparing for her day. Her hopes ran high. She was optimistic that with the sedatives and Dr. Carroll's counseling, Jerrod would be made better.

At breakfast, she could see apprehension on the faces of her children. She smiled at them and said, "I know you're both wondering if Mommy's doing the right thing in getting Daddy released from jail. Please trust me. We want Daddy to get better, don't we?"

"Yes, ma'am," they said together.

"Haven't we prayed and asked Jesus to make Daddy better?"

"Yes, ma'am."

"Well, I believe Jesus is going to use Dr. Carroll to make Daddy better. So let's cheer up and be happy."

James and Molly Kate smiled for their mother. Her optimism made them feel better.

"James," Dottie said, "I know this whole horrible thing has interfered with your school work, and I won't punish you for letting it slide. But you really need to buckle down now that things are getting better. Understand?"

"Yes, ma'am," he said.

"I want you to take your *McGuffey's Reader* and your arithmetic book to Grandma Reeves's house and do your lessons. You know which ones."

James nodded.

The morning sun was lifting off the eastern horizon into a few scattered white clouds when Dottie and the children climbed into the family wagon and pulled out of the yard. Twenty minutes later, Dottie left the Reeves place and pointed the team eastward. The birds were singing in the trees that lined the road, and she hummed along with them. She would arrive in San Bruno around 8:15, which would give her plenty of time to get Jerrod released and have him in San Francisco before the 11:30 appointment with Dr. Carroll.

A little before eight, Sheriff Donner ambled down the boardwalk and entered his office. Since the door was unlocked, he assumed his deputy had already fed the prisoners. Myron always came in at 7:15 when there were prisoners to feed. He picked up their breakfast at the café across the street, then did his janitorial duties.

The sheriff approached his desk and noticed trash in the wastebasket and that the floor needed sweeping. Puzzled, he walked to the door that led to the cell block, opened it, and listened. Silence.

"Myron!" he called. "You back there?"

"Yes!" came the reply. "I'm...I'm locked in a cell!"

Donner hurried into the cell area to see his deputy standing at the barred door of cell number two. There was dried blood on the side of his face.

"What happened?" Donner asked as he unlocked the cell door.

The deputy told him the story. Donner was angry at Hall for letting the prisoners trick him and fumed at the thought of Tillman and Harper working together to escape. Hall apologized for being so gullible and received half-hearted forgiveness.

"We've got to get on their trail," Donner said. "I'll go fetch Clancy. We'll have him watch the office while we're chasin' those two."

Clancy McBride had been sheriff of San Mateo County before Max Donner. He had retired some seven years previously and often filled in for Donner when both sheriff and deputy had to be away from the office.

It was 9:10 when McBride stood at the door of the office and watched the two men swing into their saddles. He heard Donner say how sorry he felt for Dottie, who was going to be extremely disappointed in her husband. He gave them a wave as they rode out of San Bruno, hoping to find some sign of which way the escapees had gone.

14

THE CRACK OF THE .44 CALIBER WINCHESTER resounded among the jagged peaks on the eastern promontories of the Sierra Nevada Range. Wayne Feaster, K. D. Wilhite, Les Pate, and Brad Cahill stood over Feaster's dead horse. The chestnut gelding had just stepped into a hole on the steep incline halfway up Luther Pass, breaking its leg and throwing Feaster from his saddle.

Feaster swore, cursing his luck. He turned his burning eyes on the other three and hissed, "Now, what're we gonna do? We'll never make Placerville in three days ridin' double."

The four were on their way westward over the Sierras to pull a series of bank robberies with another gang headed by an old prison mate of Feaster's, Chick Dubb. The two leaders had run onto each other in Carson City, Nevada, in late August. Dubb revealed a plan he had been working on for several months to make a fortune hitting California banks from Placerville to San Francisco, but he needed more than his three men to pull it off. He had inside information on cash deliveries, and would know when to hit which banks to make the best hauls.

Feaster and Dubb decided to join forces. Because of prior commitments, the two gangs would meet in Placerville in early October to begin their robbing spree. Feaster knew that Dubb was not a patient man. If they were late arriving in Placerville, Dubb would find other men to help him.

Brad Cahill, the youngest of the bunch, saw the frustration on his boss's face, and said, "From what I've heard about this pass, boss, it's traveled quite a bit. Maybe while we're climbin', we'll run into some travelers comin' down who've got a good saddle horse. All we'll have to do is throw our guns on 'em, take the horse, and keep movin' west."

Feaster swore and said, "I don't like *maybes*, Brad. If we don't make it to Placerville in time, Chick'll find somebody else to help him. We'll miss out on all that money."

"Wayne, I've been over this pass before," Les Pate said. "There's a California Stagelines way station right at the top of the pass. There's always a few good-lookin' saddle horses in the corral there."

"Well, I hate to wait till we reach the summit to pick up another animal," Feaster said. "We're still losin' valuable time. But...all we can do is keep movin'."

"You can ride my horse, Wayne," Cahill said. "I'll double up with one of these guys."

"My horse is a little bigger than the others," Pate said. "You can ride with me."

"Okay, Brad, I'll take you up on it," Feaster said. "Let's go."

Saddle leather creaked and horses blew as the outlaws mounted up. When K. D. Wilhite swung into his saddle, something on the trail below and behind them caught his eye. He sat still and peered eastward, studying the rocky, tree-lined ridges that swept downward to the level ground, now far in the distance.

"See somethin', K. D.?" Feaster asked.

"Yeah. I seen somethin' move down there a few seconds ago.

See, look. It's a wagon train comin' this way."

"Sure enough," Pate said, lifting his hat to shade his eyes against the brilliant sun.

Wilhite hipped around in the saddle, unbuckled a saddlebag, and pulled out a pair of binoculars. "I think I saw a couple of men on horseback out in front."

Feaster was squinting, trying to make out the line of wagons as they moved slowly along the winding trail amid towering pines and massive, protruding rock shelves. Only part of the train was visible at any given moment.

A gusty wind swept over the side of the mountain, flapping the wide brim of Wilhite's hat as he peered through the binoculars. He grinned when he caught a glimpse of the first wagon, because just ahead of it were two riders. He guided his mount to where Feaster sat astride Cahill's horse and handed him the binoculars. "Take a look, boss. Right ahead of the lead wagon."

Feaster placed the binoculars to his eyes, searched for a few seconds, then focused on the two riders. "Either one looks like good horseflesh to me!" he exclaimed.

"What have they got, boss?" Pate asked.

"Looks like a big black. The other's a white-faced bay. Both geldings, I'd say." He handed the binoculars back to Wilhite and grinned broadly. "Looks like I'm about to get me a good horse, fellas!"

The outlaws dismounted and led their mounts a ways off the trail. Together they studied the layout of the land below them.

Wilhite was still using his binoculars. "I think I see the perfect spot to surprise 'em, Wayne."

"Yeah? Where?"

Wilhite handed the glasses to the gang leader and pointed.

"Look right past that outcroppin' of rock down by that patch of blue spruce. See that open spot right where the trail makes a sharp curve?"

"Yeah, I see it. Sure enough. That's where I'll put my hands on that big black!"

"Perfect spot," Cahill said. "We can put our guns on the riders and the first wagon or two as they come around the bend. We'll have the black and be gone before the other people even know what's happened."

A bright autumn sun and a cloudless sky looked down on the wagon train as it climbed slowly into the Sierra Nevadas. Luther Pass was lined with trees whose fall-colored leaves danced in the wind. Small animals scuttled across the trail in front of Curly Wesson's wagon. From time to time, hawks were seen on the wing, climbing toward the sun, then coasting on the currents, wheeling in delightful patterns, then swooping down and floating above the treetops.

Sitting next to Curly Wesson, Breanna Baylor shaded her eyes with her hand to watch three hawks put on a show. When the great birds had disappeared, she let her glance drift to the two riders a few yards ahead. John Stranger and Rip Clayson were in some kind of discussion about the Scriptures, for John had his Bible in his hand and was reading from it to Rip.

Breanna smiled to herself as she studied the broad back of the man she loved. *Thank You, Lord. Thank You for bringing that wonderful man back to me. My life is full, Lord, because of the salvation You've given me...and it will be complete the day I can become John's wife.*

While the wagon train climbed higher and higher into the Sierras, Breanna let her thoughts run to her sweet sister. Her heart thrilled as she pictured the moment she and Dottie would first see each other. Breanna envisioned that it would be on the front porch of the big three-story house Dottie had so carefully described for her in a letter. And she was eager to finally meet Jerrod after all these years. And her niece and nephew. Breanna wondered if Molly Kate could really look as much like her mother as Dottie's letters had indicated.

"What's that your playin' with?" Curly Wesson's voice intruded on her thoughts.

"Hmm?"

"Pardon my inquisitiveness," Curly said, "but at first I thought that round thing in your hand was a silver dollar. I can see now that it ain't. It's got a star in its center and some words engraved around the edge. What is it?"

"Oh, this," Breanna said, and raised the silver disk up so he could get a good view of it. "It's a medallion. Pure silver, all right. Here, take a look at it."

Curly took the medallion in his hand, squinted, then extended his arm to its full length.

Breanna giggled. "Before long, Methuselah, you're going to have to break down and either buy a pair of spectacles or get an extension built on your arm."

Curly snorted. "Methuselah, eh? Well, I may be gittin' a li'l gray and wrinkled around the edges, missy, but I ain't *old!* I'm just *mature!*"

Breanna laughed. The dear old man had been such a blessing to her. She had led many people to Christ since she had become a Christian, but none more enjoyable to be around than Curly

Wesson. Curly had grown so much in his faith since he had been saved on the trail in Wyoming, and Breanna had experienced much joy in helping him to grow.

Curly held the medallion so it did not catch the sun's rays and read the inscription aloud. *"THE STRANGER THAT SHALL COME FROM A FAR LAND—Deuteromony 29:22."*

"Deuteronomy," she corrected him.

"That's what I said."

"No, you said Deute*rom*ony."

"Well, you may be barely into your thirties, honey pie, but your ears are a-failin' ya."

"All right. First mistake I made today. You said it right."

"That's better," he said with a smile. "Curly Wesson don't make mistakes."

"Oh, is that so?"

"Well, I guess I should admit that I made one mistake once."

"Only one?"

"Yep."

"And what was that?"

"I thought I was wrong, but I wasn't."

Breanna laughed. "Your a case, Mr. Wesson."

Curly showed her his nearly toothless grin. "We're both cases, honey. It's just that your case is a lot perttier than mine!"

Breanna laughed again, shaking her head. She was going to miss the old man when the journey was over.

Curly handed the medallion back to her, and Breanna answered his question before he could voice it.

"From John."

"John? *He's* the stranger from a far land?"

"John's whole mission in life is to help people. To help them believe the Bible and open their hearts to Jesus, and to help them out of trouble, often even saving people's lives."

"I done figgered that out."

"Good for you."

"But what's the medallion for?"

"Whenever John has helped people, he always leaves behind one of these medallions before he rides away. I have several of them myself."

Curly lifted his hat and scratched his head. "But what does this 'stranger from a far land' mean? And what's Deuteromony 29:22 say?"

"Well, in Deuteronomy 29, God says if the people of Israel do not obey Him, He will plague their land and bring various kinds of sickness upon them for their idolatry. 'The stranger that shall come from a far land' is taken from verse 22 of that chapter, where God says that if the people of Israel turn from Him and worship false gods, the next generation of Israelites and strangers who come there from far lands will find a land desolate and judged by Him." Breanna reached inside the wagon for her Bible and said, "Here, let me read it to you."

While the wagon rocked up the steep, winding trail, Breanna read Deuteronomy 29:22 to Curly, then followed with verses 23 through 27, teaching her new convert how much God hates idolatry and the kind of punishment he exacts on idolaters. She then told Curly that John Stranger had simply adopted the nine words from verse 22 to place on the medallion.

The old man glanced at her, furrowed his brow, and asked, "Is his name really *Stranger?*"

Breanna did not reply immediately. She let her gaze take in two hawks looking down on them from atop a giant rock pillar, then said, "Don't you think the name fits him? I mean, the way he travels about helping people out of trouble or capturing outlaws...then like a phantom, fades out of the picture and is gone?"

"I...uh...I ain't shore you're answerin' my question."

"Many people have called him Stranger when he's been of help to them, but he hasn't volunteered his name."

"Well, I'm still not sure just 'zactly what you've told me, girl. But I think it's all you're *gonna* tell me. So, let me ax ya somep'n else."

"I don't know," she said.

Curly raised his bushy gray eyebrows. "Now, wait a minute here! I ain't axed the question yet!"

"I already know what it is."

"All right, miss smarty—what is it?"

"Your curiosity is screaming to learn what far country John Stranger is from. And like I just said, I don't know."

"You're in love with that tall drink o' water an' you plan to one day be his missus an' you don't know where he's from?"

"John hasn't told me anything about his past, Curly. I figure when he wants me to know, he'll tell me."

Curly rubbed his stubbled chin. "Don't it seem sorta strange to you, all this secrecy?"

"Why do you suppose he's called Stranger?"

"Well, I—"

"Some things are better left alone, Curly. I'm comfortable with things the way they are. John's the most wonderful man I've ever met. He loves me, and I love him. I trust him completely.

198

The Lord has brought us together. I know that for sure. What else do I need?"

"Nothin', honey. Pardon this ol' fogy's curiosity. You an' that John Stranger just have yourselves a wonderful an' happy life!"

"With God's hand on us, we will!" Breanna said.

As the horses ahead of the train pressed up the steep trail, John Stranger twisted in the saddle, placed his big black Bible in the saddlebag, and said, "Well, Rip, that's probably enough for today."

"I'm going to miss these sessions, John. You've taught me so much."

"Glad to be of help," Stranger said.

The light wind continued to sweep down off the jagged, towering peaks above them. A cold chill washed over Rip Clayson. "I'll be glad when we get through these mountains."

"I'm sure it can get pretty bad when the snow flies," Stranger said. "I'd say, however, chances are we'll get through before that happens. Even if we see some snow, it shouldn't be too bad."

"Ordinarily that's so," Clayson said. "It's that slight chance that we *could* get caught in a blizzard that keeps my stomach on edge."

Stranger ran his gaze over the mountains that dwarfed them, then looked back toward where they had come from. "I figure we're up about thirty-five hundred feet right now, wouldn't you say?"

"Luther Pass tops out at just over seventy-seven hundred feet. I'd say we're not far from halfway to the top."

"Cool as it's getting at this altitude, I expect it'll be downright cold at the top."

"Cold I don't mind," Rip said. "It's blowing snow and ice that makes it dangerous on this steep trail."

They were passing through a heavily wooded area and started around a sharp curve as they came out into the open. There was a stretch of about a hundred yards before they would be in heavy timber again. Towering rocks lined the trail on both sides.

A lone man stepped out from behind a boulder and into the middle of the narrow trail. He stopped and raised both hands, signaling for Clayson and Stranger to stop.

"What do you suppose he wants?" Rip asked, turning around and motioning for Curly to draw rein.

"I don't know," Stranger said, "but we're about to find out."

15

WAYNE FEASTER'S HANDS held no weapon as he stood with his feet spread in a defiant stance. His revolver remained in the holster on his hip.

As Rip Clayson and John Stranger drew up, Feaster gave them a threatening look and said, "Stay in your saddles. If you so much as flinch, you're dead men. If you don't believe me, lift your heads very slowly and take a look in the rocks off to your left."

Clayson and Stranger could see K. D. Wilhite crouched between two rocks, his rifle pointed directly at Clayson.

"Now, take a look up to your right," said Feaster, grinning with grim pleasure.

At a level just a bit higher than Wilhite, they could see Les Pate in the cleft of a huge rock, high-powered rifle pointed directly at Stranger.

"Just what do you want, mister?" Rip demanded.

"Shut up!" Feaster said. "I'll get to that in a minute. I want you boys to know I've also got a man who's got a bead on the cute little blonde sittin' on the seat of the lead wagon."

Stranger searched the rocks and spotted a third rifle close to the man on the right. He could not see the man who held it, but there was no question the gun was pointed at Breanna.

Stranger's face mirrored his anger as he said, "If the lady is so much as scratched, mister, the world isn't big enough for you to hide."

"Tough talk for a dude who's a trigger squeeze from death, ain't it?" Feaster said.

"What do you want?" Stranger asked.

"First, I want you and your partner to ease your guns out of their holsters and drop 'em on the ground. Then I want *you*, mister, to get off your horse."

Feaster saw Stranger's face harden and roared, "You wanna bullet in your heart, mister? We ain't hankerin' to kill nobody here, but it'll happen if you give us any trouble! All we want is the black and the saddle and bridle that's on 'im. Everybody stays calm, we'll ride on, and all you've lost is a horse and some leather. Give us trouble, and somebody's gonna lose their life. Could be you, could be the woman. Now do as I say and drop those guns."

Five men came running around the bend from the wagons that were yet out of sight, guns ready. As they drew alongside the Wesson wagon, Rip shouted, "Hold it, men! Don't come any farther!"

"What's going on, Rip?" one of them called. "Who is this guy?"

"He hasn't graced us with his name," Clayson said, "but he's not alone. There are three riflemen up there in those rocks. One has his gun pointed at John, another at Miss Breanna, and the other at me. They want John's horse. Back off and lay down your guns, and don't let anybody interfere."

On the wagon seat, Curly whispered, "Just sit still, honey, and keep your eyes on John."

Breanna nodded, glanced at the rifle that was aimed at her from the high rocks, then set her eyes on John, who was half-turned in the saddle, looking at her. When their eyes met, he gave her a steady look. There was something in those iron-gray eyes. She knew John was telling her to keep her attention on him. When he saw in her expression that she understood, he straightened around in the saddle.

Rip and John slowly drew their revolvers and let them fall to the trail.

"That's good, boys," Feaster chuckled. "Cooperation here will be well worth the effort. Now, *you*, cowboy…off the horse."

Stranger swung his leg over the saddle and stepped down. Ebony pulled his head around, eyed his master, and nickered.

"It's all right, boy," John said, patting Ebony's neck. "This man wants to take you for a ride."

Feaster stepped up and said, "Move away, mister. You don't need him nearly as bad as I do…believe me. You can pick up another horse at the way station on top."

Stranger stepped back and watched as Feaster moved up beside Ebony and took hold of the reins. The big black gelding swung his head around again and gave a short whinny.

Under his black broadcloth coat, John Stranger wore a .36 caliber Navy Colt pistol in an obscure shoulder holster. He glanced again at Breanna, then at the hiding place of the man who had her in his gunsights.

Wayne Feaster gripped the reins and raised his left foot to slip it into the stirrup. Ebony sidestepped, causing him to miss. Feaster cursed and tried it once more. Again, the big black danced sideways, blowing and whinnying. The outlaw swore angrily at Ebony and went at him again, this time swinging aboard from ground to saddle in one leap. The big black shook his head and whinnied, but stood still.

Feaster glared at Stranger and said, "I'm ridin' outta here, and my men are gonna keep their guns trained on the three of you for five minutes. If nobody does anything crazy, my men will disappear, and nobody will get hurt. But I'm warnin' you, don't try to come after us. First man we see on our trail will die." Feaster looked up at his men and shouted, "Okay, boys, I'm off! If one of 'em flinches, let 'em have it!"

Suddenly Ebony arched his back and lowered his head. He released an angry whinny and exploded under his would-be rider. Feaster went straight up into the air, then came down hard on the saddle. The impact knocked the wind out of him, but he swore and hung on. Ebony did a full circle, head down, rear hooves kicking.

Wayne Feaster gripped the saddlehorn with one hand and clung to the reins with the other. He had always considered himself an expert horseman. He had broken many horses to the saddle, but he had never climbed on the back of one like this. Feaster went up again and came down with a jolt that jarred his teeth. Ebony bucked and turned in a tight circle, throwing Feaster off balance. The outlaw came down once more, this time biting his tongue. The brassy taste of blood filled his mouth.

Ebony laid his ears back, snorted angrily, and gave another violent buck. Feaster took flight and landed hard on his head and shoulder. He didn't move.

High up in the rocks, Wilhite, Pate, and Cahill looked on wide-eyed. Cahill rose up a few inches, his attention fixed on Feaster, who lay unconscious on the ground. The muzzle of his rifle, however, had not left Breanna. The other two still held their weapons on Rip and John, but their eyes were riveted on Feaster.

Stranger's right hand plunged inside his coat for the Navy Colt. At the same time, he shouted, "Breanna, go!" Breanna dove inside the wagon just as John fired at Cahill.

Stranger's slug tore into Cahill's right shoulder, knocking him down. The other two outlaws cursed and headed for Cahill, keeping low. Les Pate bent over him and examined the wound. "C'mon," he said, helping Cahill to his feet. "Wayne's not movin' down there. He's either dead or hurt real bad. We gotta get outta here in a hurry!"

Wilhite picked up Cahill's rifle, took hold of him also, and they stumbled their way toward their horses.

John Stranger holstered the Navy Colt inside his coat and picked up his .45 as Rip Clayson slid quickly from his saddle. The men who had gathered at Curly's wagon searched the towering rocks while hurrying toward Stranger and Clayson. Others had come from the stalled wagons and were right behind them.

"Rip, I'm going up there," John said. "I think I hit the one who had his rifle trained on Breanna."

"I'll go with you," Clayson said, moving toward him. "In fact, I think it would be best if we took a half-dozen of these men with us. Those no-goods just might be waiting up there to shoot whoever sticks his head in amongst those rocks."

"I doubt it," John said. "I'd wager the other two took off. But choose your half-dozen, and let's go."

Clayson quickly picked out six men, telling the others to stay on guard. Then they followed John Stranger up into the rocks, keeping their eyes peeled for any sign of the gunmen. When they reached the top, the outlaws were nowhere to be seen.

Stranger made his way to the perch where Brad Cahill had held his rifle on Breanna, and as he suspected, his bullet had found its mark. There were blood spots on the rocks and on the ground. The others soon gathered around.

"That's pretty good shooting," Rip said. "Sharp angle, small target. Looks like you got him good. Quite a bit of blood."

"There's more over here, Rip," one of the men called. "He's leavin' a trail."

"Let's follow it," Stranger said.

A few minutes later, they found the place where the three horses had been tied. The gunmen had fled. The ground was quite rocky, and there were no hoofprints to follow.

When John, Rip, and the six men reached the lower level, they found Breanna and Carolyne Fulford kneeling over the injured outlaw. Everyone in the wagon train was gathered in the open area. A few clustered near Breanna and Carolyne, curious to see how bad the man was hurt.

John and Rip went to Breanna and Carolyne, and the others filled the crowd in on what had happened. The outlaw lay flat on his back. He was conscious, but obviously in a great deal of pain.

"How bad is he hurt?" John asked.

"Broken collarbone and a dislocated shoulder," Breanna said. "His head took a pretty good blow, and he's got a big knot under all that hair. There's a slight cut on his scalp, too."

"I assume you haven't given him anything for the pain, nor tried to put the shoulder back in place."

"No. He only came to about two minutes ago."

Stranger nodded, then set his piercing gray eyes on the injured man. "What's your name? And why did you want my horse?"

"Ain't there somethin' you can give me to ease the pain? Whiskey, maybe?"

"No whiskey on this wagon train," John said. "However, this lady whose life you threatened is a nurse. I think she can help you."

Feaster gave Breanna a pleading look with his pain-filled eyes. "I'm sorry, ma'am. We didn't mean you no harm. Please...can't you give me somethin' to take this pain away?"

"She can do more than that, mister," John said. "She can set your shoulder and bind you up so your broken collarbone will heal properly."

"Please, ma'am, do it!" Feaster begged, looking at Breanna again. "I can't stand to hurt like this!"

"First, I want your name," John said. "And don't lie to me."

"My name's Edgar Wilson."

"Where you from?"

"Arizona. Phoenix."

"What's the name of the mountains forty miles east of Phoenix?"

"Uh...Dragoons."

"You're lying, mister. You're not from Phoenix. Forty miles east of Phoenix are the Superstition Mountains. I want the truth. Tell me your name."

"Man, I'm hurtin', can't you see that?"

"Yes. And I'm waiting."

"Okay, okay. Name's William Becker. I'm from Carson City, Nevada."

"How long you lived there?"

"I don't know—'bout twelve years I suppose."

"Twelve years? Then you know that the town wasn't called Carson City until just over ten years ago. What was its previous name?"

Feaster gave him a blank look.

"You're not getting any relief till I hear the truth, mister. What's your name, and in how many states and territories are you wanted by the law?"

"What're you talkin' about? I ain't no outlaw!"

"No? Then why did you put guns on us, threaten our lives, and try to steal my horse?"

"Well…I needed the animal to get me down to Placerville. Got a business appointment there."

"You must like that pain," Stranger said.

"I ain't lyin'! I'm a legitimate businessman."

"Legitimate businessman? Would a legitimate businessman run with skunks who hide in rocks and threaten innocent people? Looks like you're going to have to just keep hurting."

"No! Please…let her do somethin' to help me!"

"Sure. When I get the truth."

"All right! All right!" he gasped. "I'm Wayne Feaster. Wanted by the law in Idaho, Nevada, Arizona, and California."

"For what?"

"Robbery."

"What kind? Banks? Stagecoaches? Trains? Little old ladies?"

"Banks and stagecoaches. C'mon, mister, what more do you want—I need help!"

"So what's your business in Placerville?"

Wayne Feaster gave in and spilled it all to Stranger and the few gathered near.

Stranger eyed him with disdain. "So you were going to make a big haul with Chick Dubb, eh? I know about Dubb. Bad company for you, Wayne. You should've learned that in prison. Now look what he's got you into. We're taking you with us, and I'm going to turn you over to the law at Placerville."

"Right now, all I care about is this pain. Please let the nurse—"

"In a minute. What about your three cronies? Will they go ahead and meet Dubb in Placerville?"

"How should I know? They ran out on me, didn't they? Maybe they'll meet up with Chick at Placerville and maybe they'll go somewhere else. Please! This pain is killin' me!"

Wayne Feaster was carried to the rear of Curly Wesson's wagon and laid on the tailgate. Breanna put him under with chloroform, and with John's help, snapped the shoulder back in place. Using what material she had, she bound up his arm and shoulder and suspended the arm in a sling. When Feaster came to, he was placed in one of the wagons. Breanna gave him laudanum to dull the pain, and soon he was in a deep sleep. Breanna left Feaster and found the people of the wagon train gathered in a circle, listening to John.

"Feaster's henchmen just might look in on us further along the trail and decide they want their leader back. I don't have to tell you they'll use force if it serves their purpose. I want all of you—men, women, and children—to keep on the lookout. If you see anything that looks like Feaster's pals are near, give a holler. We're all in this thing together, and we've got to watch out for each other. Since one of the three is wounded, they may be trying to find medical help for him. If so, they might be too busy to bother us. Besides, they don't know whether their boss is dead or alive. But we need to stay alert in case they show up."

The people agreed to keep their eyes open for any sign of Feaster's men, then the gathering broke up so they could get ready to roll out.

Breanna moved up to John, smiled, and said, "I'm proud of you, darling. You really handled Feaster well. I hated to see him suffering so, but you did the right thing in making him tell you the whole story." There was a pause, then she said, "I love you, John."

John embraced her. "I love you, too, sweet lady. Now let's get you into the wagon."

Stranger took her by the hand, walked her to Curly's wagon, and lifted her onto the seat. Before he backed away, Breanna leaned forward, looked into his eyes, and said, "Thank you for making sure that man up in the rocks couldn't get a shot at me."

John grinned. "Don't have to thank me for protecting the greatest treasure I have in this world."

Breanna watched as John strode to his big black horse. Ebony nickered at his master's approach.

Stranger stroked Ebony's long face, then patted his neck and said, "Good boy. You sure took care of that outlaw."

The magnificent animal bobbed his head and whinnied as if he understood what his master had said.

16

THE THREE OUTLAWS reached the place where their horses were tied, and Les Pate and K. D. Wilhite helped a wincing Brad Cahill into his saddle. Pate pulled a dirty bandanna from his hip pocket and handed it to his wounded friend. "Here, use this," he said. "We'll get higher up, then stop and take a better look at the wound."

The trio rode hard up the steep slopes for a half hour, then pulled into a enclosed area that was out of sight from the trail. Cahill was dizzy and needed to rest. Wilhite and Pate laid him on the ground and examined the wound carefully, tossing the bloody bandanna away.

"The slug's buried in your shoulder about an inch above the armpit, Brad," Pate said. "If we don't get it outta there, you'll either bleed to death or die of lead poisonin'."

Cahill licked his dry lips. Fear showed in his eyes. "Either of you know anything about diggin' a bullet out?"

"Not me," Wilhite said, shaking his head.

"Me, neither," said Pate. "But I know somebody in these mountains who does. Remember I told you about the way station at the top of the pass?"

"Yeah."

"Well, it's not just a way station, it's a general store too. Tough old woman runs the place. I've heard her tell how she patched up a lotta gunshot wounds when she ran a store down in Placerville durin' the gold rush days back in the fifties. I've met a couple men she patched up. They swear by her…say she's good as some doctors they've known."

"Well, let's do what we can to stop his bleedin'," Wilhite said, "and head on up the mountain."

"There's a spare shirt in my saddlebag," Cahill said. "You can use it…to wrap around the wound."

While Wilhite tied the shirt around Cahill's shoulder, he said, "Les, this old woman…she run the place by herself?"

"Yeah. She's a widow. Her name's Judy Charley. Her husband was a Mohave Indian they called High Mountain Charley—I guess 'cause he used to run the station at the top of the pass before he met the old girl and they got married. She's tough as they come. Wears men's clothes, chews tobacco, and wears a Colt .45 on her hip."

"Sounds like a real doll," Wilhite said.

"You won't forget her," Pate chuckled.

"All I care," Cahill said, unable to cover his pain, "is that she can save my life."

Pate and Wilhite hoisted Cahill into his saddle, then they rode hard up the steep pass, pushing the horses as fast as they could go. Pate told them they could make the top by midnight if they kept moving at a good pace. From time to time they had to stop for Cahill's sake. After a few minutes rest, they would push on. A clear sky and a nearly full moon gave them enough light to stay safely on the trail.

It was two o'clock in the morning when they topped Luther Pass and hauled up in front of the large log building that was fronted with two signs:

Charley's General Store
Judy Charley, Prop.

California Stagelines

A stagecoach was parked between the log building and the corral, which was situated forty yards away, sided by a large barn. The silver moon showed them several horses behind the split-rail fence in the corral.

"We gotta make up a story about Brad gettin' shot," Wilhite said. "What'll we tell her—it was a huntin' accident?"

"You must be slippin' in your old age, pal," Pate said, helping the wounded man from the saddle. "That bullet's from a small caliber pistol, not a rifle. This old girl is no fool. She'd pick up on that lie the instant she dug the slug out."

"Then let's tell her we were comin' up the pass and some robbers jumped us. We fought back, but before we drove 'em off, one of 'em shot Brad."

"That's better," Pate said, steadying Cahill, whose knees were about to give out. "The old girl lives in a shack out back. Let's sit Brad down on the porch, here. You stay with him, and I'll go wake her."

Les Pate hurried behind the building and up to the small, unpainted shack that stood in the shadow of a massive pine. He pounded on the door several times. When there was no response, he pounded on it again. He was about to bang on the door a third time when lantern light flickered against the old lace curtains that adorned the windows on either side of the door.

There were footsteps as the glow of light grew brighter, then the door rattled and came open. A short, skinny form clad in a man's woolen nightshirt and wearing men's work shoes was outlined against the yellow flare of the lantern. "What is it, young feller?"

"You probably don't remember me, ma'am," Pate said. "I've been over the pass and in your store on several occasions."

"Shore I remember you, sonny. Cain't recall your name, but I never fergit a face. It's a little late…er should I say it's sorta early? Anyway, since ya done got me outta bed, what do ya want?"

"I remember you tellin' about some doctorin' you done on miners who got shot up back in the gold rush days when you were runnin' a store in Placerville."

"Yep. Done that. Took out a lotta bullets. Some of 'em made it, an' some of 'em kicked the bucket. Done the best I could. Weren't no doctor around them parts fer quite a spell. You got somebody shot up needs doctorin'?"

"Sure do, ma'am. Good friend of mine. He's in pretty bad shape too, or I wouldn't have woke you up."

"All right. Gimme a minute, an' I'll git some proper clothin' on."

The wagon train made camp on the steep incline of Luther Pass about a mile above the spot where Wayne Feaster's horse lay dead on the trail. Since there was no open area large enough for the wagons to form a circle, they were strung out snake-like at an elevation of about forty-five hundred feet.

People built campfires along the line and huddled around them, wearing heavy coats. The temperature had begun to drop sharply when the sun went down, and the night wind had a bite to it.

Carolyne Fulford volunteered to feed the outlaw so Breanna could eat her supper with John. Rip Clayson stood at the rear of the wagon where Carolyne sat beside Wayne Feaster and fed him broth with a large spoon. The laudanum Breanna had given him made his stomach sour. Broth was all he could tolerate.

After their meal, John and Breanna walked through a stand of wind-swept pines to the edge of a massive canyon. They could see the white foam of a river far below. Breanna wore a scarf to protect her ears from the cold wind, and though she was in a heavy coat, she felt a chill seeping to her bones.

John put an arm around her, pulled her close, and said, "Maybe this will keep you warm."

She looked up and smiled. "I feel warmer already."

He bent down and planted a soft kiss on her lips.

"Mmm," she said. "Now I feel even warmer."

"I love you, Breanna," he said. "I always will. You know that, don't you?"

She reached up and stroked his scarred cheek. "Yes, I know that. You're so different than Frank Miller was. I'll never doubt your love, darling."

Huddled together, they let their eyes roam the granite walls of the canyon sprayed silver by the moon. The stars twinkled like windows in a fairy palace overhead. The sweet scent of pine was on the wind.

"Isn't that a beautiful sight?" Breanna said, snuggling close.

"I was just thinking—*In the beginning God created the heaven and the earth.*"

"Mm-hmm. And Solomon says in Ecclesiastes, *"He hath made everything beautiful in his time."*

John grinned. "And He saved His finest work till it was time for you to be conceived and born."

Breanna stood on her tiptoes, kissed his cheek, and said, "You say the nicest things, John Stranger."

"I just speak the truth, Miss Baylor."

Tears moistened her eyes. "I'm going to miss you so much when we part in San Francisco."

"Well, maybe I'll be heading east with you."

"What?"

"I've been thinking. Unless the Lord directs me differently, I'll just buy a train ticket for Ebony, put him in the stock car, and ride back to Denver with you. I'm sure Marshal Duvall can use my services. He always has some kind of problem to solve or an elusive outlaw to track down because he's short-handed."

"Oh, John, that would be wonderful! Just think of it...riding the train together all the way from San Francisco to Denver!"

"It'd be all right with me," he said. "I'll just have to wait and see if the Lord directs differently by the time we reach the coast."

They returned to the camp arm in arm. John walked Breanna to the wagon where she slept, kissed her goodnight, and climbed into his bedroll under a towering pine a few feet away.

Three days had passed since Les Pate awakened Judy Charley in the middle of the night. It was now ten minutes past noon in the high Sierras. The normal stiff wind was blowing over the top of Luther Pass.

The old woman had just sent a Nevada-bound stagecoach on its run down the east side of Luther Pass. She was sweeping the porch when she saw the wagon train top the crest of the pass, led by two men on horseback. The train formed a circle in a wide space among the trees across the road.

Judy stepped to the edge of the porch and said under her breath, "Whoopee! Oughtta sell a whole lotta stuff to that bunch!"

Curly Wesson left the rest of the travelers and crossed the road. He was getting low on beef jerky and wanted to buy some more before the others swarmed the store. As he drew near, he was jolted a bit by the sight of Judy Charley. Her back was slightly humped, and she stood no more than five feet tall. She had coarse gray hair that stuck out in strands of varying lengths. Her homely face was deeply lined, and she had a jutting, tobacco-stained chin. Her large eyes seemed to look right and left at the same time, and the man's shirt and overalls she wore looked as if they were hanging on a scarecrow. On her feet were a pair of men's work shoes, and on her narrow hips hung a Colt .45 in a black leather gunbelt.

Judy grinned at Curly as he drew up. All of her teeth were missing except one that protruded from her upper gum at the front of her mouth. Her wrinkled lips were sunken in around the hollow place where her teeth used to be. She had a large wart on the lobe of her left ear, and one that matched it between her eyes at the top of her thin, humped nose. Under her left cheek was a telltale lump of tobacco.

"Howdy, good-lookin'," Judy said. "Don't recollect layin' eyes on you afore."

"Well, I been over this here pass a few times, ma'am, but never took time to stop. You carry beef jerky, I assume."

"I shore do," she nodded, then spit with the wind. "C'mon inside."

The store was quite spacious and stocked with a good supply of everything a general store was known to carry. There were shelves built into every wall, and the floor was well-covered with more shelves and glass cases. The twenty-foot counter where items were paid for was stacked with merchandise of every description.

Judy led the old man to the end of the counter and pointed to a large box full of beef jerky strips wrapped in paper. "Right there, honey," she said. "Just pick out all ya want."

Curly grabbed sack after sack and stuffed them under his arm. Judy went behind the counter, picked up an empty coffee can, and spit into it. She set the can back down and said, "There's a special price on jerky fer the man what knows how to talk right."

"Is that right?"

"Shore 'nuff. What's your name, handsome?"

"Curly Wesson, ma'am." He set the jerky on the counter and asked, "What's the damage?"

"Well, ord'narily them sacks is twenty-five cents apiece. But since you're such a sweet-talker, they's fifteen cents apiece."

"Well, thankee, ma'am. That's mighty nice of ya. I seen your name on the sign. You're Judy Charley, right?"

"You got it, Curly," she said.

The wagon train crowd poured through the door, and Judy Charley happily had her hands full, collecting money from her customers. John and Breanna browsed until everyone had been taken care of, then they approached the counter. Judy used the coffee can, then grinned at the couple and asked, "What kin I do fer you folks?"

"I assume you're Mrs. Charley?" John said.

"Yep."

John was trying to look her in the eye, but he couldn't tell which one was focused on him. "Mrs. Charley, in the past three days have you seen three rough-looking men come through? One of them has a gunshot wound in his shoulder."

"What do ya wanna know fer?"

Stranger quickly explained what had happened on the trail and told Judy they were taking the gang's leader to the law in Placerville. He made sure she understood that the three men he was looking for were killers and needed to be apprehended.

"Well, mister," Judy said, "the one ya shot is in a back room right now, layin' on a bunk. I took the bullet outta his shoulder when they come in here in the middle of the night. They told me they was hit on by robbers, an' Brad got shot in the fracas."

"Do you know Brad's last name, ma'am?" Stranger asked.

"Nope. Just Brad. Others is K. D. an' Les."

"Are K. D. and Les back there, too?"

"Nope. They left here a li'l while ago, sayin' they'd be back soon. Come to think of it, I did notice they been awful nervous the last day or so. They was wantin' to git on the move, but Brad's been so sick and weak, he couldn't travel. He ain't doin' good atall. I done the best I could, but I ain't no doctor."

"Well, ma'am, this young lady right here is a nurse. Could we go back and see him?"

"A nurse, eh? What's your name, honey?"

"Breanna Baylor, Mrs. Charley."

"And this is *Mister* Baylor?"

"No," John said. "We're not married. My name is John Stranger."

"*Stranger?* Your name's John *Stranger?* Never heard of such a name."

"Well, now you have, ma'am. Could we see Brad?"

"Shore, c'mon. I'll take ya back."

John told Breanna to go on back with Judy. He would tell Rip Clayson that the wounded outlaw was here and that the other two could show up at any time. He would also bring Breanna her medical bag.

Judy took Breanna into the room where Brad Cahill lay. There were dark circles under his eyes, and his skin was pallid. When he saw Breanna's face, he recognized her as the woman he held in the sights of his high-powered rifle from atop the rocks. His eyes showed it.

Breanna pulled up a chair and sat down. "I see you recognize me, Brad."

He said nothing.

"I'm a nurse. I want to see what kind of job Mrs. Charley did on you."

Judy left Breanna, saying she needed to get back to the store. Breanna removed Judy's bandage and examined the sutured wound.

"Am I…gonna be all right, ma'am?" Cahill asked.

"You've lost a lot of blood," Breanna said. "Has Mrs. Charley been giving you lots of water?"

"Yes."

Breanna looked up as John Stranger came through the door and stood by the bunk. "How's he doing?" he asked.

"Mrs. Charley did a good job taking the bullet out and sewing him up. He's lost a lot of blood, but I believe he'll make it."

"Can he ride in a wagon?"

"It won't be easy for him, but he should be able to."

"Did you tell him about Feaster?"

"No."

Cahill's eyes widened. "Is...is Wayne still alive?"

"Yes. Banged up, but alive. He's in one of the wagons. We're taking him to the marshal in Placerville, and we'd love to have you join us. You're both going to prison for a long time."

Cahill swallowed hard.

Stranger leaned down and lanced him with his steely eyes. "You put a gun on this lady, mister. You can be real thankful you're wounded. If you weren't, I'd take you out behind the barn, and I don't think you'd like what I'd do to you."

Stranger stood straight again, handed Breanna her medical bag, and said to the outlaw, "I want to know where your pals went."

"I have no idea," Cahill said. "I didn't know they'd gone anywhere."

"Well, as soon as Miss Baylor gets some laudanum into you, we'll be pulling out. I'll be back to get you in about half an hour."

K. D. Wilhite and Les Pate were listening outside the window of Brad Cahill's room. They had saddled up to ride down the eastern slope of the pass and see how close the wagon train might be. Brad's condition had kept them from moving on, but they wanted to be gone by the time the wagon train arrived. They had barely ridden away from the store when they saw Clayson and Stranger leading the train to the crest of the pass. They had galloped into the forest to avoid being seen.

The outlaws hunkered beneath the window and eyed each other.

"We ain't lettin' 'em take Wayne or Brad to the law in Placerville!" Wilhite said in a low whisper.

Pate nodded. "Best bet is for us to grab the nurse and put a gun to her head. We'll hold 'er hostage and tell 'em to get their wagon train outta these mountains. Once they're gone, and Wayne and Brad can travel, we'll leave the nurse here and head for parts unknown."

"Sounds good to me," Wilhite said. "Let's move."

John Stranger passed through the store and saw Curly Wesson talking with Judy Charley. He caught Curly's eye and wiggled his eyebrows. Curly got the message. His face crimsoned. Stranger grinned and walked out the door.

"What was that all about?" Judy asked.

"Aw, that young whippersnapper was just givin' me a hard time. Anyway, Miss Judy, as I was sayin', I used to have that terbaccy-chewin' habit meself."

"Ya say *used to.* What happent?"

"Well, I got saved."

"Ya got *what?*"

"I met Jesus Christ, God's Son. He changed a whole lotta

things in my life. But the best is, I know I'm goin' to heaven when I leave this ol' world."

Judy grinned. "I've heard about this gittin' saved stuff, Curly, an' I've often wondered where ol' Judy was gonna go when she kicked the bucket. But I didn't know if there was a way to really know where ya was goin' when your time come. Ya mean a person can really *know* they's goin' to heaven?"

"Shore can. I'll go git my Bible. You'll believe it if'n it's in the Bible, won't ya?"

"Well, of course."

"All right, then. Be back in a jiffy."

John Stranger had been talking with Rip Clayson and several other men at the wagon train when he saw Curly Wesson leave the store and head toward his wagon. Curly grinned at John as he moved past him. He was about to climb over his tailgate when a sharp voice cut the air.

"Hey, you there in the black! Your name John Stranger?"

Every eye swung to the man who stood at the front corner of the store, his gun drawn and aimed at John Stranger. Stranger recognized the face immediately. It was the gunman who had aimed the rifle at him from the rocks back on the trail!

John took a couple of steps in the outlaw's direction but halted when the man blared, "Hold it right there!"

"How'd you know my name?" John asked.

"Your little girlfriend told me," Les Pate said, grinning. "My partner's got her in Brad's room...and he's got a gun to her head."

"You harm a hair of her head, and I'll—"

"Shut up and listen to me!" snapped Pate. "I want you to bring Feaster into the station, then move the wagon train out. We'll keep the little nurse and your two saddle horses here. When we know the train's long gone, and Wayne and Brad can ride, we'll be on our way. Do as I'm tellin' you, and the little nurse won't get hurt. Cross me, and she'll get her head blowed off."

Inside the store, Judy Charley had heard Pate yelling at John Stranger. She peered through a side window and saw the outlaw standing near the corner of the building with his gun drawn. She hurried toward the back of the store, picked up a heavy cast-iron skillet that was on display, and headed out the back way.

"So, what's the word, tall man?" Pate said. "You gonna bring Wayne in and get the wagon train movin' down the mountain? If I don't show up at that back room in another coupla minutes, my partner's gonna blow your girlfriend away."

More than once on this wild frontier, John had faced a man holding a gun on him, drawn, and shot him before he could pull the trigger. It crossed his mind to try that now, but he was afraid the sound of a gunshot could get Breanna killed.

Stranger's mind was racing for a solution when he saw the old woman creeping up behind Pate. He hoped none of the people looking on would give Judy away.

"I'm not producing Feaster till I know Breanna's all right, mister," John said.

"You can take my word for it, Stranger. She's okay at the moment, but she won't be okay much longer if you don't bring Wayne out."

Judy Charley was almost there. Curly watched from beside

his wagon, urging her under his breath to swing hard. Judy tip-toed up behind Pate and drew the skillet back.

"I don't like your terms!" Stranger said.

"Well, you ain't got no choice! It's gonna be the way we say, or—"

The skillet met the side of Pate's head with a meaty, sodden sound, making a dull ring. He went down like a brain-shot steer. The crowd started to cheer, but John hushed them, not wanting to alarm the outlaw holding Breanna.

John, Rip, and Curly hurried to the old woman, who stood over the unconscious outlaw, ready to hit him again if he needed it.

"Good job, ma'am!" Stranger said with a smile. "Thank you."

"Tweren't nothin' to it," Judy said.

Stranger looked at Clayson and said, "Tie him up, Rip. I'll be back shortly."

As the tall man hurried away, Clayson called, "Don't you want some help?"

Stranger was rounding the building, heading for the rear. "No! I'll take care of it!"

When he reached the rear of the building, John flattened himself against the back wall and edged up to the window of Brad Cahill's room. He removed his hat and stole a peek inside. K. D. Wilhite stood over Breanna, who was still seated beside the cot, his revolver pressed against her head. Stranger slipped inside, moved down the hallway to the room, and tapped lightly.

"It's me. I'm back," he said, making his voice sound like Les Pate's. "Open the door."

Heavy footsteps sounded, the key rattled in the door, and it came open. Wilhite never saw the fist that connected with his jaw. He went down in a heap.

John stepped over him, and Breanna hurried into his arms. He held her for a long moment, then said, "Go tell Rip to send a couple of men to carry Brad to the wagons."

"All right," she said, looking down at Wilhite, who was beginning to stir. "What about him?"

"Bring a rope, and I'll tie him up."

Breanna hurried down the hall into the station office, then passed through the store. She saw Curly Wesson and Judy Charley in a corner behind the counter, looking at an open Bible. Breanna looked on with curiosity, but didn't have time to stop.

Rip Clayson, John Stranger, and a couple of men from the train loaded Brad Cahill, Les Pate, and K. D. Wilhite into separate wagons. Breanna and Curly stood by the old man's wagon, talking to Judy Charley. Rip Clayson called for everyone to take their places as he mounted his horse, which stood next to Ebony.

Stranger walked over to the Wesson wagon and found a beaming Curly standing beside Judy. The old woman was showing her snaggletooth in a wide smile.

Curly's eyes sparkled. "I just got my first convert, John! Miss Judy here done got saved!"

"Wonderful!" Stranger exclaimed. "I'm so happy for you, Miss Judy!"

"An' guess what," Curly said. "She's done throwed her coffee can away already...an' I've got a personal invite to come back and...uh...maybe do a li'l courtin'!"

John laughed heartily. "Well, that is good news, Curly! Congratulations!"

Moments later, the wagon train pulled out. Curly Wesson had Breanna hold the reins so he could stand on the wagon seat and wave to Judy Charley till she passed from view.

17

PLACERVILLE, CALIFORNIA, was a busy town. Though the gold rush that began in 1849 and lasted through the early 1860s had been over for nearly ten years, the town had continued to grow. Hundreds of men who failed to strike it rich fell in love with the area, stayed there, and went into the logging business. There were more than a dozen mills in and around Placerville, which provided dependable employment for men willing to work hard. This drew more people, and new business sprung up as a result.

It was early October, and summer's heat was being replaced with cool breezes off the mountains.

Placerville's deputy marshal, Bert Watson, was returning from delivering a court summons to a man who lived in the foothills of the Sierras just east of town when he spotted a wagon train wending its way down Luther Pass. The youthful lawman trotted his horse toward the line of wagons, adjusting his hat against the noonday sun.

He met up with the two horsemen who rode point as they neared level ground. He raised his hand in a friendly signal for them to stop and reined in, smiling. "Howdy, gentlemen. I'm Deputy Marshal Bert Watson from over here in Placerville. I assume you're part of the wagon train that's behind you."

"Sure are," said the man on the bay gelding. "I'm Rip Clayson, wagon master. Something I can do for you, Deputy?"

"Well, maybe, sir. Is there a man named John Stranger in your train?"

"That's me," said the man on the big black horse.

"Oh, good," Watson said. "I believe you're acquainted with Chief U. S. Marshal Solomon Duvall in Denver."

"Sure am."

"Well, Mr. Stranger, he wired my boss, Marshal Jack Abner, early last week. Said you had sent him a message a few weeks ago from Fort Bridger saying you were traveling with a wagon train on the California Trail. Marshal Duvall asked us to keep an eye out for any wagon trains that showed up, and to find you, sir. He wants you to contact him as soon as possible. The telegraph office is right next door to our office and jail."

"All right," Stranger said. "It just so happens we'd be knocking on your door anyway."

"Oh?"

"We've got four wanted men tied up in the wagons. It's a long story, so I'll save it till I see your boss. Got some room in your jail?"

"Sure do. Just built a whole new office and jail house. We've got room for sixteen prisoners, and right now we've only got five locked up."

"Fine. Why don't you ride on in and tell Marshal Abner we're coming. We should be there…how long would you say, Rip?"

"About thirty-five, forty minutes."

"Will do," Watson replied. "When you come into town and reach Main Street, turn right and go three blocks. You can't miss us."

"Fine. See you in a bit," Stranger said.

As Bert Watson galloped westward toward the town, John said, "Rip, I want to tell Breanna what's up. Be right back."

Stranger wheeled Ebony about and trotted him toward the lead wagon. As he drew up, Breanna had a curious look on her face. "Did I see a badge on that man's chest?" she asked.

"Yes. His name's Bert Watson. He's deputy marshal in Placerville. He and the marshal have been watching for the wagon train."

"They knew we were coming?"

"Only because Marshal Duvall wired them that I was on a train that should be coming down out of the mountains some time soon. The wire came last week, he said. Duvall wants me to wire him."

"I know what it is," Breanna said, disappointment in her eyes. "There's somebody somewhere, probably a lawman, who needs help. And Marshal Duvall wants you to go help him. You won't be riding the train back to Denver with me."

"You're probably right."

"I don't mean to be selfish, John," Breanna sighed, "but I was really looking forward to our train ride together."

"Yes, so was I," John said. "But if Chief Duvall says I'm needed somewhere, I have to go. It's my duty before the Lord."

"I know, darling. But it's been so wonderful to be with you on this journey, and I...well, I wish it could last forever."

"Aw, c'mon you two!" Curly Wesson said, laughing. "You're breakin' my heart!"

John Stranger gave him a mock look of scorn and said, "You ornery old cuss! A lot you know about it! You fell head-over-heels for Judy Charley, and you're going to turn right around, go back up there, and court her. And unless I'm way off my rocker, you'll end up marrying her, and you'll be in the general store and way station business for the rest of your life!"

Curly eyed him with suspicion. "What *are* you, anyway? A prophet of some kind? How'd ya know what I was plannin'?"

"Doesn't take a prophet to figure *you* out, pal. All I had to do was watch you and Judy together and use a little arithmetic. One plus one equals two. Wedding bells for Curly equals matrimony and money."

"Aw, g'wan. I ain't plannin' on marryin' her fer her money! No, sir! I just plain fell in love. It ain't my fault if'n she's got a coupla lucrative businesses goin'!"

The wagon train soon ground to a stop at the eastern edge of Placerville. Breanna and Carolyne accompanied John and Rip when they took the four outlaws to the jail and turned them over to Marshal Abner. Abner assured them he would see that the outlaws were turned over to the proper authorities for prosecution.

Rip and Carolyne mingled with the other people of the wagon train as they stocked up in the stores.

Breanna went with John to the telegraph office next to the jail and waited while he sent his wire to Chief Duvall. The two of them took a twenty minute stroll, then returned to the telegraph office.

The agent, an elderly man wearing a green visor, was waiting behind the counter with a smile as they moved through the door. He extended a folded sheet of paper and said, "Reply came back 'bout ten minutes after I sent it, Mr. Stranger."

The tall man thanked him, then opened the door for Breanna and they stepped outside.

Breanna watched John's eyes as he read the message and knew it meant he would not be riding the train with her to Denver. When he finished reading it, he said, "I have to leave right away, sweetheart."

"Where will you be going?" Breanna asked, fighting to hold back the tears.

"Apache Junction, Arizona. Duvall says the marshal there is getting on in years. His name's Ben Clifton. Some of the gold miners working the Superstition Mountains close by are trying to run Ben off and take over the town. The man's got trouble. He needs my help."

"I understand, darling. How…soon does 'right away' mean?"

"As soon as I can resupply the necessities for my saddlebags."

"I see. Then we'd best get that done."

An hour later, the people of the wagon train gathered near the Wesson wagon to say good-bye to John Stranger. Breanna waited patiently, her heart hurting and her emotions in a storm. The last ones to say good-bye were Rip Clayson, Carolyne Fulford, and Curly Wesson. John wished Rip and Carolyne a happy marriage, and teased Curly one more time about Judy.

John then led Ebony away from the group while holding Breanna's hand. They stopped when they were out of earshot. John looped the reins over the saddlehorn, took Breanna in his arms, and held her for a long moment. Then he looked into her tear-filled eyes and told her again of the undying love he held for her. She said the same to him.

They kissed tenderly, then he said, "I'll find you in Denver or wherever you are when I finish my job in Arizona."

Again they kissed, and then the tall man swung into his saddle. He smiled at her, then trotted away. When he was better than a half-mile across the rolling land, he looked back and waved, then put the big black into a gallop.

Breanna watched John through a wall of tears until he passed from view.

Dottie Harper stood stunned in the San Mateo County sheriff's office, looking at Clancy McBride as if he had slapped her in the face.

"Mr. McBride, I don't believe it!" she said.

"Well, Mrs. Harper, it's so. Sheriff Donner and Myron are after both of them right now."

"No!" she cried, shaking her head and placing her fingertips to her temples. "Sheriff Donner can't possibly believe Jerrod would plot an escape with Marty Tillman! Jerrod's not that kind of a man!"

"But, ma'am, they're both gone. They were in separate cells. Tillman could have just gone off and left Jerrod where he was, but he didn't. From the way Myron explained it, the two of them were workin' together to trick him so's they could make their escape."

"No!" Dottie said. "I know my husband. He's not a criminal, Mr. McBride. He's not!"

"Maybe when he's in his right mind he's not, ma'am, but from what Donner and Hall told me, your husband can be real bad when he's havin' one of his spells."

"Yes, but when he's in a spell, he's not rational at all. There's no way he could have plotted an escape with Tillman when he was in one of those. And when Jerrod is in his right mind, he's such a good man. I'm telling you, he wouldn't do anything like that."

"Well, how else do you explain it, Mrs. Harper?" pressed McBride. "Your husband's gone, isn't he?"

"Yes, but not of his own free will."

"You mean you think he was *forced* to escape?"

"You *did* say Tillman had the deputy's gun, didn't you?"

"Yes'm."

"Well, that explains it."

"You mean you think—"

"I'm sure of it. That man put the gun on Jerrod and made him go with him."

McBride scratched his hoary head. "Well, if it happened that way, it'll be the first time I've ever seen such a thing in my forty-odd years of law enforcement."

"If the sheriff and deputy find them, Mr. McBride, you'll see that what I'm saying is true. Like I said…I know my husband. He would not go along with anything Marty Tillman did. I'm staying right here until they return. I've got to know if they find that no-good outlaw and my husband."

Dottie paced the floor of the office, praying. Only God could protect Jerrod and bring him safely back to her. When midmorning came, she left the sheriff's office long enough to send a wire to Dr. Matthew Carroll, canceling the appointment.

Dottie returned to the sheriff's office and was about to enter when she saw Jerrod coming down the sun-bleached street. He was shoving Marty Tillman in front of him.

"Jerrod!" she cried, drawing the attention of people on the street. They watched her as she ran to meet the two men who were walking in from the east side of town.

When she reached them, Dottie could see that the outlaw had been severely beaten. He was bleeding from his nose and mouth. Dottie wrapped her arms around her husband, and said, "Sheriff Donner thinks you plotted the escape with this...this criminal. He and his deputy are out looking for you right now!"

"But you told him I wasn't in on it with him, didn't you?"

"I haven't seen him nor his deputy yet, Jerrod. But I told Clancy McBride you weren't in on it. They left him to watch the office. You remember him. He used to be the sheriff."

"Yes, but I've never met him. Does he believe you?"

"No, he doesn't." A smile broke on her lips. "But your coming back with him in tow will show them all they were wrong."

With Dottie at his side, Jerrod continued to prod the stumbling outlaw down the street. As they went, Jerrod told Dottie how Tillman had engineered his escape and taken him along, intending to kill him, and how he was able to catch Tillman off guard and subdue him.

Tillman remained silent. Jerrod had pounded him so hard, he was dizzy and nauseous. He had nothing to say.

When they reached the sheriff's office, Clancy McBride stood with his mouth open when he saw Jerrod Harper shove Marty Tillman through the door. Clancy locked Tillman up in his cell, and the Harpers sat down in the office to wait for Donner and Hall to return.

Jerrod told the entire story to McBride, and as the hours passed, they discussed Jerrod's mental problem. The sun was setting when Donner and Hall finally rode up in front of the office and dismounted. The instant the two lawmen entered, surprise showed on their faces.

"Jerrod!" the sheriff exclaimed. "You're...you're back!"

"Yes, sir," Jerrod nodded. "I never would've left if Tillman hadn't forced me to go with him. He was gonna kill me when we got far enough away from town. I caught him off guard and...well, you'll see. He's back in his cell and not feelin' too good."

Donner took off his hat and hung it on a wall peg. He looked at his deputy and said, "Well, Myron, looks like we owe Jerrod an apology."

"We sure do. Both of us assumed you'd plotted the escape with Tillman."

"Apology accepted," Jerrod said with a grin. "Can I go now?"

Donner's gaze swung to Dottie. "He is going to see Dr. Carroll?"

"Yes, Sheriff," she said. "I had to wire his office and cancel the appointment today, of course, but we're going first thing in the morning. I'm sure Dr. Carroll will work him into his schedule."

The last shadows of twilight were on the land as Jerrod and Dottie pulled up in front of the Reeves house. James and Molly Kate were on the front porch with Grandpa Will, who sat in his rocking chair.

Molly Kate was playing with two of her dolls. When she saw that her father was at the reins, she picked her dolls up, placed one under each arm, and moved close to the old man.

Will rose to his feet, laid a hand on her shoulder, and said in a half-whisper, "Don't be afraid, honey. Your daddy won't hurt you."

James also pressed close to the old man. Will laid his other hand on James's shoulder and squeezed it tight.

Jerrod helped Dottie out of the wagon, and Maudie came out

the door as they were mounting the steps. "Well," she said with a wide smile, "how did it go with Dr. Carroll?"

Dottie said that Jerrod had not yet seen the doctor, then between the two of them, they explained what had happened. Maudie invited them to stay for supper, but Dottie graciously declined, saying they needed to get on home. There were things Jerrod needed to tend to before morning, and he could do some of it while she was preparing supper.

An hour and a half later, the Harper family sat down to eat. Jerrod could see that his children were afraid, and he spoke calmly to them, telling them that he loved them and that they didn't need to be afraid of him. Dottie reminded them that their father was going to begin seeing Dr. Carroll, who would help make Jerrod better.

Both children tried to relax. Molly Kate sat on Jerrod's right, holding a doll in the curve of her left arm while attempting to eat with her right hand. The fear that her father might go into one of his spells at any moment had stolen her appetite. She picked at her food with her fork.

Jerrod noted it and said in a firm voice, "Molly Kate, you're not eating. Lay your dolly down beside your chair, and sit up and eat your supper. You haven't even touched your milk."

Molly Kate's hands trembled as she lowered her doll to the floor. Then to please her father, she reached for her glass with both hands, as she had been taught to do. But she was shaking so bad, the glass slipped from her fingers and overturned.

Dottie jumped up and rushed to the cupboard for a cloth. James's eyes were fixed on his father, whose face went suddenly red. Jerrod shoved his chair back and stood, glowering at the terrified child.

"Molly Kate, why can't you be more careful?" Even as he

spoke, he backhanded her across the face, knocking her off the chair.

James left his chair and backed up until he ran into the wall. Dottie dashed to her daughter and picked her up. Molly Kate was dazed and glassy-eyed. Dottie held the child close and glared at Jerrod, who was moving toward her.

"Jerrod!" she screamed. "Stop!"

"Put her down, Dottie!" he roared. "She spilled her milk! She needs to be punished!"

"Jerrod, no!" Dottie cried, backing away. "She dropped the glass because she was frightened of *you!*"

Jerrod grabbed his chair and threw it across the room. He started for her.

James ran in front of him, wailing, "No, Daddy! Don't hurt Mommy!"

Jerrod fixed the boy with wild eyes and knocked him out of the way. James hit the closed pantry door and fell to the floor.

Jerrod bore down on Dottie and raised a hand to strike her.

"Daddy-y!" Molly Kate screamed.

The high-pitched little voice stopped Jerrod short. He blinked and looked at the hand poised to strike. Then he turned and bent over the table and wept.

Dottie put Molly Kate down and helped James to his feet. "Go up to your room, children," she said above the sound of Jerrod's weeping.

"But, Mommy," argued Molly Kate, "Daddy might hurt you!"

"No, honey. He's the real daddy again. He won't hurt me. Go on now, both of you."

When the children were out of the room, Dottie went to Jerrod, put an arm around him, and said, "Here, honey. Sit down."

Jerrod slumped sideways onto James's chair and wrapped his arms around his wife. Dottie stood there, holding his head in her arms. He sobbed over and over that he was sorry, begging Dottie to forgive him. When his sobs had subsided, she stroked his hair and said, "I love you, Jerrod."

"I don't deserve you, Dottie," he said, his voice breaking. "I don't deserve those wonderful children. Oh, why doesn't God just kill me!"

"Sh-h-h," she said, laying her head down against his. "You can't help it, darling. That old war did this to you. Dr. Carroll will help you. I just know he will."

The next morning, James and Molly Kate were once again with the Reeveses as Jerrod and Dottie pulled up in front of Dr. Matthew Carroll's office in San Francisco.

Jerrod slid from the wagon seat and hurried around to the other side to help Dottie down. Holding hands, they stepped onto the boardwalk and approached the door of Dr. Carroll's office.

Suddenly Jerrod froze.

Dottie looked up at him with concern in her eyes. "What's the matter?"

"I can't go in there!"

"Jerrod, you *must!* You've got to have Dr. Carroll's help."

"No, Dottie! He'll put me in the asylum. I know it! That jail was bad enough, but there's no way I could stand bein' caged in the asylum!"

Desperate and frightened, Dottie gripped both his arms as hard as she could. "Jerrod, listen to me! He's not going to put you in the asylum! Remember what you did last night? Do you remember what you did to your children?"

When he didn't answer, she shook him. "Jerrod, are you listening to me?"

He licked his lips and met her gaze. "Yes. Yes, I…I'm listenin'."

"Jerrod, if you won't let Dr. Carroll help you, I have no choice. I'll have to take James and Molly Kate and leave you. Those children have suffered enough! I cannot…I *will* not let them go through another episode like last night's! Do you hear me? I must protect my children! If you don't go in there right now, I'm taking them and leaving!"

Jerrod grabbed Dottie by the hair, yanked her head back, and yelled, "You try to take the kids and leave, *I'll kill you, Dottie!* Do you hear me? I'll kill you!"

Passersby stood and stared. Someone spotted a police officer crossing the intersection on horseback at the end of the block and called to him.

Suddenly the earth trembled. The boardwalk began to undulate, and Jerrod and Dottie grabbed hold of each other to keep from falling. By the time the police officer skidded his horse to a halt, the quake was over. As he dismounted, people pointed at the couple and told him the man had just manhandled the woman and threatened to kill her.

The policeman moved up quickly, pulling his night stick from his belt. He scowled at Jerrod and snapped, "Let go of her, mister!"

"Officer, this man is my husband," Dottie said. "He's having some emotional problems, and I'm taking him in here to see Dr. Carroll. He got a little upset, but he's calmed down now. May we go on in?"

The policeman eyed Jerrod sternly and said, "You going in to see the doctor?"

"Yes, officer," Jerrod said, wiping sweat from his face.

"Okay, I'll just go in with you."

As the Harpers moved inside the building, Jerrod looked down at Dottie and said with a quaver in his voice, "I'm sorry, Dottie. I didn't mean it when I said I'd kill you and the kids."

Dottie squeezed his hand and said, "I know you didn't."

Flora Downing greeted Dottie and told her the doctor was just finishing with a patient. He would be able to see them in a few moments. While they waited, Dottie explained the presence of the officer to the receptionist, telling her what had happened on the street. They talked for awhile about the brief quake, and soon the patient came out of Dr. Carroll's office. Flora went in and told Dr. Carroll the Harpers were there and why the police officer was with them.

Dr. Carroll came out with Flora and smiled at Dottie, then extended his hand to Jerrod. The big man shook hands with the doctor, but his nervousness was showing. Dr. Carroll said Flora had told him of the incident on the street, and he thanked the policeman for his presence.

"Mrs. Harper," Dr. Carroll said, "before I sit down with Jerrod, I'd like to talk to you alone for a few minutes."

Fearful Jerrod would bristle at that, Dottie looked at him and said, "It's all for your good, darling."

"Yes, I can assure you of that," Dr. Carroll said.

"I understand," Jerrod said. "I'll wait right here."

"And so will I," the officer said.

"After the way I acted out there on the street, I can't blame you," Jerrod said. "Don't worry, Dottie. I won't give him any trouble."

18

DR. MATTHEW CARROLL leaned on his elbows and looked at Dottie Harper as she sat in front of his desk and worked some more to get her hair back into place. Again his heart went out to her. She was such a sweet and lovely woman. She didn't deserve the kind of treatment she had been subject to, being married to Jerrod Harper.

"All right," he said. "I want you to tell me everything that has happened since we talked last. I need to know in order to better help your husband."

Dottie spilled it all out, almost breaking down a couple of times.

When she was done, Dr. Carroll sighed, eased back in his chair, and said, "Mrs. Harper, Jerrod has to be locked up."

"But, Doctor, you said—"

"That was before he threatened to kill you. He's dangerous. *Very* dangerous. It wouldn't take much for him to kill you with his bare hands. He's got to be locked up."

Tears welled up in Dottie's eyes. Her lower lip quivered as she said, "Can't you at least try using the sedatives, do the counseling here in your office so Jerrod can live at home? It would be so.

much better for his state of mind. He—"

"No," Carroll said flatly. "He's too dangerous."

"But if the sedatives would do as you thought, I'm sure Jerrod won't be dangerous…and the counseling."

"Mrs. Harper, I deeply appreciate the magnificent love you have for your husband and your unceasing faithfulness to him. But if Jerrod isn't placed in the asylum, your faithful heart is going to get you killed." Dottie stared at him, wiping tears. "Until it's done, you and the children will not be safe. It's not only best for the three of you, but it's best for Jerrod. You must see that."

Dottie bit down on her lower lip, blinking against the tears in her eyes. She stared at the floor for a long moment, then looked up at the psychiatrist. "I'm terrified, Doctor. I'm afraid of how Jerrod will react when he's told he must go to the asylum."

"Well, Officer Felton is out there. The best time to tell him is right now. We'll have the officer escort us while we walk Jerrod to the asylum."

Dottie drew a shuddering breath and said, "All right, Doctor. I will go along with you on this…but you'd better be ready to see Jerrod go into one of his spells."

"I'll tell Officer Felton to stay near, okay?" Carroll said, rising from his chair.

"I'm not sure he'll be enough."

"Well, I'm here, too. Certainly between the two of us we can handle him."

The doctor opened the door and stepped into the outer office. There were no other patients present. Flora was at her desk, and the two men sat opposite each other in the waiting area.

Jerrod rose to his feet. "You ready for me now, Doctor?"

"Yes, please come in."

The doctor let Jerrod move past him and told him to sit next to Dottie. Pulling the door shut, he whispered to Felton, "Stay close, will you? I may need you." The officer nodded.

Carroll left the door open about an inch and returned to his desk and sat down. Before he could say anything, Dottie laid a hand on Jerrod's arm and said, "Honey, I've told Dr. Carroll everything that's happened since he and I last talked…and we've come to a conclusion as to what's best for you and for the children and me." She paused. "That is what you want, isn't it? What's best for all of us?"

Jerrod gave her a wary look. "And just what is this conclusion?"

"Before we tell you, Jerrod," the doctor said, "please understand that this decision is really mine, based on many years of experience in my field. Mrs. Harper would like it another way, and so would I if it were possible. But there is only one way you can really be helped. You must consider your family. Certainly you realize that your problem has placed your wife and children in a very perilous position."

Storm signs showed in Jerrod's hazel eyes. "I knew it," he rasped. "I knew it."

Dottie took hold of his hand. "Please, Jerrod, don't—"

"It's the asylum, isn't it?" he gusted, standing up.

When neither Dottie nor the doctor denied it, he yelled, "No! Nobody's puttin' me in a cage!"

Dr. Carroll rounded the desk and said in a calm, level voice, "Jerrod, there is no alternative. If you ended up killing your wife or one of your children, it would be my fault. I must insist—"

"No-o!" Jerrod roared, and struck out at the doctor.

Carroll was able to dodge the punch, but stumbled against a bookcase and lost his balance. Jerrod whirled and yelled at Dottie. "You're plannin' to take James and Molly Kate away from me if I don't go in the nut house, aren't you?"

Dottie was paralyzed with horror. She tried to speak, but the words locked in her throat.

Just then, Officer George Felton bolted through the door, nightstick in hand. "Back off!" he warned.

Jerrod ignored him and railed, "I'll kill you, Dottie! That's what I'll do! You and this doctor plotted against me! I'll kill you!"

Dottie put out a hand, as if to touch him. She still couldn't find her voice.

Jerrod's fist lashed out and caught her on the jaw. She landed hard against the desk and lay motionless. Felton's night stick caught Jerrod with a glancing blow, enough to stun him. The policeman pushed him to the floor and was pulling his handcuffs from a hip pocket when Jerrod rolled over and struck out with his fist. It caught Felton on the mouth and knocked him over.

Dr. Carroll shouted for Flora to run to the street and call for more officers. As she was heard running from the outer office, Jerrod rose to his feet and struck Carroll on the jaw. The doctor went down in a heap.

Officer Felton's mouth was bleeding as he picked up his billy club and went after Jerrod again. Jerrod dodged it and caught the policeman with a blow high on the head, knocking Felton off his feet.

Jerrod Harper was wailing like a wild beast as he plunged in-to the outer office and through the door into the hall. Felton scrambled to his feet and went after him. Jerrod had just reached the street when the officer tackled him from behind.

The two men wrestled and rolled off the boardwalk and into the dust of the street. A policeman's whistle blew, and two officers came running toward the scene of the fight. Three more appeared on horseback. All five drew their revolvers as they converged on Jerrod Harper, who was now standing with an unconscious George Felton at his feet. One of them pointed his gun at Harper and bawled, "Hold it right there, big fella!"

Jerrod Harper was back at Wilson's Creek facing enemy soldiers and enemy guns. The blue uniforms faded to gray. These were Rebels, coming to kill him. "Shoot 'em down, men!" he shouted, fixing them with eyes of hatred. "Let those dirty Rebels have it!"

Jerrod heard no gunfire from behind him. He whirled about and looked for his men, expecting to see their familiar faces behind guns that blazed at the enemy. There was no one.

The five officers swarmed him, trying to take him alive. Jerrod yanked Felton's revolver from its holster, snapped back the hammer, and fired blindly into the oncoming uniforms. The bullet struck one of the officers in the chest, but the others were on him, swinging the barrels of their revolvers as clubs.

Jerrod Harper went down unconscious.

Dr. Carroll staggered from the office door, blinking to clear his vision. He saw Jerrod down, along with two officers, and said to the others, "This man is a mental patient. I heard a shot. Was someone hit?"

An officer who knelt over the one who had taken the bullet looked up and said, "Your patient put Officer Felton down and used his gun to shoot Sergeant Dover. He's dead."

Dr. Carroll leaned back against the building and closed his

eyes for a moment. Then he asked the policemen to handcuff Jerrod and take him to the asylum. "Tell my people at the asylum that I'll be there shortly. They are to put him in chains in a padded cell."

"He's a killer, now, Doctor," argued one of the officers. "We're taking him to jail."

"This man is my patient, sir," Dr. Carroll countered. "I will take full responsibility for him. Tell your captain I will come to the station and sign the necessary papers to declare my patient insane. You know the law. He cannot be tried if I declare him insane."

"All right, Doctor, we'll take him to the asylum as you requested…but we'll need you to come to the station within an hour to sign the papers."

"I'll be there," said Carroll, wiping blood from a split lip. "But first, I have to see about the man's wife. She's in my office and seriously hurt."

George Felton was now on his feet. Dr. Carroll thanked him for what he had done and went inside as the officers carried their dead comrade and a groggy, handcuffed Jerrod Harper away.

Flora was bending over Dottie, whom she had laid on a couch. A wet cloth was across Dottie's brow.

"She's conscious now, Doctor," Flora said, "but I don't think her mind is clear enough yet to understand what's happened."

"I'll take care of her. We've got more patients due in, don't we?"

"Yes, sir," Flora said, standing up straight.

"You'll have to reschedule them. First thing, get an ambulance over here. I want Mrs. Harper examined at the hospital. Once I've taken care of that, I have to go to the police station and sign papers declaring Jerrod Harper insane. The officer he shot is dead."

Flora gasped and her hand flew to her mouth. Then she hurried out of the office and headed for the street to find someone who would run to the hospital and summon an ambulance.

The doctor drew up a chair, sat down, and looked at Dottie as she rolled her head and tried to focus on his face. He wished he didn't have to give her the bad news.

"Mrs. Harper," he said, "do you know me?"

Dottie licked her lips and nodded slowly. Her voice was weak. "Yes. Dr. Carroll."

"Good," he smiled, taking hold of her hand. "Listen carefully. I—"

"Doctor," she interrupted. "My legs. I can't move them. I can't even feel them!"

Carroll let go of her hand and quickly untied and removed her shoes. He squeezed her feet and asked, "Can you feel this?"

She waited. "Feel what?"

He pinched the sole of her right foot and said, "Can't you feel me pinching your foot?"

"No," she said, a look of fear on her face. Then there was breathless panic as she gasped, "Doctor, I'm paralyzed! I can't feel a thing below my waist!"

Dr. Carroll's own heart thudded his ribs as he forced calm into his voice, took hold of her hands, and said, "Now, Dot— Mrs. Harper. When Jerrod hit you, the force of his punch knocked you into the desk awfully hard. But this doesn't mean your paralysis is permanent. Sometimes it takes a while for your body to recover from an impact like that."

Dottie squeezed down on both his hands. "Are you sure, Doctor?"

"Yes. I've already sent for an ambulance to take you over to the hospital. I didn't know about the paralysis, of course, but I just wanted to have you checked over. Since you know Dr. Glenn Olson, I'll ask that he see you. Would you like that?"

"Yes, thank you," Dottie said. "Doctor, where's Jerrod?"

"Jerrod's at the asylum," he said quietly. "We'll talk about him after Dr. Olson has examined you."

The sounds of the ambulance attendants coming through the door of the outer office met the doctor's ears. He pulled his hands free from hers, stood up, and said, "The ambulance is here."

Dr. Carroll told the attendants about Dottie's paralysis so they would be extra careful when they placed her on the stretcher. He also told them to notify Dr. Glenn Olson that Mrs. Harper wanted to be in his care. He once again assured Dottie that he would be at the hospital as soon as he could.

At City Mental Asylum, the policemen delivered Jerrod Harper into the hands of Dr. Verle Huffman, the assistant to Dr. Carroll. When the officers gave Huffman Dr. Carroll's instructions, he immediately led them down the hall that was lined with padded cells.

Jerrod heard the screams and cries coming from the cells and strained against the handcuffs that held his arms behind his back. "No-o!" he yelled. "You're not puttin' me in here! No-o!"

Dr. Huffman called for help from his attendants. It took four of them to wrestle Jerrod into a padded cell, hold him so an officer could remove the handcuffs, and then put both his wrists and ankles in shackles. When the police officer and the attendants backed out of the cell, Jerrod lunged at them, but fell hard when the chains reached their length. Jerrod strained against the chains, his eyes wild as they closed the door.

"I'll get outta here!" he roared. "I will! And when I do, I'll kill her! Do you hear me? I'll kill her!"

Dr. Olson had just emerged from Dottie's hospital room and started down the hall when he saw Dr. Carroll coming toward him. He stopped and waited for Carroll to draw up.

"Hello, Glenn," Carroll said. "Have you examined Mrs. Harper?"

"Yes, Matt, and I've got good news."

"I can use some of that."

"Her spine has been bruised, but from what I can tell, not permanently injured. I'm reasonably confident she'll get all the feeling back below her waist. As for walking, it will take some therapy, but I believe she'll walk as good as new in time. She already has some feeling back in her legs and feet."

"Well, praise the Lord!" Carroll said. "That dear lady has been through so much."

"I understand that her husband's been placed in the asylum?"

"Yes. She brought him in for me to begin treating him. Has she told you what he did last night?"

"Yes. Awful."

"Well, I told Jerrod that for the sake of his family *and* himself, he needed to be admitted to the asylum. He went crazy. Mrs. Harper doesn't know yet, but before it was over, we had to call for several policemen to subdue him. Jerrod managed to get his hands on a gun and shot and killed one of the officers."

"Oh, no."

"I just came from police headquarters. I had to sign papers declaring him insane. Otherwise, as you know, he would hang."

"Yes," said Olson, shaking his head slowly. "Poor man. That Civil War was an awful thing. It left so many men scarred in both mind and body."

Carroll sighed and rubbed the back of his neck. "Now I have to go tell that dear woman that her husband will be in the asylum for the rest of his life."

"You want me to go in there with you? She's in room thirty-one."

"Would you? This won't be easy. I can use all the help I can get."

"All right."

The two doctors entered the room, and Dr. Carroll told Dottie how happy he was with her prognosis. She was able to smile and tell him about the feeling she was already getting back in her legs and feet.

Dr. Carroll then told her that Jerrod had killed a police officer. When she got over the initial shock of it, he explained about signing the necessary papers for the police, declaring Jerrod insane…and that Jerrod would be kept in the asylum for the rest of his life.

Dottie wept as if her heart would break. Both doctors held her hands and tried to be as much comfort as they could. When her emotions settled down, Dr. Carroll prayed with her, asking the Lord to give her extra strength and to watch over her and the children.

Dottie then asked if someone could notify Will and Maudie Reeves that she was in the hospital. She wanted to see James and Molly Kate. She also asked if they would let her pastor know what had happened.

Dr. Carroll told her it would be taken care of immediately.

It was early afternoon when Reverend Howard Yates arrived at the hospital, along with Will and Maudie Reeves and James and Molly Kate. Mother and children had a tearful reunion, and Dr. Olson came to assure them that with therapy Dottie would soon be well.

Dottie wept as she told them about Jerrod killing the policeman, and that he would be a permanent resident in the asylum. Yates read Scripture and prayed with them, doing what he could to bring comfort.

Maudie assured Dottie the children were welcome to stay with them until she was out of the hospital and able to care for them. Will told her he would get their neighbors to join in and take care of her crops. He would take the animals to his place and keep them fed.

Dottie cried as she thanked them for their kindness.

Will and Maudie told Dottie they would bring the children to see her as often as they could. Reverend Yates assured her that he would look in on Jerrod, for which Dottie thanked him.

James and Molly Kate were given a few minutes alone with their mother. After hugs and kisses, they were taken by the elderly couple to the Reeves wagon, and they headed for home.

✧

It was almost suppertime when Will Reeves entered the house to find James and Molly Kate helping Maudie set the table. The kitchen was filled with the scent of food cooking.

Will breathed deeply through his nose and said, "Smells like fried chicken to me!"

"You're right, Grandpa!" Molly Kate laughed.

Will winked at Maudie, who was standing by the stove, and said, "James…Molly Kate…I have a surprise for each of you."

The little girl clapped her hands. "What is it, Grandpa?"

James grinned from ear to ear, expectantly.

"Well, I have them out here on the back porch, but before you see them, I want to say something. C'mere."

He put an arm around each child and said, "Grandma and I love you both very much. You know that, don't you?"

Both nodded, sending smiles to Maudie, who stood looking on with tears in her eyes.

"Well, because we love you so much, Grandpa's been in his workshop making something very special. You've both had…a lot of sorrow in your little lives lately, and Grandma and I want to give you something to be happy about."

The children looked at each other and smiled.

"All right," said Will, heading for the back door. "Ladies first. We'll give Molly Kate her present first."

"Give James his present first, Grandpa. He's the oldest."

"You sure?" Will said with a chuckle.

"Uh-huh. I want James to get his first."

The old man looked at James. "What ya say, boy?"

James shrugged and said, "Who am I to argue with a woman?"

Maudie laughed.

"Okay!" said Will, opening the door. "Oldest first!"

The children waited with anticipation dancing in their eyes while Will went out on the back porch, closing the door behind him. Seconds later he came back in, pulling a bright-red wagon by the tongue. White lettering on the side said: *James Harper Express.*

The boy's eyes lit up and bulged from their sockets. "Wow!" he exclaimed, running to the old man and throwing his arms around him. "Thank you, Grandpa! Thank you, thank you, thank you!"

Molly Kate looked on with joy to see her brother so happy. James ran his hands over the smooth wood of the wagon, then ran to Maudie and embraced her, expressing his thanks all over again.

He returned to his new toy and looked at Molly Kate. "I'll pull you around in it," he said with a grin.

"Thank you," she said, then looked at Will, who was back at the door.

He smiled at her and said, "Molly Kate, I know you love dolls. You must have a dozen or more at home. You always have at least two with you when you come to stay with us. You *do* love dolls, right?"

"Oh, yes, Grandpa," she said, trying to imagine what he had for her out there on the porch.

Will looked at Maudie, winked again, then set his eyes on

Molly Kate and said, "Well, sweetheart, I've got something for you like you've never even seen before. Are you ready?"

"Yes!" she said, nodding rapidly. Her little heart was racing.

Will slipped through the door and closed it behind him. Maudie was about to burst, knowing what was coming.

When the door came open, there was nothing but darkness on the back porch. Then suddenly Will came around the edge of the door carrying the biggest doll Molly Kate Harper had ever seen. The sight of it stole her breath and made her eyes pop.

The doll was the same size as Molly Kate and had hair the same length, style, and color. The dress she wore was exactly like one Grandma Maudie had made for Molly Kate on her last birthday.

What captivated the child the most, however, was the doll's face. Will had carved the head from the wood of a balsam fir and had captured the features of the little girl. The doll was a near-perfect replica of Molly Kate.

Molly Kate stood in breathless wonder. She couldn't believe her eyes. Her little hands were pressed against her cheeks.

Maudie moved up behind her, put an arm around her, and said, "What do you think of her, honey?"

"Oh, she's wonderful, Grandma! Grandpa's an artist!"

Both grandparents received hugs and kisses and excited words of thanks.

Will then went to the porch and returned with a stand he had made for the doll so Molly Kate could stand her up anywhere she wanted. James sat in his wagon, toying with the tongue, and Molly Kate held her doll.

"What are you going to name her, honey?" Maudie asked.

The child looked up sweetly and said, "Well, since she's my size and looks just like me, there's only one name that would fit. I'll call her *Molly Kate!*"

Grandpa, Grandma, and big brother all had a good laugh.

19

IT WAS MIDMORNING the next day when Breanna Baylor drove out of San Francisco with a rented horse and buggy and headed for San Bruno. She was filled with mixed emotions. More than anything, she missed the man she loved and thought of him riding southward toward Arizona.

The good-byes to her friends in the wagon train and to her namesake, baby Breanna, had been extremely difficult, and she was still feeling the pain of parting from them. On the other hand, excitement ran through her with the anticipation of seeing her sister once again and meeting Dottie's family.

Since Breanna did not know the location of the Harper farm, she decided to drive to San Bruno and ask around until she found someone who knew the Harpers and could tell her how to find them.

It was almost eleven o'clock when she turned onto San Bruno's main street and guided the horse to the hitch rail in front of the San Bruno Bank. Two elderly men sitting on a bench stopped their chatter to watch the young woman as she stepped out of the buggy and approached them.

"Good morning, gentlemen," Breanna said. "I wonder if—"

"Why, Dottie Harper!" said a woman emerging from the bank. "How are you, dear? It's good to see you."

"Myrtle," her husband said, "that's not Dottie."

Myrtle studied Breanna's features. "Well, it has to be."

"No," Breanna said smiling. "I'm not Dottie Harper. I'm her sister, Breanna. I arrived in San Francisco this morning in a wagon train and rented this horse and buggy. Dottie doesn't know I'm coming. I was going to ask these two gentlemen if they could direct me to the Harper farm."

"Well, we can do that, ma'am," said Myrtle's husband. "By the way, we're Clarence and Myrtle Nolan, friends of Dottie and Jerrod. Our farm is about three miles south of theirs."

Clarence and Myrtle shook hands with Breanna, then Clarence said, "We've got more business to take care of here in town, Miss—are you a miss or a missus, ma'am?"

"I'm a miss, sir. Breanna Baylor."

"Oh, yes," Myrtle said. "Dottie did tell me her maiden name was Baylor."

"Anyway, as I was sayin'," proceeded Clarence, "we'd lead you to Jerrod and Dottie's place if we were goin' back right now, but we've still got business to tend to here in town."

"That's all right," Breanna said. "If you can tell me how to get there..."

"Oh, sure."

Clarence Nolan drew Breanna a map on a slip of paper Myrtle had in her purse. Breanna thanked him, bid them goodbye, and headed out of town. She followed the map, passing fields and orchards, and was soon guiding the horse down the road that led to her sister's farm. She finally caught sight of the big three-story house she recognized from photographs Dottie had sent her. She had admired the turret with the cone-shaped roof and the wide, sweeping porch in the pictures, and now actually seeing them was a thrill.

Breanna liked the big trees that towered over the house at the back and both front corners. It looked like a pleasant and comfortable place to live. She longed for the day when she and John could have a house and a family of their own.

Breanna was a bit surprised when she pulled into the yard. There was no one in the fields or anywhere around the house. Perhaps they were all inside. She climbed down from the buggy with her heart in her mouth, mounted the porch steps, and knocked on the door. When there was no answer after a time, she knocked again.

Still no response.

Breanna left the porch and walked around to the back of the house. There were no animals in the corral. She knew from Dottie's letters that they had a cow, a couple of riding horses, and a team of work horses. When she looked in the barn and found no trace of the animals, an uneasy feeling came over her.

She stepped onto the back porch and tried the door. It was unlocked. She opened it slowly, peered into the kitchen, and called out, "Hello! Anybody home?"

Silence.

It wasn't in Breanna to enter someone's home without an invitation, not even her own sister's. She closed the door and walked back to the front of the house. The horse bobbed its head and nickered at her.

Before climbing back into the buggy, she looked around and saw the nearest neighbor's house. She could see part of the road that led to it and could tell that the road she had come in on would have to connect with it on the other side of the peach orchard she had passed.

She put the horse to a trot and headed that direction.

In Molly Kate's room at the Reeves house, Grandpa Will was attaching the big doll to her stand so the little girl could place her at the window. Molly Kate wanted the doll to be able to look outside.

Maudie was in the kitchen baking pies, and James was in the front yard playing with his wagon. With one leg inside the wagon and the other on the ground to propel it, James was having a grand time running it in a wide circle, guiding it by the tongue.

Movement caught his eye. He stopped and scrutinized the horse and buggy coming his way at a good trot. He could tell there was only one person in the buggy, and as it drew closer, it was obvious that it was a woman. A few seconds passed, and James's eyes widened.

"Mommy! It's Mommy!" he shouted.

He dashed to the house and into the kitchen. "Grandma! It's Mommy! She's coming up the road in a buggy!"

Maudie looked up from the pies she had laid out on the cupboard and said, "Honey, it can't be your mother. She's still in the hospital and will be for some time."

"But it *is!*" he insisted. "I saw her! Come and see for yourself!"

Will and Molly Kate entered the kitchen.

"What's all the excitement about?" Will asked.

"It's Mommy!" the boy said. "She's coming up the road, driving a buggy!"

"Let's go see about this," said Will. "You sure it's her?"

"Yes!"

Molly Kate was wide-eyed. "Really, James? Is Mommy really coming?"

"Yes. C'mon, I'll show you!"

Will and Maudie followed the excited children out the front door and reached the porch just as the wagon was pulling into the yard.

"See there!" James cried. "I told you it's—" Suddenly he realized it was not his mother, but the lady was almost his mother made over. Then it struck him.

"Molly Kate," he said, "you know who that is? It's Aunt Breanna! It has to be her! It's Aunt Breanna!"

Molly Kate stood in a mild state of shock, gawking at the pretty lady. Maudie and Will watched James dash off the porch and run up to the buggy, shouting, "Hi! I'm James! You're my Aunt Breanna, aren't you?"

Breanna stepped down, opened her arms, and said, "I sure am, James!"

While hugging the boy, Breanna looked at the little girl and smiled. "Hello, Molly Kate. Do *you* have a hug for your Aunt Breanna?"

Suddenly Molly Kate bounded off the porch. Breanna let go of James and took her into her arms. After she had hugged her for a moment, Breanna put an arm around both children and looked at the older couple. "I think I can name you two. You're Grandma and Grandpa Reeves, right?"

"Right," Will and Maudie said together, smiling broadly.

"Dottie had told me about you in her letters. I just didn't

realize you lived so close to them."

As the elderly couple stepped off the porch, Maudie said, "Dottie has told us so much about you, my dear. My, don't you two look alike? You could almost pass as identical twins!"

Will shook hands with Breanna, and Maudie embraced her. Then Breanna said, "Dottie has no idea I was coming to California, so this is going to be a real surprise. I went to their place and couldn't find anyone home, or even any animals in the corral. Where are Dottie and Jerrod?"

James and Molly Kate looked to the old couple, who exchanged glances.

"What's wrong?" Breanna said. "I know something's wrong! What is it?"

Maudie took Breanna's hand. "Come on inside and sit down, dear. What we have to tell you isn't good."

"Has…has something happened to my sister? Tell me!"

"She's in San Francisco's City Hospital," Will said. "It's serious, but she'll be all right."

"Please," Maudie urged, "come in and sit down. We'll explain it to you."

James and Molly Kate stayed close to Breanna as she sat down in the parlor. Both children were amazed at how much their aunt resembled their mother, not only in appearance but also in her mannerisms.

Interrupting each other at times, Will and Maudie told Breanna the whole sordid story that started nearly six months earlier when Jerrod's disorder surfaced and began to grow worse. They brought her up to the minute, explaining that they were keeping the children until Dottie could come home.

Breanna was stunned. "I knew about Jerrod's problem. Dottie

wrote about it. I just wasn't aware it had become so serious." She stood and said, "I'm going to the hospital right now. Can you tell me how to find it? I must see my sister."

"I'll do better than tell you how to find it, Breanna," Will said. "I'll take you there myself."

"Oh, that's not necessary, Mr. Reeves. I'll find it if you give me directions."

"You sure? I'll be more than happy to take you."

"I'm sure you have plenty to do. I'll be fine."

While Will wrote down directions, Maudie said, "Breanna, you haven't said how long you'll be here, but we have a bedroom upstairs that isn't occupied. You're welcome to stay with us."

"Thank you, Mrs. Reeves," Breanna said. "I'm scheduled to take a train day after tomorrow and head back for Denver. But with this unexpected situation, I may change my plans. We'll talk about it after I see Dottie."

"Aunt Breanna," Molly Kate said.

"Yes, honey?"

"Before you go see Mommy, would you like to see my new doll Grandpa made for me?"

"Well, I sure would!" Breanna said, pulling the child close to her. "Where is your doll?"

As Breanna Baylor drove to San Francisco, she marveled at the love the elderly couple had shown the Harper children. Molly Kate's life-sized doll was indeed a work of art, and Will had put a lot of work into James's wagon. Breanna thanked God that Dottie had Will and Maudie. She was going to need them to help her through the days ahead.

Breanna swung onto Clay Street and pulled up in front of the hospital. She stopped at the reception desk, learned that her sister was in room thirty-one, and headed down the hall. As she drew near the room, her nerves tensed and her heart quickened pace. It had been ten years...

The door to room thirty-one was closed. Breanna stopped in front of it and was taking a deep breath when a nurse came out of an adjacent room and moved down the hall toward her. The eyes of the two women met, and the nurse cocked her head, blinked, and came to a stop.

"Pardon me," she said, "but you've got to be Mrs. Harper's twin sister."

Breanna smiled. "No, just her sister. I'm from Denver. Dottie doesn't even know I'm here."

"Well, I'm sure she'll be plenty happy to see you. I was just in there. She's asleep right now."

"Should I wait?"

"Oh, no. I spent quite a bit of time with her this morning. She didn't sleep well last night, but I'm sure seeing you will perk her up. She's having a hard time with her husband's situation. You do know about it?"

"Yes."

"Well, she's quite upset about his being in the asylum."

"I can understand that," Breanna said. "It's got to be a horrible thing."

"You can say that again. Anyway, you go on in there and wake her up." With that, the nurse headed down the hall.

Breanna took another deep breath, pushed the door open,

and stepped into the room.

There were two beds, but one was unoccupied. Dottie was asleep in the bed next to the window. Breanna moved quietly to the side of the bed and looked down at the pale face of her sister. Memories flooded her mind. How many times during their childhood had she seen her little sister sleeping peacefully like this and lovingly kissed her forehead?

Breanna couldn't resist. She bent over and kissed Dottie's forehead. The patient stirred, rolled her head, and opened her eyes. They were dull at first, but when they focused on the face of the woman who stood beside her, they sharpened immediately.

Breanna smiled and said softly, "Hello, Dottie. I love you."

Dottie's mouth dropped open and her eyes widened. Her lips began to quiver as she gasped, "Bre-*Breanna!* Oh! Am I dreaming?"

Breanna took hold of her hand and kissed her forehead again. "No, you're not dreaming. It's me. In the flesh."

"But how...?"

"I'll explain it all in a minute."

Dottie raised her other arm and started to cry. "Oh, let me hug you!"

Breanna released her hand and bent down so Dottie could wrap her arms around her neck. The sisters clung to each other and mingled their tears for several minutes. Then they looked at each other and laughed and wiped their faces dry.

Breanna drew up a chair, took Dottie by the hand, and said, "I found your precious children at the Reeves house, and Will and Maudie told me the whole story. I'm so sorry, Dottie. It hurts me to know you've been through so much."

"It's been very hard, I'll admit," Dottie said. "But Breanna, my Jesus has been so close to me. I've had a hard time sleeping at night, but His presence has been so real, so precious. I think maybe He's kept me awake just so He could commune with me in my heart. This whole thing with Jerrod—especially his killing the police officer—is like a nightmare. But somehow I have peace like I never knew was possible."

"That's the kind of peace Jesus said He would give, didn't He?"

"Yes. But you know, Sis, Christians can't really experience this kind of peace until they face the storms of life where He can prove Himself to them. I know that now."

"You're right. How can we know Him as our Mighty Fortress unless we get into a battle? How can we know Him as the Rock that Is Higher Than I unless we get into a storm? We cannot know Him as the Prince of Peace until life robs us of our peace."

Dottie squeezed Breanna's hand. "Now, I want to know why you're here in California. You didn't make the trip just to come and surprise me, did you?"

"Well, I wish I could say that was the case, but it isn't. Not that I haven't wanted to come and see you, but you know how it is in my line of work."

"Of course. So what brought you here?"

For the next hour or so, Breanna told Dottie all about the wagon train journey that started at South Pass, Wyoming. She told her about delivering babies and fighting off Indians. She told her about Curly Wesson and the joy she had in leading him to the Lord. She told her about the death of Frank Miller, whom Dottie remembered as the man who had jilted Breanna. She told her about Chief Red Claw—and about John Stranger.

Once she had brought Dottie up to date, Breanna told her she had a train ticket for Denver and was to leave day after tomorrow.

"Oh, so soon? Can't you stay longer?"

"Well, when I learned about all this from Mr. and Mrs. Reeves, I told them I might make a change in plans...that I'd let them know after I saw you."

"You mean you *can* stay longer?"

"Yes. All I have to do is wire Dr. Goodwin and tell him I'm going to be delayed, and why. I don't want to leave you until you're out of the hospital and well on the road to recovery."

Tears spilled down Dottie's cheeks. She was deeply touched and very happy with the prospect of having her sister near for a while.

Breanna told Dottie she would take the children to the Harper place so they could be in their own home. Whenever she had to be away without them, she would leave them with Will and Maudie. Dottie said it would be good for James and Molly Kate to be home, and it would give Breanna and the children an opportunity to get acquainted.

"That's the best part," Breanna said. "They seem like such wonderful children. I'm looking forward to getting to know them."

Dottie's eyes filled with tears once again. "Breanna, would...would you do me a real big favor?"

"Of course. Just name it."

"Would you go to the asylum and see Jerrod for me? Tell him I'm doing better and that I'll be there to see him as soon as I possibly can...and that I love him with all my heart?"

"Will they let me in to see him?"

"I'm sure they will. Our pastor said he was going to go see him. I would think if they let him in, they'd let family in, too. If they give you any problem, show them your nurse's credentials and see him professionally."

Breanna brushed a lock of hair off Dottie's forehead. "You really love Jerrod, don't you?"

"Yes. With everything that's in me."

"I admire you, Dottie. You've been so loving and faithful to Jerrod in spite of all that's happened."

"How could I be anything else? When I took my marriage vows, it was for better or for worse. I meant what I said that day, Breanna. I'll love that man till the day I die...or he dies."

Breanna stood to leave, then bent and kissed her sister's forehead once more. She told Dottie she would take the children home, go see Jerrod in the morning, and come to the hospital and tell her how it went.

After supper at the Reeves house that evening, Breanna took her niece and nephew home. James put his new wagon on the front porch, and with Aunt Breanna's help, Molly Kate placed her doll in her room on the second floor of the house. The doll was positioned at the window so she could "look" into the front yard. Molly Kate raised the arms and placed the hands against the window pane, making it appear that the doll was leaning against the window, trying to see clearly anyone who stood in the yard.

Just before bedtime, Breanna took the children outside with her, intending to lead the rented horse to the barn and give it hay and grain. When they stepped into the yard, Molly Kate backed up a few steps and clapped her hands. "Look, Aunt Breanna!" she said excitedly. "It looks like Molly Kate is looking right down at me!"

Breanna looked up at the window. The doll was silhouetted against the lantern light in the room, and her face was partially lighted. Breanna shook her head in wonderment and said, "Molly Kate, if I didn't know better, I'd think it was *you* standing at the window!"

It was nine-thirty the next morning when Breanna Baylor stood at the lobby desk in the asylum, explaining to the male receptionist that she was the sister-in-law of Jerrod Harper and wanted to look in on him for her sister, who was in City Hospital.

"Ma'am," the man said politely, "ordinarily the only people who can see the patients in the section where we have Mr. Harper are their ministers and the next of kin, not in-laws. I believe Dr. Carroll, who is our chief of staff, is with Mr. Harper right now. As soon as he comes out, I'll explain the situation and ask if you can go in."

"Thank you," Breanna said.

At that moment, the door that led to the cells came open, and Dr. Matthew Carroll entered the lobby. The receptionist was about to speak to him when the doctor saw Breanna. He stopped abruptly, smiled, and said, "For a second there, I thought you were Dottie Harper, ma'am. I'm Dr. Matt Carroll. You *have* to be Dottie's sister. Am I right?"

"Yes, I'm Breanna Baylor, doctor, and I've come to look in on Jerrod for my sister. This gentleman said you would have to give your approval for the visit."

Carroll grinned at the receptionist. "I'll take her in myself, Leonard."

"Yes, sir."

The doctor ushered Breanna through the double doors and said, "I need to explain some things to you before you see Jerrod, Miss Baylor. My office is right here. Let's go in and sit down a moment."

Breanna eased onto a straight-backed wooden chair in front of the desk. Carroll moved behind it, and as he sat down, he said, "Has your sister told you anything about me?"

"No, sir. We haven't had a lot of time to talk. I was only with her a short while at the hospital yesterday."

"I won't bore you with a long spiel, but I want you to know that I am a Christian. Dottie—your sister has told me all about you."

"Well, I'm glad to hear this about you, doctor. I know Jerrod is in the best of care, then."

"Thank you. I assume you understand about Jerrod's *dementia praecox*, which was brought on by the shell shock he suffered in the War."

"Yes, doctor. The split personality—the good Jerrod and the bad Jerrod."

"And your sister has told you everything that has happened?"

"Yes. All of it."

"All right. I was just with him. We have him in chains in a padded cell. The dementia has almost completely taken over. He has moments now and then when he's his old self, and when that happens, he's very sorry for what he's done. Weeps over it. But those moments are fewer and farther between, and becoming more brief all the time. Just now, he was fighting his chains and screaming that he was going to get out and kill your sister."

Breanna looked the doctor square in the eye. "There's no

hope he'll ever be any better, is there?"

"None. There's nothing we can do. I've tried sedatives since we've had him in here, hoping to at least calm him, but they don't do a thing. As for a cure...never."

"It's hard to say this, Doctor, but since Jerrod is a Christian, it would actually be better if the Lord would just take him home."

"I agree. But, of course, his life is in God's hands."

There was a brief pause, then Breanna said, "May I see him now?"

"Of course. Come with me."

Dr. Carroll led Breanna down the hall past several padded cells. She shivered at the horrible cries and moans that met her ears.

When they came to Jerrod's cell, the doctor stopped, nodded at the small window, and said, "He's in there. You can move up close. He can't reach you."

Breanna leaned up to the window and looked at the man who had married her sister. Jerrod was on his feet, staring directly at her. A piteous look captured his face and tears filled his eyes. His voice was soft as he said, "Dottie. Oh, Dottie, you've come to see me. Please...forgive me for hurtin' you. I didn't mean to. I'm sorry, honey. So sorry. I love you so much."

"Jerrod," Breanna said with compassion, "I'm not Dottie. She's still in the hospital from what you did to her. I'm her sister, Breanna. Dottie wants me to tell you—"

"Stop lying, Dottie!" Jerrod shouted. "I know it's you! Why do you say you're not you?"

Breanna looked back at the doctor, who whispered, "That's how fast he can change."

Breanna peered through the window again and said, "Jerrod, I am Dottie's sister. She wants me to tell you that she loves you and—"

"Shut up!" Jerrod said. He backed up and slapped his hands over his ears and shut his eyes. "Liar! Liar! Liar!" he shouted. His face twisted grotesquely. His mouth opened wide and he screamed a wild, primal scream. Saliva sprayed from his mouth as he yelled, "I'll kill you, Dottie! You hear me? I'll get outta here and kill you!"

Dr. Carroll took Breanna by the arm and escorted her back to the lobby and outside to her rented buggy, talking the situation over as they went.

"The thing that touches me most about this, Doctor, is Dottie's unswerving love and faithfulness to Jerrod," Breanna said.

"Yes, me too," he replied. "In fact, I recently told her if she wasn't careful, that faithful heart of hers was going to get her killed. It almost did."

20

WHILE BREANNA BAYLOR was driving from the asylum to City Hospital, there was a brief but strong tremor. Windows broke in some of the buildings, street lamps were loosened in their moorings, and there were a few places where the boardwalks split.

When she entered the hospital, Breanna heard some of the staff talking about the "big one" scientists were predicting. A white-frocked doctor said, "I sure hope the seismologists are right, that it won't come till after the turn of the century…if it has to come at all."

Dottie was happy to see her sister, and after the two briefly discussed the tremor, she wanted to know about Jerrod. Breanna softened the report as much as she could without lying. She didn't want Dottie upset more than necessary.

For the next week, Breanna visited Dottie every day. Will Reeves had brought the wagon team back to the Harper place, and Breanna turned in the rented horse and buggy. Every other day, she brought James and Molly Kate with her to see their mother. Will and Maudie visited her a couple of times during the week, as did Reverend Howard Yates.

Dr. Carroll came to see Dottie often. Breanna thought more

often than necessary and didn't like it, but she kept those thoughts to herself.

At the beginning of the second week, Dr. Glenn Olson had Dottie sitting up in bed, and by the end of the week, she was sitting up in a chair. On Saturday of that week, Breanna came to town alone and stopped at the asylum first to ask about Jerrod. She met Dr. Verle Huffman, who told her Jerrod was about the same. Once in a while he was rational, but most of the time he was in a rage.

Breanna then went to the hospital, where she met Dr. Olson in the hallway. He was now positive there was no permanent damage to Dottie's spine. With some therapy she would walk again as good as new. Breanna's face showed her relief as she thanked the doctor for how well he was taking care of her sister.

Dr. Olson told her he would start Dottie's therapy the next day, and if all went well, she could go home in another week. She would need someone to bring her to town every other day for therapy until she was walking normally. Breanna said she would bring her until the time she had to return to Denver, but she was sure Will Reeves would bring her in after that.

Breanna thanked Olson again and proceeded down the hall to Dottie's room. When she walked in, she saw Dr. Matthew Carroll sitting beside Dottie, who was in a chair. Both turned and smiled at her. Breanna smiled back, but it was for Dottie, not the doctor.

"I've just come from the asylum," Breanna said. "Jerrod's about the same."

"I appreciate you doing that, Sis," Dottie said. "Dr. Carroll has kept me informed about Jerrod and says the same thing. Oh, I'll be so glad when I can go see him."

The doctor rose to his feet and said, "Well, I've got to get back to my office and see some patients. Flora will have my head if I'm late for that first appointment."

Matthew Carroll prayed as he drove his buggy from the hospital to the office. *I feel as though I'm carrying a torch inside me, Lord. You know I don't want to sin against You in this. Lord, help me. Please help me.*

Breanna sat down next to her sister when Dr. Carroll left the room. "I just talked to Dr. Olson," she said. "He says he's starting you on therapy tomorrow, and if you respond well, you can go home in another week."

"Oh, yes!" said Dottie, almost laughing. "Won't it be wonderful? I'll get to see Jerrod when I come to town for my therapy…and it will be so good to be in my own home with James and Molly Kate!"

"Oh, Dottie, I'm so glad for you," Breanna said, taking her sister's hand.

Dottie had not been with her sister for ten years, but she knew her well. The look in Breanna's eyes did not match the happy moment. She fixed her with a steady gaze and asked, "Sis, is something wrong?"

"Of course not. I think it's wonderful that you're doing so well and can look forward to going home. I only wish I could stay and take care of you, but I do have a job, and I'll have to get back to Denver before much longer."

"Oh, so that's it. You're worried about what's going to happen to me after you're gone. You needn't worry, Breanna. I'll be all right. I have Will and Maudie, lots of friends at church who'll look after the children and me, and neighbors who'll share in taking care of my crops. Don't you worry now, you hear? The Lord will see that we're taken care of."

When Dottie's words did not remove the look in Breanna's eyes, Dottie squeezed her hand and said, "Okay, big sister. There's something else bothering you. Out with it."

Breanna looked her in the eye, then at the floor, then in the eye again. "Oh, it's...it's nothing. On *your* part, at least."

"On *my* part? What on earth are you talking about?"

"Honey, it's Dr. Carroll."

"What about him?"

"Well, the way he looks at you."

"I don't understand."

"Dottie, I've been in this world long enough to recognize love in a man's eyes. I see it in Dr. Carroll's eyes every time he looks at you."

"What? Oh, Breanna, you're mistaken. He's just a kind and compassionate man. He's a Christian, and a very dedicated one, too."

"Yes, and he's also a married man. I saw in his office a wedding photograph of him and his bride. And there was another of her taken in a studio. It was signed, 'To my darling husband.'"

"Would you feel any better if I told you Dr. Carroll is a widower?"

"Oh, well, perhaps. But you're still a married woman, Dottie. He ought to—"

"Breanna, let me tell you something. You already know how I feel about Jerrod. We've discussed that."

"Yes."

"Well, I have never seen what you saw in Dr. Carroll's eyes. And he has *never* made any kind of a move that would make me think he's any less than a gentleman, or has designs on me. I mean it…*never.*"

"Well, I'm sure he must be a very lonely man," Breanna said. "I can't blame him if he has fallen in love with you."

"Maybe what you see is nothing more than admiration. He's told me a few times how much he admires me for the way I've stayed by Jerrod through all of this."

"I know he admires you for that. He told me so himself. But when he looks at you the way I've seen it here in this room, it's not admiration. It's love."

"Then he'll just have to get over it," Dottie said. "As long as Jerrod is alive, he alone will have my heart."

There was much rejoicing at the Reeves home that evening when Breanna picked the children up and told them the good news. James had told his mother about his new wagon, but he was eager for her to see it. Molly Kate had also told her mother about the doll, but she wanted her to see it at the upstairs window, looking down at her when she rode into the yard.

The next day was Sunday. During the church service, Reverend Yates's sermon was interrupted by a mild earthquake that lasted less than half a minute. Yates paused during the tremor, then went on with his sermon.

When the last prayer was offered, and the congregation began filing out the door, they found Sheriff Max Donner standing in front of the church. He was telling a group of townspeople that he had just received word by wire that the quake had hit the downtown area of San Francisco hard. Several buildings had been seriously damaged, and had it not happened on a Sunday morning, there would have been a great many more people injured and killed. The wire had not given any count of the dead and injured, nor had it identified any of the damaged buildings.

Donner's words quickly passed among the worshippers. When Breanna heard them, she turned to Will and Maudie and said, "I've got to go see about Dottie! I *must* know if she's all right."

"Of course," Will said. "Maudie can drive our wagon home with the children. I'll go with you."

"Oh, you don't need to do that, Grandpa Will. I'll make it fine."

"Breanna, I hate to say it, but what if you get there and find out…well, find out that it's bad news? You'll need someone with you."

Breanna bit her lower lip. Nodding, she said, "All right. Let's go."

Will Reeves was at the reins in the Harper wagon as he and Breanna raced toward San Francisco. As they neared the outskirts of the city, they came upon two wagons that stood back to back in the middle of the dusty road, blocking traffic. Teams were still hitched to the wagons, and one saddle horse stood close by.

"Looks like they're keepin' folks from goin' into town," Will said.

"Oh, Grandpa Will," gasped Breanna. "Do you think the quake was *that* bad?"

"We'll soon find out," he said, the strain in his voice revealing his apprehension.

The old man slowed the team, and as they drew near the roadblock, the four lawmen who manned it stepped forward. There were two sheriff's deputies and two policemen. One of the deputies raised both hands, signaling for Will to stop. Will drew the wagon to a halt, and the deputy who had raised his hands stepped up on Will's side of the wagon.

"I'm sorry, sir, but we can't let you through. You're aware we just had a bad quake?"

"Yes, deputy," Will said. "We were in church in San Bruno when it happened. Felt it pretty good for a few seconds. Understand it did some damage downtown."

"Yes, sir. Real bad. There are buildings that are still standing, but might collapse. There's no danger in the residential area between here and downtown, but we've got to keep curiosity seekers out of the area. We've got fire wagons and ambulances racing up and down the streets, and we don't need people in the way."

"I can understand that," Will said. "This young lady has a sister who's a patient at City Hospital. Can you tell us if the hospital was damaged?"

"The hospital escaped any serious damage, ma'am. No one there was hurt. I'm sure your sister is fine."

"Oh, thank the Lord," Breanna said.

"Folks weren't so fortunate just a few blocks east," said the deputy. "There were four square blocks that were hit pretty hard."

Will's face lost color. "Was the mental asylum damaged?"

"Yes, sir. Real disaster at the asylum."

"Do you know if anyone was injured or killed?" Breanna said. "I ask because I know someone who's there."

"Well, Sergeant O'Neill just rode in from that section, ma'am. He was about to tell us what he knows about it when we saw your wagon coming." He turned around and said, "Sergeant O'Neill, what can you tell us about the asylum?"

O'Neill stepped forward. "The asylum was damaged real bad. One whole wall collapsed and fell on some of the inmates. I think they presume something like ten to fifteen are dead. Others are injured. I don't really know how many. That's about all I can tell you."

Breanna covered her mouth with her hand and squeezed her eyes shut.

"Now let's not panic before we know the facts," Will said, putting an arm around her shoulder. Then looking at the lawmen, he asked, "Do you gentlemen have any idea how soon we'll be allowed to enter the city?"

"It'll be a couple of days at least, sir," Sergeant O'Neill said. "It really depends on what the building inspectors tell us about the extent of damage to the structures that are still standing. Right now, every road into the city has been blocked. Come back day after tomorrow, and we'll know a whole lot more than we do right now."

"All right, Sergeant," Will said. "Thank you." He gave Breanna a tight squeeze, then took hold of the reins with both hands and wheeled the wagon around. "Best thing right now, Breanna, is for you and those two little kids to be together. You can tell 'em for sure their mother's okay. Thank the Lord for that."

"Yes," Breanna responded. "Thank the Lord for that."

❧

Dottie Harper was sitting up in bed with her Bible in her hands. The quake had hit an hour earlier, and all she knew about the damage at City Mental Asylum was that it was severe. A nurse had told her that much. No one else in the hospital knew any more.

Was Jerrod all right? What about Dr. Carroll? Had he been on duty when the quake hit? She knew that sometimes he had to be there on Sundays.

She gripped the Bible and closed her eyes. "Oh, Lord," she whispered, "You're the Maker and Ruler of this universe. Nothing can happen to any of Your children unless You deem it so. I don't know whether Jerrod is dead or alive. If…if You've seen fit to take him home to be with You, help me to accept it, and give me the strength that only You can give. If he's still alive but injured, I ask You not to let him suffer. I love him so much, dear God. Please—"

Dottie's prayer was interrupted when she heard the voice of Dr. Matthew Carroll outside her door. He was saying something to a nurse. The nurse gave a short reply, then the door came open. Dottie was thankful to know Dr. Carroll was all right, but when she saw his face, she was afraid he was about to give her bad news.

"Hi," he said, closing the door and trying to smile.

"Hello."

"Nurse Wilkins tells me you've been informed that the damage at the asylum was pretty bad," he said, moving up to the bed.

"Yes. Were…were you there when the quake hit?"

"No. I was in church."

"Oh, I'm so glad. I was afraid it might have been your Sunday to be on duty. Have you been there? Is…Jerrod all right?"

Dr. Carroll took hold of Dottie's wrist, cleared his throat nervously, and said, "Mrs. Harper…Dottie…as you know, the asylum was built of stone. And—"

"Doctor, is Jerrod all right?"

Carroll bit his lower lip, closed his eyes, then opened them and said, "No. The entire east wall collapsed. My staff told me it teetered for about twenty minutes. They were dashing into the cells and freeing patients from the chains, trying to get them all out. They were able to get all but eleven. There was an aftershock, and the wall came down. Jerrod…Jerrod was one of the eleven buried in the rubble of the wall. It'll be days before the city workers can get the bodies out."

Dottie's eyes filled with tears and she choked back a sob. The tears spilled down her cheeks, her anguish tearing a gaping wound in her heart.

Matthew Carroll fought his own emotions. He wanted to take her in his arms, but was afraid to let himself get that close.

"Oh, Jerrod!" Dottie cried, and broke into heavy, heart-rending sobs, burying her face in her hands.

The doctor could resist no more. He sat on the bed and wrapped her in his arms. "Dottie, I'm so sorry," he said.

Dottie took refuge in the security of the doctor's embrace and gave in to the storm of grief. She pressed her face into his shoulder and wept.

Dr. Carroll held her until her weeping diminished to quiet sniffles, then eased back and tilted her chin up. "Dottie…I hope you don't mind if I call you *Dottie.*"

"No. Of course not."

He smiled thinly. "At least you have this consolation. Jerrod's not shackled in a padded cell anymore. He's with Jesus. And in heaven, nobody has mental problems. His shell shock is gone."

Dottie closed her eyes and nodded.

"If you want, I'll be with you when you tell your children," he said.

"That's thoughtful of you," she said. "I appreciate you being so kind to me."

Carroll wanted to tell Dottie that he loved her, but knew this was not the time.

Dottie thought for a moment, then said, "Certainly they know about the quake in San Bruno by now. Word will spread to the farms. I know what Breanna will do. She'll come racing in here to make sure I'm all right, maybe even bring James and Molly Kate with her. I would really like to have you with me when I tell them about Jerrod, but you have things to do at the asylum. You can't stay here just because of me. I'll have Breanna. She'll be a great help, I know."

"I'm afraid there's another problem," Dr. Carroll said.

"What?"

"On my way over here, I was told by a policeman that all roads into San Francisco have been blocked by the authorities. They'll remain blocked until the damage in every downtown building has been assessed. I imagine Breanna has already been turned back."

"I hadn't even considered that possibility. I guess we'll just have to wait till she's allowed to come to the hospital, and hope she brings the children with her."

"Seems we don't have any choice. But if at all possible, I want to be with you when you break the news to the children."

Jerrod Harper's first indication that he was still in the world was the sound of fire wagons racing up and down the streets. He shook his head and opened his eyes. There was dust in his eyes and in his mouth. When the fire wagon bells faded away, he heard excited voices close by. He tried to remember what had happened, then it all came back at once.

The earthquake.

Jerrod's thoughts were invaded by excruciating pain in his left leg. Chunks of stone from the collapsed wall lay around him, making dark shadows. But there was light coming from just above his head. He tried to move the leg, fearing that it might be pinned under some massive stone. He was able to move it, and heaved a sigh of relief.

He thought of what had happened just before the wall collapsed. Two attendants came into his cell, saying the wall was threatening to come down. They released him from the chains and were about to lead him out when an aftershock shook the wall, and it began to topple. The attendants sprang away to save their own lives, and the wall came down, breaking apart as it fell. Miraculously, the tons of stone formed a pocket of protection above and around him, and only injured his left leg.

Jerrod lifted himself to his knees and nearly passed out from the stab of pain in his leg. Gritting his teeth, he crawled toward the opening in the rubble above him. When he stuck his head up, he looked back to what had been the interior of the building and saw attendants helping inmates out through the front doors.

He was free!

Jerrod climbed carefully out of the rubble and into the alley. There was noise everywhere. He could smell smoke. A building was on fire somewhere near. With all the traffic on the streets, he decided to find a place to hide until dark. In spite of his injured leg, he would sneak to the edge of town and make his way through the ditches and fields to the farm. The fire of revenge burned in his brain. Dottie was going to pay dearly for what she had done to him!

Limping on the bad leg, he made his way down the alley till he came to a small horse barn. Inside he saw a pile of hay in one corner and crawled in behind it. He grinned to himself in spite of the pain. "Just sit tight, Dottie. Your loving Jerrod's coming to you. And after I kill you, I'll find that doctor and kill *him!*"

As twilight faded into night at the Harper farm, Breanna lighted kerosene lanterns in the kitchen, the parlor, and the hallway. She then went to the second floor and placed a lantern on a hall table. She told the children she was going to give the entire house a good cleaning before their mother came home in a few days. She wanted to get started on the third floor tonight. James and Molly Kate quickly volunteered to help.

Breanna had told the children about the roadblock when she and Will returned to the Reeves place. She assured them the hospital had not been damaged and that their mother was all right. The children had asked about the asylum, and Breanna told them their father could be injured...or worse. They would just have to trust him to the Lord. They accepted that and had talked about both parents during the ride home.

Breanna was glad the children were eager to help clean. It would keep their minds off the disaster in San Francisco.

When Breanna said they would start on the third floor first and work their way down over the next couple of days, James told her that his mother only cleaned the third floor twice a year. They hardly ever went up there, so it didn't need to be cleaned now. Breanna insisted they at least clean the corner turret room with the cone-shaped roof.

The large windows were not dirty enough to bother with, but together Breanna and the children dusted the furniture, mopped the floor, and cleaned around the fireplace. Breanna was amazed at how heavy the old poker was that leaned against the fireplace. They didn't make them that heavy any more. She noted the age of the wood stacked on the hearth and realized it had been a long time since there had been a fire in that room.

It was late when they finally had the turret room polished clean, but before going to bed, the children wanted Aunt Breanna to read them a story. They chose a book from the shelves in the parlor, then turned up the parlor lanterns and sat down, one child on each side of the aunt they had come to adore.

21

IN THE PARLOR OF THE HARPER HOME, Breanna Baylor was reading to James and Molly Kate when a gust of wind slapped the side of the house. She cut off in the middle of a sentence and looked up. A second gust rattled the windows.

James saw the surprise on his aunt's face and said "It's all right, Aunt Breanna. We get wind like this every now and then. Daddy says it comes from the ocean."

"I wouldn't think it would be so forceful this far inland," Breanna said. She looked back at the book. "Now, where were we?"

"The big ol' giant was about to crush the poor farmer's house," Molly Kate said.

"Oh, yes."

The wind seemed to be getting stronger as Jerrod limped into the yard. He paused and studied the house. Lantern light showed in the parlor and in the kitchen. On the second floor, he could barely make out a faint light in the window of his and Dottie's bedroom.

He grimaced from the pain in his leg as he limped toward the side of the house. He stumbled and fell once, but scrambled to his feet again and soon drew up to the window.

The wind now lashed the house unmercifully. In the parlor, Breanna had to raise her voice slightly to be heard above the howl of the wind as she finished the story.

She closed the book and said, "All right, sweet dumplings, it's time for little boys and girls to go to bed."

"Will you come in my room and pray with me before I go to sleep, Aunt Breanna?" asked Molly Kate.

"Me, too?" asked James.

"Of course," Breanna said, rising from the couch.

Suddenly James gasped and pointed to the window. "Look! It's Daddy!"

The lantern light made Jerrod's features look ghastly through the glass. Molly Kate screamed and grabbed for Breanna. Jerrod ejected a wild, beastly roar and smashed the window with his fists. Glass showered the parlor floor.

Jerrod struggled to climb through the window. The desire to get at the woman he thought was his wife was so powerful he didn't realize he was cutting his hands on the shards of glass that still clung to the window frame.

The children stood frozen with terror, eyes bulging.

Breanna grabbed a heavy wooden chair that stood beside the window and swung it in a full arc. The chair caught Jerrod square in the face and knocked him out of the window. Breanna heard him hit the ground hard. She dropped the chair and said,

"James, take your sister and go out the back door! Quick! There's enough moonlight. Run to Grandpa Will's house!"

The wind shrieked through the broken window, making the curtains fly. James and Molly Kate stood against the far wall of the parlor, their white faces stark against the dark tapestry.

"Aunt Breanna, you come with us!" James said.

"No," she said, taking their hands and leading them to the hall. "None of us can outrun your father. He's out of his mind, and your lives are in danger, too. The only hope is for me to stay and keep him occupied while you two run to Grandpa Will and ask him to bring help!"

Breanna could hear Jerrod mumbling angrily. He was going around to the front of the house. She ran to the front door and shoved the bolt home, then hurried back to the children as she heard heavy footsteps on the porch.

"Hurry, James! Go!"

"But Aunt Breanna, he'll kill you! Please come with us!"

"No! We can't outrun him, James. He'll kill all three of us if I go with you. I must stay and try to hold him off while you run and get help! Now go!"

James took his little sister by the hand and ran down the hall. Jerrod was throwing his weight against the door and screaming Dottie's name. Breanna heard the back door open and close, then wheeled to see the front door splintering.

Her mind racing, Breanna prayed for God's help and ran down the hall into the kitchen. She had to find a weapon. *Butcher knife. Where's the butcher knife?* She had used it yesterday. Or was it the day before? Both children had helped her clean up the kitchen after their meals. *Where had they put the knife?*

She heard the front door bang open, then heavy footsteps

coming down the hall. She frantically opened drawers in the cupboard, one after the other. Her hands trembled as she pushed utensils aside, trying to find the knife. At the same time, she detected the uneven sound of Jerrod's footsteps. Was he limping?

Suddenly the big man appeared at the kitchen door, bracing himself with both hands against the frame. His eyes were wild and his face flushed as he yelled, "Where are my children, Dottie?"

Rolling pin. There it was on the cupboard. She held his glare with her own and inched her way along the cupboard toward the rolling pin.

"You wicked witch!" Jerrod roared. "Where are James and Molly Kate? Don't tell me they aren't here! I saw 'em through the window! Where are they?"

"What do you want with them?" she asked with a shaky voice, trying to delay whatever would come next.

"Where are they?" he bellowed. He let go of the door frame and lunged across the kitchen for her. His faltering gait gave her time to grasp one handle of the rolling pin. When she picked it up, she saw that it had been lying against the knife.

Just as Jerrod came within arm's reach, she brought the pin down on his forehead, ejecting a wordless cry as she did it.

He staggered and blinked, then lunged at her again. This time he was able to grasp the hand that held the rolling pin. His strength was ox-like. Breanna knew he would kill her if she didn't get away from him. She swung around and grabbed the knife with her other hand. Before Jerrod could prevent it, she stabbed the sharp blade into the arm that held her.

Jerrod howled and let go. He staggered backward, swinging the wounded arm madly, as if to fling the pain out of it. His hand hit the kerosene lantern on the cupboard, knocking it to the floor. The glass bowl shattered, as well as the chimney, and kerosene spread every direction. Flames licked through it, sending black smoke toward the high ceiling.

Jerrod backed toward the door that led to the hallway, avoiding the flames. Breanna thought of the rear door of the kitchen, which led to the back porch. It was closed. Could she get to it, and *through* it, before he caught her?

Jerrod came toward her again. The knife was her only hope. The horror she was experiencing made the knife feel unreal, as if the hand on the end of her arm belonged to someone else. Her knuckles were white, she was clutching the knife so hard.

She scurried around the end of the kitchen table to put it between her and Jerrod. She held the knife pointed at him and cried, "Get away from me, Jerrod, or I'll cut you again!"

Smoke stung her eyes, and she began to cough. Both felt the searing heat of the flames as they burned their way across the floor and up the sides and doors of the cupboards. In seconds, they would be crawling up the opposite wall and engulfing the door that led to the hall. The heat was becoming unbearable.

Breanna dropped the knife and shoved the table at Jerrod with all her might. It struck the thigh of his bad leg, and he screamed in pain and fell on top of the table.

Breanna raised her skirt and ran through the flames and into the hall. She started to run for the front door, but felt heat at her ankles and realized her skirt was on fire. She stopped and beat at the flames with her hands. It took only seconds to squelch the flames, but those same seconds gave Jerrod time to recover and limp through the flames toward her.

Breanna ran for the door. Jerrod picked up a kitchen chair

and threw it at her. The chair hit her on the backs of the legs, and she fell on her face. Jerrod limped around her and slammed the door shut. Though it was severely damaged, he was able to ram the bolt into its groove. He turned slowly and lanced her with a murderous look.

Suddenly the kitchen window exploded. Wind swept into the hall and rushed through the parlor to the window Jerrod had broken earlier, carrying sheets of flame with it. Fire licked up the walls of the hall and rushed across the parlor floor with frightening speed, as if it were alive and intent on devouring all in its path. Smoke filled the parlor.

Breanna struggled to get up as Jerrod reached for her, eyes wild and full of hate. "Get away from me!" she screamed as she drew her legs back and kicked both feet at his injured thigh as hard as she could. Jerrod screamed, grabbed his thigh, and fell to his knees.

Breanna struggled to her feet. The way the bolt on the front door had screeched when Jerrod shot it home told Breanna she would have trouble getting it open. She would have to go the other way. She turned to run for the back of the house, but the hallway was a solid sheet of flame.

She had no choice. She would have to climb the stairs and go out a window from the second floor. "Please, God! Help me!" she cried as she ran through the smoke and groped her way, coughing, to the staircase and started to climb.

A fist closed around her ankle and gave a violent yank. She came down hard on the stairs, striking her chin. The taste of blood filled her mouth.

Breanna fought desperately, grasping for something to hold as Jerrod dragged her backward. Her fingers closed around the posts of the balustrade and she hung on. She thrust her left leg out, and her heel struck Jerrod's cheekbone. The force of the kick snapped his head back, and he fell.

Breanna ran up the stairs as fast as she could.

Great tongues of flame leaped through the broken windows at both ends of the house, climbing upward on the outside walls. The yards—both front and back—were alive with an angry glow, and the wind carried sparks skyward.

Breanna reached the second floor and could hear Jerrod on the stairs behind her. She ran down the hall, staggering slightly because of the pain in her legs. She would go into James's room, bolt the door, and climb out the window onto the back porch.

Suddenly one leg gave way, and she fell to the floor near the table that held the lantern she had lighted earlier. She struggled to rise and looked back to see Jerrod top the stairs, screaming Dottie's name.

Breanna used the wall to steady herself as she struggled to her feet. Jerrod stumbled toward her, his eyes wild. She took a large painting from the wall and brought it down on his head. The canvas ripped and the frame settled on his shoulders. The impact sent him reeling into the small table, and the lantern crashed to the floor, shattering the glass bowl. Kerosene pooled on the hardwood floor. Hungry flames followed the pools edges, then swept across the surface.

Breanna turned and headed for James's room. Jerrod lifted the frame off his shoulders and flung it away and started after her. Just as she reached the door, he grabbed her by the shoulders, spun her around, and jerked her up into his face. She struggled, but her frantic efforts only increased the force of his grip.

"Lock me up in the crazy house, will you?" he blared, and clamped a bloody palm over her mouth. "You're goin' in the fire!"

Jerrod forced Breanna back up the hall toward the flames. The suffocating pressure of his palm kept her from screaming, but she still had plenty of fight left. Jerking her head sideways, she was able to free her mouth enough to close her teeth on his little finger. She bit down as hard as she could, and Jerrod ejected a shrill cry and released his hold. He raised his other hand to strike her. Breanna saw it and let go of the finger. She dodged his fist, then struck his injured thigh again.

Jerrod groaned and staggered against the wall. Breanna slipped past him, intending to run toward the stairs, but the flames were too fierce to chance it. There was only one way she could go. She ran to the staircase that led to the third floor and bounded up the stairs and into the turret room. She was able to get the door closed and locked before Jerrod hit it with a bang.

"Dear Lord, help me!" she gasped.

Jerrod bellowed and hit the door again. It began to splinter. Breanna looked around and saw the heavy iron poker leaning against the fireplace. She hurried to it and hefted it to a swinging position. The lock on the door gave way, splinters flying, and the door banged open. Jerrod came stumbling into the room, trying to gain his balance. Breanna swung the heavy poker with all her might. It caught Jerrod solidly on the side of the head, and along with his own momentum, helped propel him across the room and headlong into the large curved windows. He crashed through them, fell to the roof of the wide porch below, then pitched like a rock to the ground.

Breanna dropped the poker and hurried to the window. Jerrod lay in the yard and did not move.

The howl of the wind and the roar of the flames filled her ears. She ran from the turret and down the stairs to the second floor. The hall was alive with flame. She remembered that one of the large oak trees spread its limbs close to the house on the back side next to the attic. She hurried back up the stairs to the third floor and into the attic. Light was coming through the attic window from the fire on the outside of the house. She opened the window, crawled out, took hold of a limb, and began working her way to the ground.

22

JERROD HARPER GROANED, shook his pounding head, and raised up on his knees. He had hit the ground on his right shoulder, and the impact had broken his arm and dislocated the shoulder. The pain was as excruciating as that in his left thigh.

Jerrod looked up at the blazing house. The wind-driven flames leaped skyward, and billows of smoke rode the wind, speckled with fiery sparks. Suddenly Jerrod's attention was drawn to Molly Kate's room and the figure silhouetted in the window.

"Molly Kate!" he screamed, rising to his feet. "Molly Kate!"

Jerrod summoned all his strength and limped toward the front door of the house. "Daddy's comin', honey! Daddy's comin'! Don't be afraid! I won't let the fire get you!"

Breanna heard Jerrod's words above the roar of the blaze as she came around the corner of the house. She saw him limping toward the front porch with his right arm hanging limply from the shoulder.

"Jerrod!" she shouted, running after him. "Jerrod! It's not Molly Kate in the window! It's just a doll!"

But the roar of the fire, the howl of the wind, and Jerrod's powerful desire to save his daughter blocked out Breanna's cries.

She ran to catch him before he plunged into the house, but she was too far behind him. He crossed the porch and hit the door, breaking it open for the second time.

The heat was intense, and Breanna backed away, using her arms to protect her face. She saw Jerrod enter the parlor and head for the stairs. She withdrew further from the house, weeping for Jerrod, and in a few moments saw him come up behind the doll and wrap his arms around her. His clothes were already on fire. The window shattered from the heat, and Breanna heard Jerrod Harper's last cry: *"Molly Kate!"* And he was gone.

There was a deep rumble. The house began to quiver, then it collapsed within itself in a gigantic roar. Breanna backed away to avoid the rush of heat. Smoke and fire billowed toward the night sky.

Breanna's attention was drawn to a team and wagon coming toward her out of the night. It was Will Reeves. Behind him came five other wagons. He had rallied neighbors for Breanna's rescue, but her God had brought her through safely.

A week later, Dottie Harper sat in the family wagon beside her sister and looked at the black rubble that had once been her house. James and Molly Kate were in the bed of the wagon, looking on sadly.

Tears coursed down Dottie's cheeks as she remembered what Breanna had told her about Jerrod giving his life to save the doll he thought was Molly Kate. "He couldn't help what happened to his mind, Breanna," she said, sniffing, "but he proved what the *real* Jerrod was like. He died a hero."

"That he did," Breanna said, patting her hand.

"Let's go," Dottie said shakily. "I had to see it, but I don't want to look at it any more."

As they drove away, Breanna said, "Dottie, I know Dr. Carroll has spent a lot of time with you at the hospital, especially since the fire. Has he ever told you how he feels?"

Dottie brushed tears from her cheeks. "Yes. Yes, he has. Yesterday he…told me he's in love with me. He knows I'll need time to grieve for Jerrod but, Breanna, he's so good. He has offered to move to a boarding house and let the children and me live in his house on Nob Hill. All he asks is that in time, I give my heart a chance to love him back. He said if and when I find that I can love him, we will marry, and he will adopt the children."

Breanna took Dottie's hand and smiled at her. "You already like him a lot, don't you?"

"Yes, of course. I liked him the first time we met. But I never had any other kind of feelings toward him."

"I know," Breanna said. "But since he's a fine Christian, and you already like him a lot, you should give the Lord a chance to work it out."

Dottie looked at her sister for a moment, then said, "Breanna, what do you think? Should I take him up on the offer to live in his house? He said he has a housekeeper who lives in. She could help me with the children while I'm in therapy and unable to take care of them properly."

"Dottie, I think the Lord is going to put love in your heart for him and give you a wonderful life. Besides, you can't live with Grandpa Will and Grandma Maudie forever."

Dottie smiled to herself, but said no more.